Books by Lucy Woodhull

Samantha Lytton

The Dimple of Doom
The Dimple Strikes Back
The Wrath of Dimple

Single Titles

667 Ways to F*ck Up My Life

667 Ways to F*ck Up My Life

ISBN # 978-1-78686-022-4

©Copyright Lucy Woodhull 2016

Cover Art by Posh Gosh ©Copyright 2016

Interior text design by Claire Siemaszkiewicz

Totally Bound Publishing

Published in 2016 by Totally Bound Publishing, Newland House, The Point, Weaver Road, Lincoln, LN6 3QN, United Kingdom.

667 WAYS TO F*CK UP MY LIFE

LUCY WOODHULL

Dedication

This book is for every woman who has been taught that perfection is obligatory.

What a load of bullshit. You are fabulous — warts, burps, trips and all. Give 'em hell, my courageous sisters.

And to our beautiful, bad-girl cat Paprika, who left us recently. Seventeen years ago, we were put in a dank room and interrogated mercilessly in order to adopt you.

Totally worth it.

Chapter One

F*ck-Ups One through Four
Come on, Mel, Let's Just Give Up

If there's anything more calamitous than being fired by a scumbag, it's having to be polite about it. I bit back all manner of choice words, lest a barrage of 'screw yous' and 'blow it out your asses' smack the venerated editor Carmichael Burns in his florid face. He was the king of choice words, after all. What could I say to him that he hadn't already spewed across the *New York Times* bestseller list?

Besides, sweet Dagmar Kostopoulos never, ever used words like that.

"But... But..." I did manage to get out, my mouth as dry as his pretend ennui. "You're promoting Jazmine into my role? How can that be? I have a Masters in English from Columbia." And she had a certificate from the Brooklyn Irony Emporium.

Carmichael laughed at my earnestness, as he always did. He pitied me because I actually did my job studiously and worked hard, even as he told me I kept him honest. And why shouldn't he chuckle? Jazmine had banged this ponytailed ball of pretension the moment she had gotten the job as his secretary, and now she'd 'earned' mine as editorial assistant. She wouldn't know a good nonfiction book platform if it bit her on the butt. She'd let *him* bite her butt, though. I cracked a mirthless smile at my stupid inner monologue, then sucked in a breath because...horrors—I had just lost my job.

The whole room went hazy. My head spun like water down a toilet bowl.

"You're too expensive for me, Dag," declared the man who'd given me a raise not a month ago. "Jazmine has a certain...flair for this work. You don't need a degree to develop *je ne sais quoi*."

I didn't know *je ne sais quoi* was French for 'showed her thong like it was 1998'.

No—I would not be angry at Jazmine. Or her thong, which had been hella cute. We'd both known how to get promoted in Carmichael's office. Hell, the entire publishing industry understood that you gave head to get ahead with him. She'd been willing to go there, and I hadn't, for I'd thought my stellar performance would bypass his editing-couch antics.

The blame lay entirely with him.

He who smirked at me anew and said, "I know you'll land on your feet, Dag. I'm really doing you a favor. You can do so much better than me." His modesty rang hollow and dull. His last four books had debuted at number one everywhere—tell-alls from globetrotting manly adventurers, over-sexed Instagram stars, and jailed politicians.

"No!" I chirped. I smiled my summa cum laude, brilliant-girl smile. "No. You need me, Carmichael. Promote Jazmine, of course"—that last bit came out a little teeth-grindingly—"but I am an essential part of this team. Now, if you don't mind, I'm going to get back to the business of selling books."

I stood and buttoned my navy blazer. Yup, in a year and a half on the job, I'd found a future bestseller myself from a long-lost Kardashian cousin with a combo sex/Mason jar recipe blog. She made great salads, although I hadn't ever tried one naked in a hot tub as Khandye had recommended.

He said, "I do."

I blinked sweetly down at him. "What?"

"I do mind. You're fired, Dag."

A thousand rational arguments crowded my brain and I had to squeeze my eyes shut to form them into dynamic sentences that showed, not told, him how absolutely necessary I was.

I—

He—

No. Nope.

This was not happening. *Not* happening!

"Carmichael—" I blinked and realized he no longer sat in front of me at the rugged desk that used to belong to Ernest Hemingway. He was now perched outside the office on the arm of Jazmine's chair. Her cackle blew into my ears on a frigid breeze.

Carmichael had called me frigid. He'd grabbed my boob at the Christmas party and called me a frigid slut when I wouldn't advance my career by screwing him. I'd asked him how one could be both frigid and a slut. Probably a bad move, since he was now firing me four days later.

Rage bubbled through my gut, into my throat, a wave of heat that nearly knocked me over. I clenched my teeth and willed myself to call him what he was. An aging hipster douche sniffing the pretention of his own backside while selling bullshit to the lowest common denominator for only fourteen ninety-five.

Not that it hadn't been super fun while it lasted.

I couldn't find the words to defend myself, to talk him out of it. I performed excellently at my job. I'd found talented writers and changed their lives for the better. I'd worked endless hours, putting aside my own personal life in the process.

All for nothing.

I squeezed my eyelids shut as I shuffled past them. Jazmine sing-songed, "Bye, Dag-marred."

The eyes of the entire floor bored holes into my back while I gathered my purse and coffee mug. Nobody said a word—the Swiss cheese would stand alone.

What the heck did I do now? I'd never gotten a B, much

less a pink slip. And my colleagues needed the largesse of Carmichael—they couldn't afford to anger him or Jazmine now. But Dagmar, well, Dag-*marred* was literary roadkill, so *Don't let the door smack your backside, darling*. I had many friends and amazing colleagues in this building, and I knew we would stay in touch, no matter the manner of my departure. I waved to them all without being able to meet anyone's eye.

Moments later, I shivered in a gently falling snow, not even remembering the trip down in the elevator from the lofty sixty-third floor. I pulled out my phone and dialed the first number, the tears already bubbling from my face. "I got fired, Blade."

"I'm in a meeting, babe, I'll have to call you back. Wear something sexy when I get home—I've got great news." The line went dead.

Snotcicles formed in my nose and I wondered what he'd heard me say. At least one of us had good news. We'd just moved into our first apartment together, and yesterday I'd thought that my life was going perfectly.

Maybe Khandye Kardashian would give me a job stuffing Mason jars with dildos.

I hailed a cab, reconsidered the expense since I'd lost my income, but decided that I would economize another day. Right now I was blubbering on Fifth Avenue while clutching my 'You Have as Many Hours in a Day as Beyoncé' mug.

Time to slink home.

* * * *

Four hours later, nose raw and eyes aching from the world's longest scream-cry-punch-a-pillow fest, I greeted Blade in my only Spandex dress. I'd never actually worn it—my friend Mel had forced me to buy it—because it was just so tight, you know? I could see a rib through it, and I wasn't really a 'revealing ribs' kind of girl. But getting dressed up for no reason had offered a little comfort. It'd been preferable to rage-stroking over Carmichael the @#&%.

Blade picked me up the moment he swept into the apartment and I clung to his wide shoulders and soft blond hair. He was a doctor, just as my dad always wanted, so I had that going for me, which was nice.

He set me down and said, "Break out the champagne, baby. I've got a new job at the hottest plastic surgery practice in Beverly Hills!"

Surprise melted my knees and I nearly collapsed onto the hardwood floor. "What?" When had he applied for this? *"What?"*

He trotted into the kitchen and I followed behind. With a satisfied smirk, he said, "Got the word this morning. I'm going to be a partner." *Pop* went the champagne we'd bought to christen our new place. He drank straight from the bottle. "Sun and fun — no more of this snow shit for me."

Blade hated the snow so much that I always had to shovel out his car for him.

I leaned against the kitchen counter for support, my stomach regretfully empty from not eating all day. "How stupendous! This is perfect timing." I laughed and took my swirling head (and the rest of me) to the cabinet to fetch our two champagne glasses. I held them out for him to pour. "Carmichael fired me today. Can you believe that? Fired me to promote *Jazmine.*" Blade knew how I felt about *Jazmine.* Even though she wore the best shoes — always tall and vibrant, like she was a *Sex and the City* character. If I were an *SATC* character, I'd probably be Miranda's work ethic.

Blade pulled a face at my news and didn't pour the champagne. "Guess you shoulda slept with him, huh?"

"Ha ha." My arms shook as they still held the empty glasses. Man, did I feel queasy. I'd skipped lunch in favor of crying. He took another pull of the booze and still didn't pour it. I put on my best happy face. "But now it doesn't matter — we're moving to L.A.!"

"I'm moving to L.A."

That queasiness seeped from my stomach to my arms, legs, throat. I opened my mouth to speak but, for the second time today, nothing came out.

He took the champagne bottle past me and into the living room. I took a deep breath. Another. He was just being oblivious, he hadn't really meant what it sounded like. He could be that way — selfish. But it was because he worked hard to save sick people. From their lumpy noses.

With a forced laugh, I followed him. "Blade, do you know how that almost sounded? It sounded like you were moving to L.A. without me."

"Oh." He turned around and tilted his head, a sheepish smile on his magazine-model features. "Yeah."

I waited for more.

I waited for more.

My heart started to race and I waited for *better*.

He nodded his head and said, "Yeah."

"Yeah, what?" It came out so shrill, and I tried never to be shrill with Blade. Guys don't marry shrill — that was one of my dad's words of wisdom.

Blade plopped onto the couch and shrugged. "I'm sorry about this, babe. But there's literally nothing I can do."

My shrill increased by twenty percent. "That's not how one uses 'literally'. Blade, I lost my dream job today. My job that I've been working years to get, and thousands of hours to keep. I've yearned to work with books since I was a little girl."

"Look at it like…it's a whole day of new beginnings for you. And for me. You're not really an L.A. kind of girl. I mean, you're a brunette." He chortled at his 'joke', and I lost my grip on reality. The world clicked into fast forward and I slipped to my knees. I fought the hot vomit simmering in my throat.

"Oh, geez, Dagmar. Why can't you be happy for me? This thing with us hasn't really been working out anyway."

What what *what what what*? "This is some kind of mad

joke. We just paid first and last on a new apartment!" I screamed.

"Ugh, I hate it when you get emotional." He thunked the champagne on the coffee table. "So you'll find a roommate. Maybe then you'll stop bitching about me doing the dishes." He held up his hands. "I told you, I can't do chores because I must save my hands for surgery." Then he disappeared into the bedroom.

Clarity. My entire existence became a camera lens shifting into focus:

My hard-nosed, perfectionist boss hadn't been pushing me to make me a better editor, he'd just been an abusive asshole, embittered that I wouldn't bang him.

My focused, intense doctor boyfriend wasn't absent because he was working hard, he'd been avoiding me and seeking a job three thousand miles away.

I cleaned up after these two men not as a supportive, brilliant helpmate, but as an overachiever desperate for the approval that was abundant in the beginning, in order to snare me, but that had stopped flowing long ago.

How could I have been so impossibly deluded?

I threw up, all over the hardwood floor that I would, apparently, be paying for solo with funds from my non-existent job.

So I heaved even more, accompanied by the plaintive cry of "Ew, gross" from the douchebag who'd had sex with me just this morning.

No telling how long I lay there next to the puke, throat on fire, while wearing my sexy dress. Blade passed me on the way to the kitchen several times, once craning his neck to look up my short skirt.

My cell phone rang. Could it be that somebody loved me? That someone cared enough to call and check on me? I got on my knees and crawled to the coffee table to answer. "Hi, Dad," I said, tears slipping out with the words.

Blade yelled, "You gonna clean this up? It's nasty! You see — this is why you'll never get a man to stay, Dag." He breezed by with another bottle of booze.

My dad sighed on the other end of the phone. "What's wrong, Dagmar?"

"I got fired and Blade is moving to L.A. without me." I sank next to the coffee table and set my forehead on it. "I can't wait to see you in a few days." Christmas was next week, and the plan was for us to take the train to Connecticut to visit. "Hey, maybe I should just come right away. I've got nothing here, anyhow."

"Well…" It was the way he said it. It was the way everyone had said things to me today—hesitant syllables with a side of two-by-four. "I'm going to Hawaii with your sister and her family. They bought me the ticket, isn't that generous?"

Without my go-ahead, my cheek slid off the table and I descended slow-mo style to the floor. This is where I would reside now—me and the floor that would never move to Southern California without me. My butt stopped fighting gravity and sank all the way down. "Dad… Can't I come?"

"They can't really afford you too, Dagmar. Not with two kids and his parents. You'd know that if you had a family."

"I do have a family. You and Vanessa are my family."

More sighing. "Dagmar, you never get it. She has children. A husband. She's doing something with her life. I just don't know why you twins turned out so different."

We weren't twins so much as actors in the sad melodrama *The Golden Child and the Scapegoat.*

I wanted to cry and hurl again, but, apparently, I'd been drained dry. The hollow ache that used to be my eyes twitched, but emitted nothing.

My loving father kept talking. "All those degrees of yours, and for what? You don't have a job anymore? Selling those vile books?" He didn't wait for a reply. "And Blade is a man, Dagmar. He wants a wife who's supportive, who will give him children. Children are the most important thing you can do in this life, not gallivant around New York doing…whatever. Reading other people's writing? What is that? Get with the program, and then you won't be alone on Christmas."

As talks went, this one ranked up there with, "At least the play was funny, Mrs. Lincoln."

"Thanks, Dad," I whispered.

"You should spend the holidays thinking long and hard about what's important in life and make the right choice for once."

He hung up. He hadn't even invited me on my own dime. Neither had Van.

I turned onto my back and stared at the ceiling. It had those little sparkles in its craggy white peaks. Laughter erupted from my dry, cracked lips. It kept coming, and coming— the cackle of the damned. I'd been fired. I'd been dumped. And I was worthless because I didn't have a husband and babies. Twenty-eight years old, and every single dude in my life had given up on me.

All my life, I'd worked endlessly in schools and jobs to achieve, just as Beyoncé (of my coffee mug fame) had told me to do. The more Dad lauded Vanessa for being prettier, the higher my GPA. The more cars he bought her, the more I volunteered at the soup kitchen. I'd been praised by guidance counselors and bosses as a paragon of hard work. Valedictorian of everywhere. I was going places!

What was the frigging point? No, to heck with being so namby-pamby. What was the cock-sucking point?

Or *non*-cock-sucking, as it were.

It was like...I'd gotten so used to the unhappiness and the withholding of affection that I thought it was normal. That I deserved it. My stomach twisted with self-hatred. Self-hatred, even now! Even when I knew I should hate them instead.

I managed to get myself to my knees. Blade called out from the bedroom, "Clean up that gross shit, Dagmar. I'm not gonna tell you again."

My eyelids closed and a peace soothed itself into my angry shoulders. My inner 'give a crap' bucket stood depleted and empty. For perhaps the first time in my life, I didn't care anymore. About anything.

And a plan formed in my vacant heart.

I walked, calmly, into the bedroom. Blade lay on the bed, texting. He didn't even glance at me. I proceeded into the closet and took stock. The back corner of his side was filled with expensive suits and cashmere. Blade had always been a snappy dresser — I'd noticed right away the night we'd met two years ago at a New Year's Eve party.

I hugged my arms around his soft, expensive sweaters and snatched them off the rack.

I returned to the bedroom.

Once again, I wasn't worthy of a turn from his noble, blond head.

I dropped the cashmere onto the floor and opened the window. We were three floors up. I leaned down and grabbed every single stitch of Ralph Lauren and Hugo Boss.

With a grin, I tossed them all out of the window. They sailed downward, colorful arms flailing in the breeze.

No sound of protest, so I returned to his expensive closet corner and started in on the suits. They seemed to plummet to the street much faster. I didn't know how much faster, because I wasn't a science person. I was a language person who'd read instead of getting married.

"Hey!"

A wide grin bloomed once again on my face, but I didn't look at him. I bolted back into the closet and went for the shoes this time. Blade had his shoes flown in from Italy.

I let his shoes fly into the setting New York City sun.

He lost his mind, screaming and yelling. Men — so emotional. He told me no one would ever want me because I was such a bitch. Dagmar the boring, the plain. Living with me was like screwing an accountant's ledger. Then he ran downstairs to reclaim his stuff.

After he left, I hollered down to the faces upturned toward me on the sidewalk. "It's the wardrobe of a douchebag! He talked me into an expensive apartment rental and now, three weeks later, is abandoning me to move to L.A.!" I spread my arms wide. "Take it aaaaaaaaaaall!"

I got applause from a group of women strolling by in suits and sneakers. They ran to grab the sweaters just as Blade made it down there.

I closed the window and sprinted into the living room. Splendid—he'd left his keys in the decorative bowl next to the front door. This was the first good thing that had happened to me all day. I slipped in vomit on the way to the deadbolt, but I deliberately chose not to care. I slammed the door—*blam!*—and shoved a wooden chair from our dining set underneath the handle for good measure.

Next, I cleaned the ick off my foot and flew to my laptop. Two months ago, he'd finally convinced me to obtain a joint bank account. We'd done it, but I hadn't closed my old, single-girl one. They were with the same bank. In three minutes, I'd transferred the bulk of the joint account into mine, then I severed the connection.

At least this money would buy me a little time. Two months' worth, perhaps, but it was better than nothing. A smile of surprise graced me—shocking that he hadn't done the same thing to me before he'd cut me loose. He rather had, though—I'd wanted to save more money before we moved into a pricier zip code.

Bastard.

Bang bang bang! He beat on the apartment door and hurled curses upon my head, but hell would freeze into Ice Capades before I did one more thing for that jackass.

His words sniveled through the door. "Dag, what the hell is wrong with you? You'll be alone forever, you bitch! I tried so hard to love you, but you're just—just a boring fucking nothing! Let me in!"

Well, that wasn't very nice.

Drink. I needed a drink. Why not? I was unemployed and alone. I'd always had a rule about drinking on weeknights, but to heck with that.

I ignored the throw-up again as I splashed his expensive, twelve-year-old Scotch into a glass. My pool of sick seemed a fitting representation of the day. Just this morning, I would have freaked over such a mess, but now? Now my insides had snapped loose and flailed about my ribcage.

I took a huge pull of the strong stuff and nearly breathed fire from it. The taste soured my whole mouth, but it warmed my gullet all the way down to slosh in my empty stomach. Why did I have a rule against this? Monday drinking was excellent, damn fine stuff. I drank another swallow, another, and finished the glass.

I poured again.

Leaning against the counter, I drank and considered the stupid rules I'd followed all my life. Be the best, the most efficient, no wasting time, no slacking off. I did my taxes on January first. I went to bed at ten p.m. I drank eight glasses of water a day. I hadn't consumed a donut in ten years. I was a serial monogamist who'd slept with only two men. Two men in twenty-eight years — what a wild woman.

I poured another drink and came to a realization — I *was* boring. Just as Blade was currently screamed in the hallway.

I'd never traveled to Vegas. I had no idea what happened there, because it stayed there. I wore khakis and sensible blazers in professional colors. My bras were all beige and black. My hair remained its natural hue. I followed every single rule from *The Basic Bitch's Guide* (a tome Carmichael had edited).

And for what?

I sank down the cabinet face, bounced off a drawer pull, and fell onto my butt. I was twenty-eight years old living like a sixty-year-old woman. Not even! Mrs. Delgado, my downstairs neighbor, was sixty-three and had two boyfriends. They played strip poker and all spent the night once a week, after *Wheel of Fortune*.

Oh, wow. My head really started to swish now. I grabbed a bottle of cleaner, a roll of paper towels and my Scotch, and crawled out to the vomit puddle. I drank and cleaned and listened to Blade rant outside. He was now threatening to call the police.

Let him. Let him call the police. Following the plan of my life had failed spectacularly — maybe if he called the police, they'd arrest him and give me a medal for Locking Out a Plastic Surgeon Who *Literally* Deserved It.

Once I'd finished with the vomit-soaked paper towels, I gathered them into a plastic bag and took them into Blade's office, namely the second bedroom. Into his gorgeous, hand-tooled leather briefcase they landed with a disgusting, wet *splat*.

My phone dinged with a text message. Hopefully, my sister calling to remind me that I was the short one with the bigger butt and the empty uterus. 'I've birthed two miracles, and I'm smaller than I was in high school, lol.' Yes. I had actually received that text. On our birthday.

Nope — thank God, it was Melanie.

Holy fuck, that piece of shit fired you?

I called her. "I'm on my way," she blurted by way of greeting. "We're gonna get you so drunk."

"Done and done," I replied. "Oh, and Blade dumped me. He's moving to L.A. to give Jennifer Aniston bigger tits. And my dad is flying to Hawaii for Christmas instead of seeing me."

She uttered a sound of total comfort and commiseration, something along the lines of "Uuuugggghhhhhrrrrrrrrrr-ooooooooohhhhhhhhh-aaacccckkkkkk."

My heart swelled. "Thank you."

"I'm one block away. We're going to order every kind of greasy food known to man, cut the crotches out of Blade's pants, and leave one-star reviews on Amazon for that asshole's books until you're too blotto to stand."

"I love you."

"I love you too. You're going to get through this."

"Be careful of Blade. I locked him out, and he's screaming and yelling in the hall."

"He needs to be afraid of me."

17

We hung up then, and I just sat there, drinking, unfeeling. Un-feeling, as in trying to 'un' my feelings.

Mel worked for another publishing house. We'd met in Columbia undergrad, and she was truly the bright spot in my existence now. I'd grown up being told that women were catty and hateful, that we were in competition with each other for only one thing—men. But I'd fallen for Mel's friendship the moment we'd been tossed together as roommates. She'd taught me that women were here to support one another. I mean, if I was smart, and she was smart, then it stood to reason that ladies were wonderful, right?

A knock sounded at the door and I scrambled to my feet to answer. When I swept it open, I spied Mel standing over Blade, rolling on the hallway carpet and clutching his balls. "He attacked me, officer," said my best friend in her most drawling Southern accent.

I cackled. I waved her in and snatched Blade's wallet from the side table. *Whap!* My tipsy aim was true, for it flopped open over his mouth. "You're staying elsewhere tonight. See, you already have clothes." Only about half of what I'd thrown downstairs lay in a pile beside him. He started to curse me more, but we slammed the door in his face.

"I've never kicked a man in the jewels," I said to Mel.

"You should totally try it! It puts the 'ball-busting' in 'feminist.'"

She threw her arms around me and I started crying anew as I sank into her embrace. Soon, her equally non-L.A. brown hair was wet with my blubbering. My every muscle screamed in tired agony and I sobbed until I'd expressed every emotion known to woman, and probably a few heretofore only available to bears.

Later, who the hell knows how long later, I lay on the couch shoving egg rolls into my mouth. Mel told me that the news of my axing had run through every editorial staff in the city. They all felt sorry for me, for I'd earned a reputation as a great editor.

"What's the point of being great?" I asked her drunkenly, and also rhetorically. "I'm tired of being Polly Perfect while horrible men use women like Kleenex and then sneeze their snot into them."

"Ew," offered Mel.

I shoved a wad of chow mein noodles into my ravenous maw. "Carmichael will go to his cushy job tomorrow. Blade will soar to L.A., straight into a model's bed, no doubt. But not Little Miss Dagmar Boring. She'll send out tasteful résumés and meet a Wall Street wanker who'll cheat on her with an artist from Williamsburg."

"It's not fair," Mel agreed, with a pat to my leg.

I sat up and leaned against the arm of the couch. I really had no choice, for my bones no longer functioned in their proper, rigid manner. "I'm done with it. Done. Every *good* and *sensible* decision I've ever made has flopped. I'm in debt up to my eyeballs from school, and my own father thinks it's a waste."

"Yeah, well your dad lives in 1952, and his treating you like shit is nothing new. Sorry to say, hon."

Mel was the only person in the universe who could call you 'hon' or 'sugah' and you wouldn't mind. She couldn't sound more Georgia if she sang about midnight trains.

I waved an egg roll. "I'm not following the rules anymore. I'm gonna get some shitty job I don't care about. Because caring only hurts you. And then—I'm gonna bang the boss."

She cocked an eyebrow. "Well...at least choose a hot boss."

"Duh." I switched to a sushi roll and pondered aloud while I chewed. "Den, I'mf gonna bang shome other guy. Wish tattoos! Mayshe *I'll* get a tattoo."

She nodded. "Careful—you're spitting tuna on the couch."

I swallowed. "It's Blade's couch. He can take it with him. No—maybe I'll keep the couch and have lots of nasty sex on it. I've never had nasty sex. I've had very polite, sensible

19

sex because that's what I learned from the book I was given about sex when I was thirteen."

She gasped as if I'd just admitted to wearing double-knit polyester.

I leaped to my feet, fell down, and got up again (more slower-ly) to find my notebook, the one I usually used for grocery lists and reminders to collect dry cleaning.

Notebook and pen in hand, I plopped next to her on the floor. I ripped out a page with a list of chores on it, and another with a packing list for Christmas.

At the top of the fresh, new page, I scrawled *Ways to Screw Up My Life*.

A giggle escaped Mel. "I like where this is going."

"Wait—girls who don't care don't say 'screw.' They say 'fuck' in a most unladylike fashion." I scratched out the 'screw' and printed in all caps *FUCK*.

"How many ways?" Mel asked. "You should aim high so you don't quit."

"But aiming is for achievers, and I'm not doing that anymore. I'm giving up, Mel. I'm giving up." I waved my notebook around. "I'm fucking giving up! No more shoes with sensible two-inch heels. No more washing my bras after only wearing them once!"

"You actually do that?"

I sniffed mournfully. "By *hand*."

"That's madness!"

She whooped, and I whooped, and we whooped. Then it came to me. "Six-hundred-sixty-six. I'm going to do six-hundred-sixty-six numbers of fuck-ups."

"Damn." She placed her hand over her heart. "That's a fuck ton of fuck-ups."

"It's the devil's number. If assholes always prosper, which they do—they always, *damn it*, do!—then I shall become one."

"Don't sell your soul, though. Gotta leave room for a deathbed recant. Just in case."

"It's what an asshole would do."

And we clinked Scotch glasses.

I added my numerical goal to the top of the sheet so it read *666 Ways to Fuck Up My Life*. Under this non-lofty title, I put the first item on my bad-girl list:

1. Get shitty job I don't care about

I left the period off the sentence, because who cares about grammar and shit? Nobody else in the world did. They abused punctuation as if it were a hard-working underling.

"Bang boss," Mel reminded me.

I added:

2. Bang the boss

3. Use him to get ahead

"What's the point of the sex if you're not also taking advantage?" I said of number three.

"That's just good sense." She grabbed the pad and scribbled a few words after number two. I turned the page and blinked until my drunky eyes focused. She'd put *and have nasty orgasms in inappropriate places* after *bang the boss*.

I crooked my arm around her head. "That's an excellent point."

"I have another one." Her green eyes danced as she offered me the last of the spicy tuna rolls. "Let's do what a dirty attention whore would do...what Carmichael Burns would do. I think you should start a blog."

4. Start attention-whore overshare blog

What could go wrong?

Chapter Two

F*ck-Ups Five through Eleven
A Hot Mess Requires Donuts and Leopard Print

Tuesday morning came like a freight train from Hell No Station. My face had bloated to infinity from crying, my body hurt from throwing up, and my soul felt...achy, angry, determined.

Determined.

To not be so determined.

(I'd have to work on it.)

I sat up on the couch and reached out for my notebook to add my newest fuck-up:

5. Tuesday morning hangover

Auspicious start to my don't-give-a-hoot palooza.

A clank sounded from the kitchen, so I stumbled there to find my blessed Mel making hangover food of eggs, pancakes and sausage. "Bring your laptop in," she ordered. "We're gonna create that blog."

"Meh. Let's get day-drunk and watch Netflix all day." I came up behind her and stole a sausage before she put them in the oven to stay warm. "But wait—you have a job."

"You have bad breath."

I covered my gross mouth. If only Blade were here to kiss.

She continued, "I called in sick. I agree to the Netflix, but I insist you set up a blog account. If I'm eventually going to sell the book of your blog, which I will, Momma needs that sweet commission as soon as possible."

I gave her a hug from behind then went to slump at the tiny Formica table and chairs in our four square feet of corner billed as a 'nook.' "Fine. But I will get drunk first."

"Hair of the dog." She set an orange juice in front of me and added a shot of vodka. We clinked glasses and began my first day as a ne'er-do-well. Although ne'er-do-wells probably do not use words like 'ne'er do well'.

"Can I just say" — she just said as she began the pancakes — "that I've been itching to tell you for two years that the name Blade is horrible, and it really should have given you a clue."

I snorfed my vodka juice. "I know. I detested his name."

"Blade."

"His mother actually spelled it with a Y — B-l-a-y-d-e — on his birth certificate."

"That's so much more awful!"

"I know!" I laughed so hard it hurt my head, but then everything hurt my head today. Time for more drinking. Sluuuuuurp. Aaaaah. "He would always ask me to call it out during sex. But I couldn't. I couldn't say, 'Oh, Blade!'"

Mel pumped her hips as she flipped a pancake. "Give me the blade, Blade!"

"It's a romance novel name for a very non-romance-novel fellow."

She turned around, spatula high in thought. "Blade definitely did not live up to his romance novel hero name. He was an aloof alpha male, but he never made the transition into loving duke husband. He stayed peacock-y. I mean, it seemed to work for you, but I never thought he treated you well enough, honestly. You forgave a lot of dick behavior as…something else."

I squeezed my eyes shut against the truth. "You mean I've let my boyfriend and my boss walk all over me."

She made a sad trombone noise but didn't answer. She didn't have to — it was true.

How was I such a moron? My whole twenty-eight years, I ignored the trees and lifted my chin toward the glorious paper forest. On paper, my life just a day ago had been perfect. Coveted position with the city's flashiest editor.

Gorgeous doctor boyfriend. And the self-will to concentrate only on the good, never the bad.

But now…

I found the wherewithal to fetch my laptop from the bedroom. The apartment was bathed in late morning glow. A light snow fell outside—the pretty kind. The kind that reminds of childhood and snow angels.

My dad had always made me shovel too. Never Vanessa, for she had delicate wrists.

At my bedroom window, I closed my eyes and embraced the quiet, punctuated only by the joyous smell of breakfast food. Glorious quiet. Blade had loved watching cable news, so a screaming pundit was usually our roommate. I wouldn't miss that one bit.

I hurried back into the kitchen and blurted, "I don't miss him. I-I'm not really sad. Shouldn't I be sad that he's moving across the country? Mostly…" I sat down and opened my computer. "Mostly I feel relief that I don't have to play girlfriend anymore. The messes will be mine, the space will be mine." I ran a hand over my dirty, makeupped face. "Until I'm forced to get a roommate, I suppose."

A plate of delicious placed itself magically in front of me. "That's not a great sign for your former relationship," saith my smart friend.

I shook my head. No. What had I been doing all this time? Checking off life bingo boxes instead of just…living. Bingo, bingo, bingo! If I checked off enough boxes, someone would finally love me!

I was this bizarre combination of rebelling against my family's wishes in pursuing a career in the arts, yet also conforming to the boyfriend they liked for approval. Because my father had adored Blade. A doctor, are you kidding? He could 'take care of me' if only I'd let him.

We gorged on breakfast as if calories didn't exist, because they didn't. Not during a hangover from booze and hard knocks, nope.

After the initial rush of so many pancakes I thought

I might barf, we crowded around my laptop screen. I let Mel do most of the work since she was the mastermind. She set up a blog for me, and a Twitter to match. At first, I didn't want to put my face on it, but she got me with the argument, "What do you have to lose?"

I had lost all the big stuff already.

So I posed with a dirty face, sunglasses, hair in a high, tangled ponytail and a middle finger in the foreground. It actually turned out amazing with the proper filter—I looked unrecognizable and pretty! Like a cokehead starlet. It gave me number six on my fuck-up list:

6. *Flip off the world*

We called the blog, naturally, '666 Ways to Fuck Up My Life', and explained the purpose in the inaugural post. I ended it with this:

It should be an idea familiar to any millennial reading — that all the hard work in the world hasn't meant shit. Student loans are impossible to pay off, even though everyone screamed "Go to college!" in an unceasing wail. There are no jobs, and the ones you do get are underpaid and underwhelming. My boss fired me for not screwing him, and there wasn't a damn thing I could do about it except to not give anyone power over me anymore.

If the low road is the true path, then I will crawl on it. I'm tired of trying. I'm tired of the fear of failure. I'm embracing failure. I'm going to fuck up, big time. And have a damn hell of a good time doing it. And now I'm done with writing this, so I'm going to day-drink with my best friend and watch Netflix. Arrested Development *seems a good choice.*

I'm going to Bluth this bitch.

I hit *Publish* and we clinked screwdrivers in celebration. We pushed the post to Twitter, and Mel jumped on hers to tell her followers to follow me. Whatever. I told Mel I didn't want to hear about social media strategy. I wasn't going to *try* for followers or readers.

I wasn't going to *try* for anything anymore.

My first day of terrifying, amazing free*dumb* flew by in a stupor. TV was hilarious. Leftover Chinese was delish. And the look on Blade's face when Mel deigned to let him in was priceless. I flipped him off, drunk as a skunk, and refused to leave while he gathered his stuff. I figured he'd rob me blind if I did. Guess he hadn't yet noticed that I'd wiped out the bank account.

He didn't take too much time in throwing his shit into suitcases. The lovely dear said he'd leave me all the furniture, which was nice, since seventy-five percent of it had been mine in the first place.

As he wheeled out the last of his stuff, Mel asked him where he was going to stay.

"I don't care!" I yelled from my new home, the couch.

Blade turned at the door and rolled his eyes. "I'm staying with Amy until I leave next week. Guess I don't have to hide her from you anymore."

Mel gasped.

I didn't gasp. I didn't care enough to gasp, really, except in that I hoped Amy was disease-free. Ugh, I'd have to get STD tested. I lumbered to my feet and went to the kitchen. At the back of the refrigerator sat his month-old container of miso soup. I'd asked him to throw it out for weeks. Good thing he'd kept it—I had a real use for it now.

I carried it into the living room and stood at the open door. In the hall, he turned amongst his suitcases and said, "Well, babe. We had some good times, huh?"

I smiled and nodded while brushing a lock of hair from his blue eyes. "Eat shit and die," I whispered lovingly as I poured moldy miso soup down his trousers.

He screamed and jumped backward, going ass-over-head across his enormous designer trunk. The soup wasn't quite finished, so I sprayed it on his bags.

Without another word, I yanked the house keys from his fist and slammed the door in his face, which gave me my next item:

7. Embrace my inner vindictiveness

"Oh, hell yes!" Mel jumped up and down, her phone pointed toward me. "I got all that on film!"

I yawned. "Do you want a coffee? I need a coffee if I'm drinking for two."

"Two?"

"Me and my failure."

"I'll get my coat."

* * * *

I hadn't brushed my hair in a day, still sported day-old Diorshow mascara, and fairly reeked of booze. For the first time in my life, I was the kind of woman SUV-stroller moms ushered their precious darlings away from.

It was *amazing*.

I imagined my sister clutching her double-strand pearls (a 'push' gift for nieceling number one), so I let loose with a string of language in line at the coffee shop that actually embarrassed Mel for half a second until she gave me a hug.

8. Do not think of the children

We got to the head of the line and I ordered a huge, caffeinated coffee full of enough caramel to kill a rhino. The insanely hot bro-ista, name tag *Hunter*, grinned at my double-extra-sugar ridiculousness with a side of donut. He had the widest, sunniest smile—like an advertisement for toothpaste at the beach—deep brown skin, and amber eyes. His dreadlocks were bleached blond and tied into a man bun on top of his head. He was a Benetton ad come to life.

"I like a girl that enjoys her treats," he said.

"*Who* enjoys her treats. And I don't care what you like," I replied.

He grinned even bigger at that.

I hadn't even considered the words before they had blustered themselves out of my mouth. But that was a huge part of the puzzle, right? How many of my achievements had been strictly for me, and how many for other people, so that they might approve of me? Part of fucking up my life

had to be not caring what other people wanted me to be…
But that was also a life *improvement,* was it not?

Wow, I was deep when Tuesday drunk.

I said to adorable Hunter, "If you dig it so much, buy it
for me."

His mouth dropped…but he reached into his pocket and
pulled out a wadded-up ten dollar bill. Behind me, Mel
said, "Well, shit, honey."

Well, shit, honey.

Maybe I'd been possessed by the spirit of Jazmine. Maybe
that wasn't such a bad thing. Maybe I just really wanted
to see what I could get away with. I was a cute girl, not
gorgeous, but with a good face I had no right to be angry
about. Dark brown hair, olive skin from my Greek heritage,
almost-black eyes. Dudes had a tendency to ask me "What
are you?" which might get them a slap from now on. Heh —
bro-ista Hunter probably got the same question.

Maybe it was about time to pursue more fun in the way I
looked. Doing my best to be a pretend WASP hadn't helped
me much.

I smiled at Hunter and stood there, as if accepting my
due, as if men bought me things all the time just because I
demanded them.

9. *Make them pay*

"Uh, I'm the manager here," said hot Hunter by way of
brag, and I knew what I had to do.

He was tall, he was buff, and he had to be an out-of-
work actor. I leaned over the counter, pushed out my ass,
unzipped the top of my sweater, and said, "Give me an
application."

He ran to the back while the other barista dude gaped.
I winked at him and sauntered away to await my (free)
coffee and donut.

Near the milk and sugar station, I started giggling, and
Mel came up behind me. "You're going to work in a coffee
shop?"

I shrugged. "I need money."

"But publishing."

"But nothing." I turned around. "I'm going to work in a coffee shop. And if I lose that job, do I care? You don't seem to be embracing the spirit of fucking up."

She flashed a wry smile. "Very well."

Hunter hurried up to us, all earnest eyes and shy smile. "Uh, here is the application. I'm in tomorrow from six a.m. to one p.m., if you want to bring it back then."

I grabbed the paper and let it flop to one side. "Yeah, morning doesn't really work for me. That's when I sleep it off."

"Oh! Okay, sure. On Thursday, I, uh, work close."

"When do you close?"

"Ten."

They called out my coffee, so I went to get it. He followed behind like a puppy. I'd never had a man slobber over me this way. It was as if the less I cared, the harder his boner grew. I took a sip of my confection and deigned to pay attention to my new toy. "I'll be in at ten on Thursday then. Probably. Where's my donut?"

"Uh..." He nodded and ran to fetch my first donut in a decade.

Mel folded in half laughing. "That's when I *sleep it off?*"

"What does he expect from a drunk girl applying to work? Geesh!" I licked foam off my lip. "Wait! That's number ten." I whipped out my phone and posted it to Twitter.

10. Apply for entry-level job while drunk

11. Also: Get free donut

Within three minutes, it had been retweeted fifteen times. I had seven hundred followers since this morning. Everyone loved a train wreck!

Instead of Netflix (which was a perfectly valid life choice), Mel and I decided to see a movie about sexy male strippers. We sneaked in a second lunch of McDonald's and had a grand old time mixing rum into our movie theater Cokes. My application for the coffee shop, JaVaVaVoom, got special sauce on it. Oops.

29

We took a late afternoon nap until about eight, then cleaned up to go out. Mel insisted that my life fuck-ups not include being too dirty. Personally, I thought there was a whole wide world of greasy hair to explore before I could truly say I didn't care... But then again, vanity was a wonderful sin. I was well and truly torn.

My goal for the evening was to bypass the line to get into a club, and then not pay for a single drink all night. I had worked my whole life to pay my own way — taken pride in it almost as a rebellion against my dad. Vanessa had never worked a day in her life. There was nothing wrong with being a Connecticut SAHM — she was terrifyingly good at it — but I'd yearned for so long to work with books in the big city...

But a fuck-up gets what she can whence she can, and no clean house in the bargain...unless I used the drink money I saved tonight to hire a cleaning helper. That would be excellently lazy and frivolous.

"A fuck-up doesn't use the word 'whence,'" replied Mel when I uttered this profundity.

If I wanted a free club experience, then I needed to look as hot as possible. Mel and I sat in my bedroom and tossed around my wardrobe. All black and blue and beige of it. Mel grimaced and said, "I guess I didn't realize how much of a Chico's kind of day you've been having. My mother has this cardigan."

I hung my head in shame.

"You need some sexy clothes, lady. And a push-up bra — these things are sad and industrial." She waved around a molded-cup beige number, a flag from the world's saddest country, Celibatopia. "I don't suppose you kept one of Blade's credit cards, did you?"

"No — I can do better." I rooted in my desk for my emergency credit card. The one that never had anything charged to it because I was a sensible girl who composed back-up plans for her back-up plans.

I spun around and held up my gold card. "This is the part

of our story wherein the heroine goes into irresponsible debt to have a makeover. Dagmar—from blah to *fuck, yah*."

Mel went for her purse. "We're going to Bebe. I'm putting you in something loud, tight, and awesomely trashy."

My heart started to beat a tattoo of happiness. "Can I wear leopard print? I've always dreamed of wearing leopard print."

Chapter Three

F*ck-Ups Twelve through Eighteen
Little White Lies Are Actually More Chartreuse Colored

I caught a glimpse of myself in a dirty window outside the hottest new club in Manhattan. It was called Mistake, and I knew it had opened just for me. Fabulous me. I tossed my hair, huge and frizzy. My brand new, too-expensive leopard-print dress slunk over my body in drapey waves that ended juuuust on the right side of 'arrested for solicitation.' My eyes shimmered dark and dangerous with glittery black eye shadow.

I felt like an impostor. An actress. I felt...sexy. I'd never been called 'sexy.' It had always been a word for other women, but now it was mine. I *owned* it. I clutched it to my nearly naked bosom like an expensive vase. And I didn't need anyone else to tell me. 'Sexy' sprang from a well inside me I hadn't known existed, and it existed for me alone.

"Who is this person?" Mel asked me, her arm snaking around my shoulders.

"Let's find out," I said, returning her hug. I took her hand and marched to the front of the line of well-dressed, attractive would-be club-goers to the bouncer at the front.

When I arrived, I took a deep breath and struck a hip-cocked, model pose in front of a huge guy in a black tee emblazoned with *Security*. His eyes widened when he shifted attention away from a group of bachelorettes to me. I executed a hair flip, and it totally rocked except for that one piece that dragged through my red lipstick. Whoops. I slid that hair from my pout and gritted down on my nervous belly flutter. It was time to act like every pretentious author I'd ever bowed and scraped to.

What would Khandye Kardashian do?

I stood in front of the enormous man and stared him down. He leaned in, waiting for me to say something, but I wouldn't. I was done with asking for favors. She who spoke last kept the power. This was a trick Carmichael used when negotiating—always let them talk first.

The bouncer asked, "Are you on the list?"

I shrugged and smiled. "Do I need to be? My friend and I are going to wait for my cousins inside. Have you read my blog? Or seen my TV show?" I snapped my fingers and Mel buried a smile while she turned her phone to show the bouncer Khandye Kardashian's website. In the dark, on a five-inch screen, if you squinted, I kinda looked like Khandye—gobs of makeup and huge, dark hair.

He blinked and his wide face burst into a smile. "I love those jar salads! I really try to watch my waistline—I'm an MMA fighter."

"Really?" I said. Hair flip. "That's so hot." Hair flip. The other way. "Could you trounce everyone in this line for me?"

"Huh?"

"Beat up."

His chest expanded like a puffer fish. "You bet, baby."

I simpered until he clicked the rope free and drew back the velvet for me. I sailed past, not looking to one side or the other, but straight ahead. The crowd parted, and I started giggling before I even got into the main room. Mel ran and bounced off my back, her laughter louder than the thumping music. "Holy crap, Dag! That was amazing!"

12. Don't you know who I am (pretending to be)?

"I'm shaking." I clutched my purse to my chest to try to hide it. I was a fakey mcfaker, but I felt fabulous, almost as if I were high. Maybe I was. Riding on a wave of pretention that made my legs weak and my breath flee.

Mel shook her head and laughed in my face. "Don't wimp

out on me now — get us some drinks, skank."

Skank. I'd come full circle with that sort of female insult. Dad had taught me that my entire worth lay in keeping my legs closed. Then, I'd grown up and learned that my value lay in my heart, in my work. Now? I knew I was lost. My cells fluttered out of control, as if my body might shake itself apart. I decided to lean into it. My value did not lay in my job title. It couldn't, because that sort of thing was fleeting and out of my control. And my body, well, having a little naughty fun didn't diminish my spirit, my soul. I'd judged women for that for a long time, and it was wrong. Experience lent a certain…something…to a woman. Why shouldn't I explore all that life had to offer?

In other words:

13. Embrace my inner skank

I marched right up to the bar and circled it until I found a victim. Two guys, pretty cute, sitting alone and looking overwhelmed. I nodded to Mel. She examined them and said, "Tech geeks."

"With money — look at those jeans. Let's go."

I came up behind them and took a deep breath…and slammed into the both of them at once. Naturally, they jumped to their feet and turned around, outraged. I put my hand over my mouth and said, "Oh, my God! I'm sooooo sorry!" My boobs in the *boing!* position, I took the one closest to me by the hand and gazed straight into his nerdy little eyes. "Can you ever forgive me? I'm…Giselle. This is Veronique. We just flew in from London and it's been a long day slash night. I'm desperate for a drink after serving first-class jerks at thirty thousand feet." I threw in a giggle so vacant it left a black hole.

Their eyes grew wide as *Veronique's* narrowed.

What? So I'd decided to be Giselle. It might sound nuts, but Dagmar wasn't the sexiest name ever given to a woman. I'd never understood how my twin had gotten alluring 'Vanessa' and I was named after a Greek parade float.

Also, what's wrong with pretending to be a flight

attendant? Flight attendants were fun, adventurous, globetrotting. Not unemployed losers having a quarter-life crisis in a dress they couldn't afford.

14. *The truth can be aspirational, which is a fancy word for bullshit*

Mel and I had free drinks in our hands in thirty seconds flat. The guys were fine, a little dull, average. But me... I was a shining star of sexual charisma. They couldn't take their eyes off me! And Mel came around to enjoying the perks of the mile-high club too — we told stories taller than the giant, dark, and handsome hunk who'd just given me a double-take on the way by. Baby, was he hot. But he disappeared into the crowd as I polished off my free drink. Oh, well. Plenty more where he came from.

"Ted, Tanner — you two are the best. You're better than a layover in Cincinnati!" I informed them. They appeared to be confused as to what this, exactly, meant. "I have to visit the powder room, and Veronique is coming with me. But we'll be right back."

As soon as we were out of earshot, I said, "We won't be right back. We can do better than the ant-farm enthusiast."

Mel followed me to the bathroom. "But I'm just *dying* to hear about their new app that rates women on a scale from one to go fuck yourself, dickbag."

We cackled — cackling was quickly becoming my new favorite way to laugh — and peed away the free liquor. After we primped and I applied enough red war paint to terrify a charging elephant, we decided to dance.

And we did. We *danced*. Like I'd never, ever danced before. A little drunken, a lot abandon. I jumped and twirled and shook my ass and got sweaty enough that I'd never be able to return this dress. Who knew (who cared?) how much time had passed when we finally dragged ourselves away from the teeming mass of bodies trying to forget their workaday lives.

"I'm a little jealous of the fun you're having," said a British accent from beside me. And I knew who it came from before I turned. Or maybe it was wishful thinking. Magical thinking, for giant, dark, and handsome from earlier stood appraising me with mischievous brown eyes. My breath caught in the fairy tale that shone therein.

"Then have it with me," I returned, a little breathy, and also a little amazed that I'd managed such a great line. If one of my nonfic authors had written that, I'd have rolled my eyes.

A smile twitched around his mouth—full, luscious— while his eyes narrowed into slivers—crinkly, adorable— the bigger the grin got. My whole body wanted to melt into the sticky floor, but, if I let it, I wouldn't be able to kiss him as quickly as possible.

He shook his head. "I'm really not much of a dancer."

"Of course you are!" I insisted. I took his enormous hand in mine and began to tug.

He stood firm, like granite, like hunk, like the muscles I fancied I could see throbbing through his thigh-hugging jeans and army-green button-down. Woo, I got a little lightheaded just imagining this six-foot slab of granite in my bed.

I hadn't ever felt such an animal—

A random dance-floor elbow landed in my ribcage, nearly knocking me from vertical to splat. How long had I been standing there swaying and drooling? "Uh," I stated, elegantly, while dropping his hand by accident. "Okay, how about a drink?"

He chuckled. "Are you offering or demanding?"

15. *Demand*

I slapped my hands on my hips and just stood there to dare him, capital D. With a hair flip for extra -are.

"All right, dancing queen. Come with me and pick your poison." This time he took my hand, taking his time with the taking. He slid his fingers light as a feather down my arm until he wrapped my tiny palm in his. I shivered from my toes to my hair and followed him like a puppy.

Mel shrugged and gave me a wave before leaping once

again into the boogying fray. Hopefully she wasn't too put out with me. Fucking up one's life probably meant not caring about that, but I refused to screw over my best lady for a dude. *Any* dude.

16. Remember who loves you. Forgetting that would be the real fuck-up

Once at the bar, my gorgeous companion commanded attention, and he placed a chilled martini in my hand before too long. It had been enjoyable admiring his butt while he waited for the drinks. Perky, round — very round — and I was still entertaining thoughts of eating bonbons off the glorious orbs when he said, "I'm Yash. Yash Majumdar."

Yash Majumdar... Why did that name ring a bell? "Giselle," I blurted. "Kostopoulos." For a terrifying breath, I wondered if I'd well and truly fucked up by not giving my real name to this amazing specimen with the familiar-for-some-reason name, but then I took a long pull of vodka and shushed my brain. No, no. I didn't want a boyfriend, anyway. Boyfriends like Blade are often simultaneous boyfriends with some girl named Amy, so to hell with the lot of them.

One-night stands, however...

"What brings you out tonight, Yash?" I yelled over the music once we'd found a dark corner to become too close in.

His long body draped itself against the wall covered in chipped gold paint. "My friend got a book deal today, so he decided that rip-roaring drunk was the way to celebrate."

OMG that British accent. Just James Bond-age me now, please. "Rip-roaring is a very writerly way to be."

"And why are *you* dancing on a Tuesday?"

Because I had nothing to lose? "Why not? We got in today from..." Oh, boy — I couldn't say anywhere in the UK because I'd never been to the UK, and he obviously had. "L.A. I'm a flight attendant. Getting out of California is always a reason to celebrate."

That earned me another low and lazy chuckle, and my

panties embroidered themselves with his name. "I'm not much for La La Land, myself. I've been there for business meetings, but was always happy to return to skyscrapers and dirt."

"What business are you in?"

"I'm a writer, like my friend."

OooooooOOOOoooOOOooohhhhhhhh. My eyes went wide. *That* was why I knew his name! Of course! I filtered through the memory files in my booze-soaked brain. Yash Majumdar. The British-Indian It Boy *du jour* a year ago when he debuted on the *NYT* bestseller list with his heartfelt, funny, gorgeously written apocalyptic satire.

I should turn around. I should turn around and flee because we probably have a hundred friends in common. 'We' as in Dagmar and Yash, not Giselle.

But he had lips carved by Satan himself.

17. Be sure to put the 'fuck' in 'fucking up'

"What do you write?" I asked, swallowing the lie, diving into the rabbit hole.

He shrugged and morphed his face into such an adorable bashfulness that I nearly leaped onto him. "I write novels. Working on my second one now — terrified of it, actually. Sophomore flop and all that."

Now I'd met many, many in the publishing industry so far up their own backsides, I doubted they could hear anything but their own digestive tracts. The fact that he hadn't immediately told me about his second printing, five-star reviews, and movie deal set my skirt ablaze. "I bet it'll be amazing," I told him in complete truthfulness. "I mean, if you wrote one, you can write another. You already know the potential is inside you — it's been proven."

I shot him a smile that he returned. I imagined those wide, parted lips murmuring over every inch of my body, and I had to have him. Had to. Like a salmon has to swim upstream —

Straight into the paws of a hungry bear.

"Your place or mine?" I asked. "I mean — how about

yours? I have the worst roommate." Crap crap crap, he couldn't come to my place. Not with piles of mail and such with the name *Dagmar* on them. The framed party photo of me and J.K. Rowling also might raise an eyebrow.

His shoulders fell. "I'm afraid I... I shouldn't tonight. I have an early meeting with my editor tomorrow and"—he took a step closer, the heat from him singeing my hair—"and I enjoy having more than three minutes of conversation before I show you my ass. So to speak." He fished in his pocket, never breaking eye contact, and passed me a card. "Please call. I'd love to take you out to a proper dinner." With that, he took my hand and kissed it.

He. Kissed. It.

The motion didn't feel like a put-on, and he flashed a dorky smile right after, as if he couldn't believe he'd just done that either. "I promise I'm cooler than that," he clarified before he turned around.

A few paces away, he swiveled to face me again. "Actually—no, I'm not."

I broke into a hearty laugh. "Good. Cool people are so boring." Blade had been the coolest of the cool.

With that adorkableness, Yash was gone.

A wave of sadness jittered my muscles and sank into my stomach. I was already bereft without him.

Something pushed me from behind and Mel's voice filled my ear. "Holy crap. That was—"

"Yash Majumdar."

"Is that his number?"

I clutched the sacred card to my too-exposed bosom. "Yes."

She squeed and danced her way around to my front. "Woo-hoo! Blade who?"

"Giselle."

"What?"

I face-palmed with his card. "He thinks I'm a flight attendant named Giselle!"

She pulled a horrid look then she corrected it like the

amazing girlfriend she was. "Well—then be a flight attendant named Giselle. And climb that man like a tree."

Okay. Okay. So what if he was, without question, the hottest, most charming and talented man I'd ever met. A tall, hot pile of dress-immolating *hummina hummina hummina*. A one-night stand would be sufficient. For sure. I definitely had not just made a huge, irrevocable, Giselle-sized mistake. Nope. Noooooope.

18. Massive lies always turn out well!

Chapter Four

F*ck-Ups Nineteen through Thirty-Four
Plastic Clothing Is Not for Amateurs

Two nights later, I click-clacked in skyscraper heels to JaVaVaVoom to slide my application to Hunter the broista. Never in a million years would I have guessed I'd be wearing a black pleather dress to try to acquire a new job. The new job, however, wasn't the only thing I hoped to *get* tonight.

Heh heh.

I meant his penis.

Hunter wasn't the man warming my thoughts on the way there, though. Yash and I had a date for the following night. We'd spent a wicked two days flirting via text. Oh, but he was even smarter and funnier than I'd previously glimpsed, more direct, and my imagination had been covered in unicorn stickers and doodled hearts.

And my engine had been revving at eleven for *days* now. Lucky, lucky Hunter, who would be the first to reap the rewards.

19. Bang two men in the same week

Nervous flutters flitted through my tacky dress. I'd only been with two men ever. Hopefully, I was good at this sex thing.

I pushed through the door to the coffee shop at nine-fifty-eight p.m. Hunter and I locked eyes immediately and he dropped a stack of paper cups. "H-hi!" he stuttered. "You came back!" Tonight his dreads flowed to his shoulders, like a sexy, surfing pirate.

"Yes, Hunter. I've come for you."

Heh heh.

I meant his penis.

"Are you all alone here?" I asked as I made my way to him.

A heavy sigh wafted from behind the counter, and a young, redheaded woman stood just to flash me the stink eye. "He's about to be." She rolled her peepers and I panged with sudden sympathy for Jazmine. This lady looked at me as if I were the whore of Sodom. "You can finish closing, dude," she told Hunter. "If you get around to it."

20. Do not let nay-sayers harsh your slut

No matter! She was entitled to her opinion. And I did resemble the whore of Sodom. Black eye shadow, black stockings ending in a garter, and the pretend strut of a woman who had not bedded a guy named 'Blayde.'

Better go for it. My pelvis was overheating, and Hunter would put me out with his hose.

(Yes, that's what I meant.)

I jumped onto the customer side of the counter and crossed my legs. My application dangled from my fingertips, painted scarlet.

21. Red nail polish makes the happy Sodom whore

Hunter finally stopped cleaning up his scattered cups and ran his palms down his black apron. "What was your name again?"

"Dagmar. But my close friends call me Dag."

"Gr-great. Why don't we meet in the back, Dagmar — "

"Dag."

"And I'll look over your résumé and…and…"

I giggled. "And my *qualifications*." I jumped off the counter and onto my heels (*ouch*). Hello, future shin splints. He led me into the tiny back office, large enough only for a wee desk, three chairs, and an ancient copier.

He sat behind the desk. I sat in front, hands on my crossed knees — prim, proper, pleather-y. His chest rose and fell in double time while he read my résumé — I don't think it was my internship at Random Penguin that caused his erratic breath.

"Well, Dagm—Dag," he began, trying in vain not to gawk at my tits. "I see you've been in publishing. Why... Why do you want to work at JaVaVaVoom?"

"I suspect that you didn't go to school to study coffee?"

His eyebrows rose. "I have an MFA in acting from Carnegie Mellon."

"Yup."

He flashed an adorable smile and unbent enough to lean back in the office chair, which appeared to be covered in my dress's cousin. "Okay, I get it. But I don't want to train someone just to have them quit a month from now."

"Look." I stood, already regretting these five-inch heels. Ugh, who the hell dressed this way all the time? Carrie Bradshaw was a lie. "I got canned from my dream job so my boss could promote his girlfriend. And I'm done. Done. So now I'm here. I want a job I can master and actually be rewarded in for performing adequately." His eyes followed my strut around the desk. "When I make a flavorful coffee or give correct change, will I be appreciated by you, Hunter?"

His eyes widened to capacity and he nodded.

"Excellent."

Now or never, Dag.

22. *Only the good die young*

I fell over him, my hands grasping the chair's arms. This put my cleavage just under his chin. Hunter the manager's mouth dropped. "Do you want to know why I chose this coffee shop to grace with my" —I dropped my gaze to his crotch—"skills?"

He squeaked.

My hand shaking (*Stop it! We're a saucy minx now!*), I grabbed the back of his head by the hair and planted a whopper of a kiss on him. He squeaked again, which I took to be positive, I guess? I came up for air and plopped one knee to the right of his. I balanced on it to bring my other knee up...u—gah the hem of this skirt was too tight, and my pleather didn't have a lot of give. Maybe I should have gone for latex?

I could be my own condom.

I gave up trying to straddle him and twisted to sit across his lap before pulling him in for another kiss. Mmm, nice. He smelled good, like clean soap. Normal soap, not like the fancy Sephora stuff Blade had used.

Hunter opened his mouth to me and tentatively kissed back confidently enough to quicken my blood. Not bad. Not bad at all! But his arms stayed rigid at his sides, and I started to wonder if I'd have to do the bulk of the work... or if he was actually gay, and my sexual harassment was worse than I thought? Or —

I crashed, hard, onto my butt — *blam!* "What the hell?" I squealed. He'd stood and, in my slippery dress made of recycled tires, I'd gone down — and not in the way I'd imagined.

"Uh... I'm sorry." He reached to me and I wiped the annoyed grimace off my face, lest my booty call flop.

He pulled me upward, but I couldn't get my spike heels underneath me. I buckled, a drunken giraffe, and we started to fall, almost in slow motion. I flailed. He flailed. We flailed! I flapped my loose hand for the desk as he yanked my other arm. We tipped backward and *timberrrrrrrr!*-ed. A rolling file cabinet, three cardboard boxes, and the ancient copier all went flying as we flopped across them.

Ow, pain, strain, ick, poke, *ouch!* What was digging into my butt? Breaths heavy — not in the way I'd imagined — I reached around — not in the way I'd imagined — to remove the copier plug from my unmentionables.

Hunter groaned and yanked a stapler from his... somewhere. He tossed it behind him with a half-smile, which I returned.

Okay. We could recover from this — Dagmar Kostopoulos was not a quitter. My skirt already bunched around my waist, and we were on the floor...half of my seduction had been accidentally accomplished!

Sexy, like a cougar—well, maybe a young librarian cougar—I crawled the two feet to his prostrate body. He held up his hands, and I gleefully grabbed them and pressed them to my pleather breasts. "Yes, Hunter!" I gasped. "Show me how you make my latte foam."

"Do what?"

"You're going to churn my foam, baby."

"That's not how foam works. Have you ever, uh, made a cappuccino before?"

Wow, romance was a difficult genre. These scenes were freaking hard to write. And I obviously didn't know how to make coffee.

Okay, so my words were terrible—*actions* would save this. I shoved him backward to the floor, the better to take advantage of him without further injury.

Ack! He bounced off the copier with a sick thud and groaned, his hand flying to the back of his head. "Dagmar, stop, please!"

"I, uh—" Oh, no. I hadn't been getting sexy with him... I was pretty sure this qualified as assault. "We got off on the wrong foot. This office is much too small for—"

"For what?" He crawled backward and stood. "We can't do this. It's against the coffee code. I want to hire you, so I can't sleep with you. If—if that's what you were trying...?"

23. If they have to ask if you're trying to hump them, you're fucking up

No. No no no! "Hunter," I purred in the best (and only) purr of my life. "Hunter, cutie. I'm not your employee yet. Let's just have a little fun." I took one step forward, he took two back. Jesus, what did a girl have to do to get some sleazy sex?

24. Sluttery should be easier than this!

He put his hands up again and I realized he wasn't trying to grope my boobs. If I wanted my boobs groped tonight, I'd have to do it myself.

25. Sigh

My shoulders slumped and tears chased into my eyes.

Tears! Over this guy I didn't even know. I gritted my teeth to keep a week's worth of emotions at bay. "I'm sorry," I told him, most sincerely. "I've really fucked this up, in the bad way."

Without more useless words, I turned and left the office, my head held high, my giraffe gait infused with dignity and grace. Well, after I pulled my plastic skirt over my thong.

"Dag!" He caught up with me in the middle of the dark, empty coffee shop. "Uh… You're hired, okay? You didn't have to do all that—"

"I *wanted* to do that." His eyes nearly bugged out. It seemed to be a common occurrence for him. "You're cute, and I'm feeling…"

26. Depressed

27. Irrelevant

28. Pathetic

29. Uncomfortably sweaty between the cheeks

30. Unlovable

"Adventurous," I lied.

Ick. I didn't want to hear any more from any man at the moment, even though it wasn't fair, as I had been the one who'd committed—

31. Semi-accidental sexual harassment

At the door, I turned and asked, "When do I start, boss?" That had sounded entirely too overachieving, so I added, "I'm not doing any five a.m. shit."

He grinned. "You can close with me day after tomorrow. Come in at four *p.m.*"

I nodded. "Hey, Hunter?"

"Yeah?"

"Coffee code?"

His hooded eyes alit. "I'll tell you all about it! Uh, see, one must always strive for the perfect cup. And designs in the foam—well, that's pretty advanced, we probably won't tackle that on the first day, and—"

With a faux-interested smile, I backed out of the door. This job already seemed eighty percent more jobby than

I'd intended, and ninety percent less naked. How was being a floozy so difficult? Jazmine made easy look so easy. Obviously I needed to give that lady more credit. She had skills I didn't understand, like a Jedi in Spandex.

I started the chilly walk toward home. Without a coat. In five-inch heels.

To hell with this—I'd gotten a job today! My perky nips and I hailed a cab. Two nearly got in an accident pulling over. At least I'd impressed someone tonight.

Perhaps I'd leaped to non-breathable fabric too quickly. It would take a week to peel myself out of this thing as it was. Or maybe I wasn't as sexy as I'd hoped.

32. Depressing realities must be avoided at all costs

I messaged Yash at the world's longest red light.

Me: I'm not wearing pleather on our date. Don't ask me why.

I spent the remainder of the trip home giggling to myself. This evening had been the worst night on my back since the time Blade had taken magic mushrooms and kept trying to 'oops' me into anal sex.

Why did men try this without an okay first? A girl notices.

A. Girl. Most. Definitely. Notices.

I got home, removed my dress using butter and pain, and settled into a hot bath with a giant glass of Syrah. I'd just begun an episode of *Miss Fisher's Murder Mysteries* on my tablet when my phone chirped.

Leaning way out of the water (no dunking expensive electronics), I peered to see who dared interrupt the fierce Miss Fisher. Yash!

Yash: I will ask. And you will answer.

I nearly snarfed my wine. Oh, boy. Oh, handsome boy. Oh, handsome, clever boy. My head swirled, and not with the Syrah.

Me: You and what army?

Yash: Dumbledore's.

Aaaaaagh no, not a Harry Potter reference! Get inside my knickers, oh, handsome, clever, British geek boy.

Me: Who?

I waited a solid thirty seconds before adding:

Me: Kidding. Did you just consider canceling our date?
Yash: Yes. I got queasy. HP is a deal breaker. What house are you?
Me: I'm a Ravenclaw…but lately feeling naughty, like a Slytherin.
Yash: Interesting. You'll tell me why tomorrow.
Me: Never!
Yash: I'm a Ravenclaw, too. But I will Slytherin your ass to make you spill your secrets.

He'd what?

Yash: …I mean.
Me: You're very confident about this date, aren't you?
Yash: Apparently.
Me: I'm in the bath, and it's getting cold, so I will sign off for the evening. Before you threaten to do any further damage to my ass.
Yash: I was going to threaten your boobs as well, but I suppose that can wait until tomorrow. Sleep well, lovely Giselle.

Giselle. Ick. For a few, perfect minutes, I'd forgotten.
33. Fuck up by forgetting one's own fuck-ups

Me: Sleep well, lovely Yash.
Yash: Stop it, I'm blushing.

I set down the phone and sank into my water once again, my brain a-whir.

One night. One-night stand. I could definitely say goodbye before any and all doom set in.

Maybe we'd have a boring date. After all, *I* was boring *ha ha ha ugh*.

Maybe he'd be lousy in the sack.

Or maybe J.K. Rowling would give me ten million dollars, I'd grow six inches overnight, and also hell would freeze into a rainbow sno-cone.

34. Maybe…not

Chapter Five

F*ck-Ups Thirty-Five through Ninety-Two
Sin Should Not Require Such Effort

While I assured my brain that tonight's date with Yash meant nothing, my stomach had other ideas. As I stood outside the restaurant, the rebellious organ flipped and thrashed and sang *Going to the Chapel* to me. How did it even know those lyrics? Maybe it was caused by the shot Mel had insisted I take, or the fact that I froze in yet another ridiculous dress. No pleather for me tonight, though—just curve-hugging red. I was a human race car.

I'd decided to keep almost all the details about myself the same as for Giselle. Background, childhood, etc. Except Giselle hadn't gone to college, but had joined the friendly skies right out of high school. I didn't know anything about any other college major besides English, so no degree was better than getting a third degree I couldn't hack.

35. This was madness

36. But a true fuck-up embraces the madness

37. So what if the date goes horribly awry?

38. I'll just blog about it

39. Get a book deal

40. Rub it in Carmichael's face

41. Profit!

Yes, really, going through the thousand lies I'd have to tell tonight would lead directly to a slot on the *NYT* list. Right.

I turned around to run away.

And ran smack into Yash.

Smack! He stumbled backward and nearly fell but for the hand I caught at the last minute. Whoa, Nellie, he was a big boy. He filled out a soft wool burgundy jacket, and his chest strained under a crisp white button-down open at the neck.

He righted himself and grinned sheepishly. "Running away?"

42. Might as well start lying

"Of course not. Just pacing to keep warm." I wore a white wool princess coat, but had more inches of skin exposed than a Kardashian. And I meant that in a good way.

He took my elbow in a commanding manner and walked me inside. Despite the reservation he'd made, we were asked to wait in the bar for ten or so. This time, his hand lingered around my waist as he ushered me through a throng of well-dressed New Yorkers.

He lit me up like a Christmas tree. Ah, to heck with dinner.

43. Let's get naked on the bar top and have people cheer us while throwing gin across our writhing bodies

Yash stepped ahead of me to grab a just-vacated stool. He held my hand as I slipped onto it and guaranteed himself a BJ for not making me stand in yet another pair of new, stupid-in-the-extreme shoes.

"Thank you," I breathed in my most sultry voice.

"Of course. What would you like to drink?"

44. Blow job blow job blow job

The idea was so naughty, I grabbed the bar and nearly dropped my clutch. His sweet brown eyes rendered my knees jelly, and I couldn't suck in enough oxygen to keep my brain afloat above all the hormones. I licked my lips, his eyes following my tongue, the wonderful man. "Champagne," I replied.

45. More drunk = more better for telling lies

He dutifully obtained alcohol and stood beside me, suddenly silent, a glass of wine in his hand. I clapped my whore mouth closed because I didn't want to blow it before I blew him. Also, before he could reciprocate, because come on.

"Did you have a flight today?" he asked.

Uh, sure. "Yes. Got in from Honolulu this morning." I'd actually been there about ten years ago.

"Fantastic. Is that usual, for flight crews to be changing routes?"

46. Uh…

I took a swig of champagne. Why why why hadn't I studied the lifestyle blog of a flight attendant? Instead, I'd:

47. Shopped for a dress I couldn't afford

48. Ditto shoes

49. And dove-gray panties and a bra that made my credit card sweat

50. But that would inspire poets to verse

51. (At least a dirty limerick)

"My job is pretty boring," I said. "I want to hear about being a writer. I Googled you."

His eyebrows lifted. "And without my consent, naughty girl."

I shrugged a shoulder adorably. "Your book is very popular."

"I got lucky."

Well, yes. Plenty of amazing writers never got read, and tons of terrible books made it to the top of the charts (like mine, I hoped!). But he was actually… "Luck usually follows some sort of talent."

52. Some of the time, anyway

"You're very kind," he replied.

"So should I read it?" I asked.

"My book?"

I smirked. "No, my date tomorrow night's book."

He flashed me a half grin. That's how his mouth moved — one half made a break for it, and the other followed along or not, as was its wont. "Who is tomorrow night's date?"

"Salman Rushdie, no big deal."

Laughing, he said, "You're about the right age for him."

I leaned closer —

53. The better to insert my tits under his gaze

— And asked, "Is that your plan? Date me until you turn forty, and then exchange me for a younger model?"

"I have to wait until forty?"

I smacked him on the arm before remembering that I had no plans to date him. Just to have him drape his various manly attributes upon me until I couldn't remember my own name. Or until I could.

54. Who am I?

55. Who is anyone?

56. I'm very deep

I slurped more of my drink. Mmmmmm, I could swear that actual courage floated in those tiny bubbles. "Forty in man years is one hundred and seventy-seven in lady years."

"It's quite sad for you."

Nodding, I said, "At least we outlive you bastards. I plan to join a *Golden Girls*-like commune."

The hostess came by then and told us our table was ready. Well, she told Yash. I could have been a pile of non-existence, but who could blame her? He'd become the only real thing in the room to me too. All rays of candlelight simultaneously led to and from his body, his beautiful brown skin, his shining eyes.

57. His magnificent butt

I called his butt a mistake because it would surely lead to...

We settled at a table toward the front of the dining room, next to a brick wall, a view of the street beside us. I concentrated on the Asian fusion menu before me, feeling nervous as hell. Obviously, I needed more champagne-bubble courage. I ordered another. I couldn't be so drunk that I didn't remember the sexing, though. He couldn't be Giselle's boyfriend, so I had to remember the nookie at all costs.

58. Too drunk to remember was not a mistake I was willing to make

Oh, this man looked at me like... Wow. He couldn't take his eyes off my cleavage. Although, *swoon*, he desperately tried to fight and/or hide it.

My breasts had never been lusted after in such a blatant manner. They perked under the attention. I'd never thought of the girls as fabulous but, looking down now, they amazed even me.

Damn, Dag.

After we both tore ourselves away from my assets, we decided which dishes to order family-style. I discovered Yash was a vegetarian. He explained he wasn't a terribly devout Hindu, but he'd grown up in a vegetarian household and really enjoyed it.

The food ordered, Yash asked me the question dreaded by all faithless liars. "Tell me about yourself."

"Not much to tell, really. I love traveling."

He set his manly chin on his manly hand and I imagined both in a very filthy circumstance. "How many countries have you been to?" asked he and his manly chin.

59. Boy, lying sure does take a lot of preparation

"Uh…twenty-thr—twenty?"

Yash blinked. "Are you asking me?"

I laughed merrily, and also covering-ly. "Of course not!"

60. Is twenty too many or too few?

"About twenty," I say.

"Which was your favorite?"

My heart began beating a wild tattoo—not of passion, but of flop-sweated panic. Dagmar had visited Canada, eh, and Greece with her dad and sister when she'd been twelve. Dad and Vanessa actually visited every other year or so, but I'd only been invited on one trip—when our overseas family had finally asked about me.

"Greece," I tell him. "My family's homeland. Well, several generations ago. Just gorgeous. I love the Aegean and the slow pace there."

"I'd love to visit."

He licked his lips and began to open them and, lest he ask me another question, I jumped right in. "Where are you from?"

A pause, then, "I was born in a slum call center in Bombay, where all Indian people come from."

I blinked. "I thought...the UK? Is that your accent?"

His shoulders fell. "Yes. Sorry—usually 'where are you from' is assuming I'm from India."

"What good English you speak!" I grinned, but he didn't return it. "That was a joke. Most of England speaks English."

"It's true." That slow smile spread from one corner of his luscious mouth to the other. "I am very articulate for an English brown person."

"And I obviously tell good jokes *for a woman*."

He chuckled and murmured, "All that and jokes too," and I fell further into my lust hole.

61. The lust hole is connected to the

62. Lady boner

"What other countries have you visited?" Yash asked.

Note to Dagmar—next time you pretend to be Giselle, say you're an accountant.

I cleared my throat. I sipped champagne. I searched in vain for the waiter to save me, but he didn't. His tip would suffer because of his lack of psychic ability.

"Let's see," I began, slowly. Very slowly. Countries I could fib about...

63. "Iceland"

"Really?" he exclaimed. "I adore Iceland! I've been backpacking or skiing there half a dozen times."

64. "Egypt"

I nearly screamed it because I didn't know anything about Iceland, except that they must have ice. Otherwise, what did they ski on?

His eyebrows raised. "My parents took me to Egypt after I graduated high school."

Oh, for the love of—

65. Why had I chosen to lie to a rich guy with a passport?

I smiled and nodded, determined to push ahead. Perhaps if I kept babbling, the sheer volume of countries would confound him.

66. *"Lapland*
67. *"Indonesia*
68. *"Jamaica*
69. *"Westeros"*

He set aside his wine and quirked his head. "Westeros?"

Oh, shit—that was from *Game of Thrones*. "Just—just wanted to see if you were paying attention."

"Westeros seems a quite dangerous place. I don't want to travel there, especially not for a destination wedding." Yowza—book nerds were the best! "I would love to visit Jamaica, though," he said.

70. *Victory!*

"Oh, it's marvelous! The beaches, the people. The...food. The jerks!"

His face slipped into confusion once again. If I didn't lie more believably, it would freeze that way.

I ran sweaty hands down my skirt. "Jerk is the spice they put on food there. It was another very successful joke made by me."

"Perhaps I'm not a very talented joke-hearer."

"Yes, let's blame you." Almost in slow motion, his mouth began to morph into what I knew was another question. No. I couldn't discuss boogie boarding in Sri Lanka. No more questions! "Tell me about your family," I demanded.

71. *Let him lie for a change*

"Wait," I said. "Hold that thought, my good man. I'm going to dash lickety-split to the powder, see?" Ugh, why was I not talking like myself? The entire night had turned into a 1930s comedy of manners. Which meant I'd end up dunked in a fountain or arrested by the coppers.

Without waiting for a response, I bolted. Once safely ensconced in an overly perfumed bathroom stall, I whipped out my phone.

72. *When telling copious lies, write them down for future reference*

I typed in Iceland...Wester—no, Jamaica... I sank onto the toilet lid, so overwhelmed by my own faithlessness that I didn't even ponder the germs. I had to stop telling lies, or else I'd never get the D! Why was his so freaking complicated?

I texted Mel.

Me: Help! I'm drowning in Giselle's bullshit backstory.

Mel: Stop talking. Men only want to talk about themselves, anyway. What is your problem?

Me: Not this one. This one is concerned about me and my feelings and history, damn him.

Mel: Oh, that's awful. What an asshole. What can I do?

Me: Nothing. I just have to stay on this date long enough to get his clothes off.

Mel: Now you're thinking like a man. Smile and nod. Ask him questions. And when in doubt, compliment his muscles.

Me: Okay, thanks.

Mel: Good luck getting boned. I hope he stops being concerned with you as a person.

Aw, she always knew what to say.

Okay. I could do this.

73. Smile and nod

74. Ask him questions

75. When in doubt, compliment his muscles

I glanced at the time on my phone—ugh… How long had I been in this bathroom? Shit, shit, shit.

76. He would think I was taking a shit, shit, shit

I hurried to rejoin him at the table. His eyebrows knit together, even as he smiled at me. "Sorry," I said. "Lipstick is so hard to apply."

There was that look again…

"So!" I said while smiling and nodding. "Do you work out? 'Cause…muscles."

He lit up. "Oh, thank you. Have you—"

"Tell me about your next book!" No author could resist that statement, no matter how polite and giving they were on an emotional level. It was like asking my sister, "So, how

57

are the kids doing?" It always bought me twenty minutes to mute the phone and not have to reply.

"It's a comedy about using time travel to prevent a hate crime."

Yes! It worked. He waxed poetic about his inspiration, main characters, themes and the plot points he considered particularly brilliant. Not that he put it that way, but an editor knows. It made me feel squishy and glowy inside, actually. That he desperately wanted to impress me with his book, even though he thought I hadn't read the first one.

By the time the delicious-smelling dishes started coming, we'd settled into a more comfortable rhythm of talking without any more background quizzes. My stomach unknit itself and came out of hiding from behind my spleen. Good thing, because I was stuffing that sucker.

I used to care about eating daintily on a date. Blade would shame me if I really went to town on a lasagna the way it deserved.

Damn. I really had put up with a lot of unacceptable crap from that guy.

Yash paused a bite of spicy green beans halfway to his mouth to ask, "What's wrong? Have I upset you?"

I broke into the widest smile. "No! No, of course not. I—" It was okay to tell this truth. I took a deep breath and released it. "I'd just been thinking about my ex. Not in a good way. Actually, I'd been contrasting him with you. That's probably weird."

He shook his head. "As long as I'm coming out on top?" He slid a bowl of basil tofu linguine toward me.

I scooped some onto my plate, the fresh basil delighting my nose and wetting my mouth. "For sure you're on top."

77. *I would be on top later*

78. *And so would he*

"Want to talk about it?" he asked.

No. This was becoming such a real date. Such a real, excellent date. "Your pants are amazing. Where did you get those?"

"Banana Republic, I think." His face softened into lines of gorgeous earnestness, and he leaned forward to take my hand. "Okay, I see, it's all right. Breakups can be so painful. You don't have to be afraid of showing emotions to me. I want the real you, Giselle."

Smile and nod. Smile and nod. Don't cry and shake your head, that's the opposite. "That's really great to hear, Yash. I want to show you the real...me."

79. As long as I didn't have to discuss Iceland

We joked and flirted and smiled the rest of the meal while I ate my weight in various pastas and rice. But even my tofu burps and lies couldn't sour my anticipation for the next part of the date.

80. Sex sex sex sex sex sex sex sex sex sex sex sex sex sex sex sex sex sex

I offered to pay for half, but he passed over his credit card.

"You don't have to pay," I assured him. "You're definitely getting lucky." It went against every instinct to say this to him. My whole life, my father had bludgeoned into my head that forward women would never get a decent man.

81. To hell with that

82. I'd go so far forward, my reverse would break

"Really?" He leaned back in his chair and hit me with a panty-melting stare.

83. They were long gone, anyway

"Are you sure we should?" he asked, dead serious but for the flicker of the right side of his mouth. "Are you only here to take advantage of me?"

"Yes. I'm sorry, were you under the impression that I cared about your hopes and dreams?"

He laughed and guilt sliced from my heart to my gut. He was on a real date with me. He didn't know I lived a horrifying lie.

I should stop this. Yash was innocent. And hot. Hot and innocent and hot. He didn't deserve a lying Jezebel—

84. OMG I was a lying Jezebel

85. Way to go, Dag!

A Jezebel who would rip out his heart and stomp upon it with her ridiculous, sexy shoes.

He signed the credit card slip and held out his hand to me. I took it. Oh, God — his hot and innocent and hot hand squeezed mine with just the right pressure. I felt it in my feet, and in various places between. I meant to say no, to leave — I did — but I followed him to the sidewalk.

Once outside, he bit his lip and stared down the street, lost in thought. Now was the moment for me to do the right thing and leave. Now. Now that his butt was facing me in a very confrontational manner.

He turned around to me, chuckling when he caught me staring at his backside. "Listen," he began. Welp. Guess I'd be dumped before I even got to Jezebel all over him. "Giselle, I like you. A lot. You're fun and beautiful — did I tell you how gorgeous you are tonight?"

Beautiful? *Me?* I was the dark twin. Only the fair twin ever had ever been called 'beautiful.'

He continued, "I want to wait. I find you to be…a little odd. And funny, and…mysterious. I don't want this to just be physical."

I took a step toward him and said seventy-five percent truthfully, "I don't feel any shame in being physical."

"I didn't say that you should."

One more step. I was closing in on him now. "Will you respect me less in the morning?"

"Of course not."

I stood on tiptoe and reached to pull on the lapels of his jacket. "Then what's the problem?"

His marvelous eyes went limpid, his lashes fluttering. I was wearing him down.

86. *With my oddness*
87. *With my mysteriousness*
88. *With my fuck-ups*

This was my moment. I wasn't a rule-following, beige-bra bore. I was Giselle, woman of mystery, strumpet of Sodom, world traveler on an airplane of lies!

I yanked harder on his lapels to drag his mouth closer to mine. His tensed at the corners. Not for long. I raked my hand through his soft, wavy hair and closed the gap. He smelled of a rich cologne and…man. Mmmmmm, man skin. I pressed my cold lips to his, and he immediately tucked me into his chest.

Too happy to be caught, I clutched him back. His firm mouth opened across mine and his warmth flooded me, blooming across my chest. He kissed like a demon and held me like a dream, and I pressed my thighs together against the ache he inspired.

89. Was it a fuck-up too far to fuck him in the cab?

"Take me," I whispered against his lips.

90. It was maudlin

91. I didn't care

"No," he whispered back.

It felt like a record scratch against my lady bits. "What?" I managed to squeak.

"God, you're delicious. You're enough to make a man sin for eternity."

I should kiss gifted writers more often.

"But I meant what I said. Let's pump the breaks, yeah?" He tucked some loose hair behind my ear and I exploded into a firework shaped like a frowny face. Leaning down all adorably, he peered into my eyes at my height. "Will you go out with me again?"

92. "Yes," I replied

Number ninety-two was probably my worst fuck-up of the entire bunch.

Chapter Six

F*ck-Ups Ninety-Three through One-Thirty
Cappucci-No

I awoke the next morning…er, afternoon…and rolled over in my empty bed. A lust hangover thumped in my head. I'd thrown myself at two different dudes this week and had achieved absolutely no naked.

93. No pecs

94. No hairy chest

95. No lovely neck smell

Blade had emanated a sub-par neck smell. It had been a sign, but I'd ignored it.

96. No amazing butt to grab

97. No dick

Hunter hadn't cut me to the quick. He was so lovely, but he'd been an experiment. A failed experiment, like a Frankenstein monster who begged anew for death.

But Yash…

I rolled onto my face and moaned his name. "Yaaaaahhhhhhhhhshshshshs." It didn't come out all that well. Also, he was supposed to be on top of me.

My phone read three hours before I had to be at the coffee shop. So, the better to be an asshole, I decided to write a blog post about my floptastic endeavors to get laid. I whipped out a post, didn't spell check —

98. spel chick is 4 old dagmer

And pushed it live. I threw a link onto Twitter, then ordered Greek food as a reward for my hard, hard work.

A bubble of excitement bounced around my tummy to be

starting a new job. Money! Money money money! Money from the type of job I would not have to ruminate about once I clocked out.

My bubble nearly performed back-flips, but then decided to burst into a yawn because I didn't need to anticipate or worry. I was smart, and I'd worked retail in high school. Certainly the muscle memory would flood back, and I'd be fine.

My phone dinged — Yash.

Yash: I made a horrible mistake last night.
Me: Why is that?
Yash: I couldn't sleep for wanting you.

Oh yeaaaaaahhhhhh. I hadn't gotten laid, but I'd left him wanting more.

99. Slut win!

100. Sometimes a failure can be a future mistake in the making

I left him to stew while I brushed away my morning breath and threw on enough clothing not to shock the delivery guy.

101. Then I took off my bra again because I was all about fucking up

102. Besides, bras are torture devices of the devil

Finally, I decided the poor, blue-balled man should suffer no longer without my witty text response.

Me: You poor man. If only some hot woman had tried to get into your knickers last night.

Knickers — I knew all the natty British slang.

Yash: Look at you using all the natty British slang. Yes, I blame myself.
Me: I blame you too.
Yash: Forgive me tonight? Preferably naked?

Argh! I had to close with Hunter tonight.

Me: I have an overnight to Maui. Won't be back for a couple of days.

If I didn't have work tomorrow, I had big plans to adopt a cat.

103. It's never too early to crazy cat lady

104. Especially to spite your cat-hating ex

Yea, though my loins were aflame with desire for a giant, bookish sex nerd, I would make him wait, for that is the price he shall pay for blue-ovaries-ing me!

105. Let's make blue ovaries a thing

106. People with ovaries get frustrated too

My food arrived, so I let Yash flail on text and contented my aching body with hummus. The kabob made me think dirty thoughts, so I bit that sucker with relish.

Far too soon, it was time to go to work, so I put on jeans, a dark tee, and comfy running shoes. I wouldn't get to bang Hunter, so I swiped on mascara and lip gloss, but nothing more.

107. Fuck big makeup

108. Except when I wanted to wear it

Whoa—I had tons of emails. People commenting on my blog post. Sixty-three comments! Most of them favorable, but enough mean ones that I was being defended by my fans.

My *fans*.

My Tweet had three hundred retweets. Going after hot men was really paying off.

109. Except for my lady parts

I told my throngs of hangers-on that I was going to work at the coffee shop, and ten of them begged to know which one.

Wow. Okay. I definitely needed to not give out too much personal info. After all, a Twitter account about the love of God was threatening to burn me as a whore.

I texted Yash that I was about to take off for my flight and left for my brand new job.

A coffee shop. How hard could this be?

* * * *

"I said soy! *Soy!* How stupid are you that you cannot understand sooooyyyyyyy?"

These words were screeched at me by a woman wearing a pip star T-shirt before she threw hot coffee at my chest. I managed to duck most of it, but boiling non-soy-maybe coffee still splattered across my shoulder and arm, and I yelled as I went down, hard, onto the rubber ground mat. Oh, hell, it burned. Buuuuurned gah it stung. Why why why?

I hadn't even made the coffee! I'd just taken the order!

Not that she should have thrown coffee at anyone, but Lacey, the redhead from the other night, had been frowning at me all day because she thought I'd banged Hunter.

I crawled away from the horrible soy banshee, her now-empty cup clutched in my hand. I'd only been here three hours. One woman had lectured me about the price of her triple shot caramel mocha dream that was a necessity she couldn't afford. Another person had thrown his credit card at me — thrown — and when I ducked to not get an Amex in the eye, he called for Hunter because I'd allowed his plastic to hit the ground instead of lodging itself in my retina.

After this latest assault, I crawled into the back office, the scene of already one failure. I examined the coffee cup. I'd written *soy* right on it. No doubt it had been made correctly. Pop star-lady just needed someone to vent her day on probably because her life was so terrible that she enjoyed pop stars.

Hunter hurried into the room. "Oh, no," he said. He passed me a plastic bag full of ice for my shoulder.

Aaaaaah. The cool felt marginally better, but a gentle peeling back of my sodden tee revealed a giant bubble of second-degree burn.

"You're a real barista now," Hunter said while sinking to

sit on the floor beside me.

"No, I'm not. I'm a passable order taker at best." We laughed, and I added, "Can you please tell Lacey I didn't sleep with you? You can omit the fact that I tried."

He smiled. "Sure, no problem. FYI"—he looked through the open door before whispering—"she tried and failed too."

"Yes!" I fist-pumped.

110. Penis-less misery loves company

Heh. Twitter would love that one.

111. That was the most vapid thing I'd ever thought

112. I'm winning!

113. Winning what, though?

Hunter passed me the burn cream from the first aid kit, and I *aaaaahhhh-ed* when I slathered it on. It would hurt for days, but I said, "I'm ready to go again." I let Hunter help me up and he followed me out to behind the counter.

I held up the empty coffee cup and made sure Lacey could hear. "Hunter, Lacey would never have messed up the drink. It was clearly marked soy, and she's the best barista you have." Lacey's red head turned, and a half-smile emerged. Yay! I wanted work friends—I missed the camaraderie of other women. Publishing was lousy with chicks, and that made it awesome.

Back at the register, I jumped into the fray again. Most customers were nice, even when I was a little slow because they threw an unusual process or ingredient at me. Maintaining speed, accuracy, and the register while smiling no matter what was damn hard. I'd forgotten how hard.

And I kept saying silent prayers for forgiveness for any time I'd ever been short with a retail employee. I'd never made a habit of it, but surely it had happened.

The demand for coffee cannot be slaked, so my fingers flew across the register as fast as I could make them for the next hour. I was getting the hang of this! Truth be told, a feeling of accomplishment sang through me, even as my shoulder throbbed. Sing, throb, sing, throb.

But then I wondered if excelling at taking coffee orders was a betrayal of my pledge to fuck up. Yes, I was caring too much.

114. Slack off

115. Be slower

116. Stop smiling

117. The coffee is honor enough

'Twas a fine line — performing well enough to keep the job, but also not caring if I got fired on the spot.

I took a deep breath, blew it out slowly, then greeted the next man in line without a smile. I'd use the same attitude I'd had at the club — I'm too good for you. "What can I get you?"

The tall, thin white guy leaned down to this kid, a ten-ish year old boy. "What do you want?" he asked the boy.

"Hot chocolate!"

I nodded. "What size?"

The dad rolled his eyes. "He's a kid, what do you think? Jesus. Small." He then shook his head at me.

Blink blink blink. I froze and just stared at him, the knot of overachievement in my belly twisting itself into a rage spiral. I'd had fifteen kids in this line today drinking coffees large enough to choke a giraffe. "So...a small then?" I asked the little boy directly.

"Medium!" he replied with a gap-toothed grin.

The dad huffed and rolled his eyes — again — and I entered the medium hot chocolate into the computer. One. Button. At. A. *Pause.* Time. I sniffed. I peered at the screen. The man's huffs became gale-force winds.

118. They don't tell you how much fun it is being an asshole

119. Society is afraid of the truth!

I asked the father, "And what would y — ?"

"Triple latte, medium, coconut milk."

He rattled it off so freaking fast. I kept looking for how to put triple shots into a medium, but I really couldn't find it. The dad started slamming his hands on the counter. My pulse shot into overdrive and I had to keep reminding myself through deep breaths that it didn't matter. Let him rage because I wasn't a mind reader or very fast yet. His first stroke at forty-five would give the city a holiday.

"Is this beyond you?" he asked so snidely I thought his last name must be Whiplash.

I grinned at him for the first time. "Obviously. Hold please." My grin still plastered on, I waved to attract Hunter's attention. He hurried over. "Hunter, how do I ring up three shots in a—"

The father spit (literally, he showered the counter with his nastiness), "Triple latte, medium, coconut milk! This woman is too stupid to use a computer, apparently." I grinned, thinking that if he didn't throw boiling coffee on me, he'd lose the race for 'worst dick munch of the day.'

Hunter took over punching up the order and I watched how he did it so I'd know next time. The father turned to his son and said, "Noah, this is what will happen if you don't go to college. You'll end up a dumb bitch in a coffee shop."

He said it loudly enough that every single worker in the place stopped and gawked, as did half the line.

I tilted my head, bared my teeth (in a smile, duh), and scooted the tip jar toward him while staring him straight in the eye. I never blinked, and, after a moment or two, he caved and backed away from the counter, his change clutched in his fist.

A quiet oath next to me sounded, and I met Lacey's gaze. "Here's his coffee cup," I said, passing it along.

She smiled and licked her lips. "Duhhhh...I hope I can manage to make it."

I put on my most sarcastic face. "Do you mean because you're just a dumb bitch who works in a coffee shop?"

"It took me fifteen minutes to figure out how to put on my underpants this morning!"

"You managed underpants? Are you a wizard?"

And just like that—boom!—friends. The asshole we'd bonded over was straining to see his cup over the counter.

He'd figured out that maybe you shouldn't insult absolutely everyone who is making your food product. Lacey saw his regard and quickly shoved the cup out of his sight.

I went to make Noah's hot chocolate—the only thing I actually knew how to put together so far. I gave him a huge dollop of whipped cream and called his name.

He trotted up to the counter to take it. "Thanks!" he said. He leaned forward, and I nearly lay across the counter to get as close as possible. "Sorry my dad's a tool," he whispered. "Don't worry about it. He says the same thing to me about college basically everywhere we go. We're not allowed in Tasti-D-Lite anymore."

120. I replied, "Just remember his behavior when it comes time to put him in the home."

Noah nodded very solemnly and rejoined a still-glaring father.

121. Corrupt them early

I meandered my way back toward Hunter to take over the register again when I passed Lacey. I whispered, "We don't spit in those people's coffees, right? That would be bad?"

"Of course not! We're professionals." She poured two shots into the coffee in front of her. "But we do make them decaf."

122. Decaf

"Whoa there, Satan," I replied, and I got a smile from her.

The rest of the evening went pretty smoothly. By the time ten p.m. rolled around, my dogs weren't barking so much as howling, and I wanted to collapse all over the filthy standing mat. "Time to clean up," Hunter declared.

I nodded and hopped to it. No sense in being lackadaisical now—the sooner we closed, the sooner I'd be joined with my darling, my love—my bathtub. No Yash tonight, as I was 'lounging on the beach in Maui.' Or still flying? Either way, I hadn't answered a text all shift.

When the counters had been scrubbed, the floor mopped and the chairs set upside down on the tables, I'd officially finished my first shift of a brand new job. It had been far more physically laborious than I'd dreamed—perhaps stupidly. My every muscle's weariness felt...good, somehow. I'd taken out my frustrations on the wet floor, in hauling garbage. And, once I learned the computer, even the taking of orders became mechanical in a lovely, brain-fuzzy way.

I'd discovered pretty quickly that I worked fast and smiley for the nice folks, and—

123. *Slow and smiley for the rude ones*

124. *A smile can mean 'fuck you'*

125. *Perhaps even more than a frown*

I took the train home and, at eleven p.m., had just crawled into the bath when my phone dinged.

Mel: Gaaaaaah! Are you up? Can I come over?

Me: Yes and yes! What's wrong?

Mel: I'll tell you when I get there.

Me: I'm in the bath, let yourself in. No matter what's wrong, my boobs will help. I've discovered that they're great.

Mel: I have always loved you, yet I love you more now that you're semi-evil.

Mel: But you can keep your great tits to yourself.

Now I worried about Mel. I sank into the water and *argh!* shot right back up again because it hurts when you submerge a horrid burn in hot water!

I ran out of the bath, splashing water all over my floors, and fetched an ice pack. Back into the bath I went, hot on the bottom half of me, cold on the top. Aaaaagggghhhh. My feet felt as if they were melting into the water, the pins and needles on my soles already beginning to ease.

Grrrrrr—I wished I could charge that horrible coffee thrower with assault, but at least Hunter had said they were banned. They take Polaroids of all Official Assholes and post them behind the counter. Obviously, I would work to memorize these people's faces immediately.

I closed my eyes for a little while until the ice pack and the bath had become roughly the same temperature. Through the open bathroom, I heard Mel at the front door. Followed by steps, indignant by the sound of them.

Mel burst into the bathroom and blurted, "I will kill the horrid man!"

I sat up, tits be damned. "I'll help! Also, which one?"

She handed me a towel and I slid my ice pack off to stand. "Holy crap, Dag! Are you okay?"

I groaned. "Yes. I need to put burn jelly on it." I'd managed to stop for some on the way to the train. But first—

"Cover up your ass," my BFF bade me.

Swish swish I swiped the towel all over me while Mel left... to root around in the kitchen by the clanking of it. I threw on a tank that avoided my horrifying, one-and-a-half-inch blister, sweatpants, and slippers. Once in the kitchen, I sat to apply my cooling cream and perked my ears for her. "Shoot," I said.

Mel poured the most dramatic glass of vodka I'd ever seen. She tipped the glass, downed half, wiped her mouth, then began to speak. "You remember Taylor?"

My stomach began to knot with hatred. Taylor Choate was a fellow assistant editor in Mel's group—science fiction and fantasy. "Yeeeeeeees?"

Swish. The other half of the vodka disappeared. Oh, wow. She really was pissed. She hadn't swigged vodka this fast since her stepmother had thrown out her framed university diploma to clear space in her scrapbooking room. "Taylor has just signed a *second* author out from under me."

"What?"

Mel slopped more vodka into her glass, set it on the counter, and brought the bottle to the table. "I thought the first one was a fluke. But the second was a lady I'd scouted from her self-published book I'd enjoyed. Without telling anyone, I emailed her to ask if she had any other work. She did, and she sent me a manuscript. I hadn't even brought her up in an editorial meeting yet! But today, Taylor brings her to our boss as his discovery…with the exact same book she'd sent me!" She took a pull straight from the bottle.

"That bastard!"

"So I email the lady, very politely asking what had happened. She said he'd called her saying how much he loved the book, and that he was taking over for me."

I reached for the vodka. "He had to know you'd find out."

"He doesn't care. Anything I say now sounds like sour grapes to Charlie." Ugh, that was tough—Charlie, their boss, was Taylor's uncle.

Mel flopped into a chair. "How? How did he know? Did I mention it to someone?"

"Did you?"

She shook her head so hard her hair frizzed. "No. I knew this time."

I gave her back the booze, as was only right. "Is he reading your emails?"

"I thought of that—I changed my work email password *and* messaged her from my personal email."

"But did you write the emails to her on your work computer?"

Her mouth fell into an O. "Yes."

I nodded. "He might have a keystroke logger sending him everything you do. Or have hacked the whole machine in some way, not just the company email system."

She breathed a screech of such frustration it nearly came out on fire. "That piece of shit!"

While she pounded my table and drank, my vision turned red and hazy. No. No! Why should the Carmichaels and the Taylors of this world always win? Mel was honest, hard-working, clever. She did the work, and that rank piece of hair gel would reap the rewards!

Not on my fucking-up watch.

Through gritted teeth, I said, "I'm going to get him for you, Mel."

"How do I prove it?"

I shook my head. "No, no. Don't prove it. Trap him with

it, or with some other scheme of his." I met her eyes. "And I mean it... I'm going to *get him*." I said the italics out loud, with a growl.

126. I would get him

127. Get him so good

128. Make him weep for his momma

129. Make his momma weep for having birthed him

130. Make the hospital he was born in spontaneously combust!

With wet eyelashes, my best friend blinked at me. I took her hand. "Yes, Mel. I'm going to avenge you."

She sniffed with happiness.

I leaned back. "Tell me everything about this asshole. I'm going to ruin his life, and he will leave you alone."

"Really?"

My eyes wide, I put on my most innocent voice. "What, am I gonna get fired from publishing?"

We both cackled the cackle of true witches, the kind they burned in the olden days.

Today, the witches would burn *them*.

Mel swiped her lips free of vodka. "Taylor comes from money—Charlie, too. Old New York real estate money. He drives a Pagani Zonda that he loves more than life itself. He only lives ten blocks from work in Manhattan, but drives every day just because."

I sat up straighter. "Really?" Oh, I had an idea for that... "What the hell is a Pagani Zorpa?"

"Zonda. I have no idea, but it looks like a spaceship you could buy an apartment with."

"Okay, what else?"

Her face hardened into self-determination. "He loves negging women into sleeping with him. Usually really young, not enough self-esteem to say no to his tiny-ass dick."

"Ha! Have I ever met him?"

She grinned. "I don't think so."

"Good. Try to find out where he'll be on a given night or two, and I'll make sure I'm not working."

She clapped in the chair with pure glee. "Fuck you, Taylor! Fuck your author-stealing bullshit!"

"Don't scout anybody else with your work computer. Don't type anything on there you wouldn't want him to read."

"Will do. Or won't do, as may be the case." She pointed to my wound and sucked on her teeth sympathetically. "What happened there?"

"Soooooooooooy!"

Her eyebrows shot skyward. "Well, I'd be angry if I were lactose intolerant, too."

My phone buzzed and Mel grabbed it. "Ooooh, Yash wants to know if you've landed yet. Where are you?"

"Hawaii. Can't you tell from my tan?"

She giggled and tossed me the phone. "You're going to have to get one, dorkus. Maybe one of your mistakes can be a tanning booth."

"Love it! I must have landed by now."

"I think you should spend Christmas in Hawaii. It's just in two days, anyhow. Make him stew before you give him some New Year's fireworks." She winked and made a graphic gesture with her hands to show me what sort of fireworks I should be repeatedly receiving...so to speak.

That was if I could ever convince a man to give me the business. Seriously—I was a lady with good knockers and a can-do attitude. Why wouldn't they can-do me?

I closed again the following night. Afterward, Mel and I stayed up late watching *9 to 5* for inspiration on how to ruin an asshole's life. Right around the time when Doralee was roping the sexist, egotistical, lying, hypocritical bigot, I informed Mel that we needed an operation name.

"Operation Taylor Goes Down Swift-ly?"

I spit out my vodka. "A+ use of T. Swift. Needs more outrage, though. Operation...Righteous..."

"Something with titties, or vaginas, since we have those things and will be hurting him."

I sat up straighter on the couch and paused the movie.

"Operation Righteous Titty Slam."

"Operation Righteous *Vagina*... Wham?"

"Dentata!" I stood and raised my slightly drunken arms in victory. "Operation Righteous Vagina Dentata. Sometimes the bitch bites you back!"

Chapter Seven

F*ck-Ups One-Thirty-One through One-Fifty-Seven
Operation Righteous Vagina Dentata Part One

Mel and I spent an amazing Christmas watching bad movies, smoking a little of the good stuff my drug dealer neighbor had gifted me by way of a yuletide present, and generally goofing off. I hadn't been able to see Yash, for he'd traveled back to London for the holiday (and through the New Year). No fireworks for poor Giselle. I despaired, for he'd probably forget all about me in the arms of a milk-skinned English lass — swarthy women such as myself have usually suffered from some blonde interloper at least once. At least he didn't have to look at the mess of disgusting that was my shoulder burn. Since that incident, my ducking skills had become epic, like those of a politician.

But neither Yash nor angry coffee customers were on the top of my mental to-do list. Lust had its place, sure — a much higher place than ever before in my life. This week, however... *Justice* reigned supreme. Justice for author stealers! For rude drivers! For people who change diapers on restaurant tables while you're trying to eat a freaking pancake! Okay, maybe not all of them at once, but once started, my retribution for grave wrongs would be unending.

Dagmar Kostopoulos used to be a sheep. A rule-follower. A beige devotee. No longer. Now evildoers would face my wrath, for I had fuck-ups to perpetuate, yet I had no more fucks to give.

131. OMG that should totally be my catchphrase for the New

Year

Yea, it was happening:

132. Operation Righteous Vagina Dentata was a go

133. And the first forward advance would happen tonight

Mel and I had quite a few facts at our disposal.

—Mel knew which New Year's party Taylor would be attending.

—He would be driving his precious car even though he would be getting 'fuckin' wasted.'

—She'd overheard him droning into his phone that he would 'fuck the shit out of some skank.'

134. I was that skank

Or so he would think. No way would I ride in a spaceship car with a gross drunk lech, so we'd obtained supplies — screwdriver, gloves (two pairs), hoodies (one — Mel already owned one because she was not khaki), sugar, and a new skank dress.

We'd auditioned all of my recent purchases, but the tackiest frock I now owned was merely Level Real Housewife — close to Level Skank, but not quite cheap enough. So we soldiered to the local teen store, where I'd found a disturbing number of elastic options for under twenty dollars. I chose the same dress as the twelve-year-old next to me.

Disturbing.

Mel and I alit from a cab two blocks from the trendy bar in Williamsburg where Taylor would experience Operation Righteous Vagina Dentata Part One. Once again, we went over the plan. Our iPhones synchronized, we hugged, and I took off toward the bar for my portion of the effort.

Mel grabbed my arm. "Maybe we shouldn't. I mean, maybe I could just start adding laxatives to his coffee. I'll probably do that anyway." Her face screwed up into a horrific mixture of smile and grimace. It was the worst smimace I'd ever seen.

I yanked her in for a hug. "We're not really doing anything illegal. Relax."

135. Well…

136. Mildly illegal at most

137. Nothing Taylor himself hadn't done

138. Probably

Pulling back, I gave her leather-clad hands a squeeze. "If anything seems amiss, just quit and walk away. We do this only if it's easy and fun, right?"

"Right. You too."

"Oh, that scumbag is not laying one finger on me."

Mel let out an outraged squeak. "If he does, honey, I will put Skinny 'n Sweet in his coffee!"

A lady passing by did a double-take and hurried away.

I said, "Skinny and Sweet was the sugar substitute in *Nine to Five*, but I appreciate the sentiment."

"Oh, yeah, whoops—I meant the rat poison."

"I love you so much."

"Me too."

We fist- and hip-bumped, and I teetered toward the bar in my stupid heels, Spandex snake-print tank dress, and faux fur. Every inch of me screamed conspicuousness. I felt like an amateur hooker.

The skeevy guy who just passed me seemed to feel that way, too.

In better news, I was starting to learn to walk in stripper heels. My gait had a lot fewer hitches in it, and I hadn't fallen in the last thirty minutes!

139. Actually, maybe I could be a stripper for my next fuck-up

140. But is it really a fuck-up to make tons of money for dancing?

141. Makes my other career seem rather stupid

I arrived at the bar and rushed in, thankful for indoor heating and the possibility of booze. After all—

142. Half of walking well in five-inch heels was being lit enough not to feel my feet anymore

Time to get serious.

I was here to get Taylor. No longer could bad people be allowed to take advantage of hard-working, honest, nice, sweet—

A guy walked up to me and slid his arm around my waist. "Hey, sexy girl."

I slammed my heel into his foot. "Take your hands off me, asshole."

He limped away.

—Young ladies!

I scanned the dimly lit room. Ugh, so many douchebags. If this place blew up right now, at least twenty percent of the tools in this city would be vaporized at once. Entire offices of investment bankers would go *poof!*

There he was. Taylor. He stood near the bar, dressed in dark skinny jeans and a sweater bedecked with a skull. Ooh, what a bad boy... If only the sweater hadn't cost a grand. I tented my fingers together in the universal symbol of evil plans—excellent.

I swished over, shoved my way to stand to his right, and let out a girly huff. "Who does a girl have to bang to get a drink around here?"

The guy to my right said, "Me," with a wide smile.

"No." I focused on Taylor, busy looking away down the bar. I gave him a sharp elbow in the ribs, and he finally turned toward me. "Oops!" I simpered. "I'm so sorry! I was just trying to get the bartender's attention."

Taylor grinned, his curly dirt blond hair wobbling atop his pointy head. "You got my attention. What would you like, lovely lady?"

I let the 'fur' slip down over one shoulder and said, "Whatever you're having."

He puffed up his bird chest. "Can you handle a Long Island iced tea?"

"Who wants to remember New Year's Eve?" I let out a long, ditzy laugh and he joined me.

Oh, yeah. I got him.

Our drinks arrived, and I fished my secret weapon, a tiny vial, out of my purse. My nice drug dealer neighbor, Dennis, had acquired it for me, as it wasn't his normal product. I would pour the contents of the vial into Taylor's

Long Island iced tea when he wasn't paying attention.

143. Mel had told me that Taylor once bragged about roofie-ing a woman

144. See? Nothing that he hadn't done

145. And I wouldn't even assault him

146. So the GHB hardly even merited inclusion on my fuck-up list

We retired to a small couch by the front entrance to the bar. "You are smoking hot!" said my gallant date. "What a great dress."

There was literally nothing great about this dress. It was a glorified tank top out of which every single body part I possessed now spilled.

147. I was totally bangin' tho

"Thanks!" I giggled. I hadn't thought that one could 'giggle' a word, but it is, in fact, possible. "You're so cute!"

He flexed his piddly 'guns,' and I nearly gagged. I covered it with another giggle. It came out like a Tommy gun—*rat-a-tat!* Taylor didn't seem to want to talk to me much, so I just kept machine-gun laughing. I did take a few sips of my drink, keeping my eye on it the whole time.

148. No way would I be roofied before I roofied him

"What do you do?" I asked him. Every moment I waited for him to look away for a few seconds so I could just GHB the drink and not have to talk to him anymore.

"Books which make tons of money—I make those happen."

"*That* make tons of money."

He froze mid-leer with a quizzical blink.

Whoops. But really—an editor who couldn't tell the difference between that and which? Shame! "Wow," I said. "Money. I like money."

He returned to leering—whew—and began droning on about his big job while trying to worm his hand under my ass. If I kept scooting forward at this rate, I'd fall on the floor. My phone buzzed. I checked the text. He didn't seem to give a shit. Nice.

Mel: I'm still at home with food poisoning, but everything is okay.

Yay! That was our code. If we got caught by the fuzz and hauled downtown at some point in the future, her texts would read that she'd been at home, and not near this douche's car.

Me: I'm so glad. Get some rest. I'm putting the noodles in your soup any minute now.

149. Noodles = GHB
150. Soup = Taylor
Although that was a grievous insult to soup.

Finally, I couldn't take his yakking anymore. I set my drink on the floor and 'accidentally' threw my purse halfway across the room. "Oh, no! I'm getting drunk and clumsy and stuff." I yanked Taylor's drink from his hand. "Will you go get my purse? All my lube and condoms are in there! Hee hee!"

"Condoms?" he said with a horrified face before he took off.

Ew.

I tipped the tiny vial into his Long Island, and he returned to the couch, my purse in tow. With a smile that didn't reach his eyes, he said, "Here you go. But you won't need this stuff with me, honey. You look clean, and I like it bareback."

151. V

152. O

153. M

154. I

155. T

I shoved his cocktail back into his hand and held my own aloft. "Let's drink!" I suggested in such a high sing-song pitch that perhaps only dogs could hear it. Taylor got the message and downed the entire rest of his in one gulp.

156. Yes!

Operation Righteous Vagina Dentata Part One complete.

Taylor got up to get us more drinks and I texted Mel.

Me: The noodles are in the soup
Mel: The barf is in the toilet

Oh, yeah!

Okay, so perhaps our codes were a little tame and/or gross, but they worked for us.

Taylor returned and I just waited. Not very long, for soon he started swaying, sleepy and spacey. "Hey, buddy," I said. "Let's go to your house."

He yawned and sat up straighter. "Yeah, okay. Finally."

It had been twenty minutes.

Now, he likely would have agreed even if I hadn't roofied him, but I knew that being very agreeable was a side-effect. Hence the popularity of the drug for raping purposes. I'd been out with Mel once when she'd suddenly began acting like a total weirdo and had wanted to go with some strange man to his hotel room for what he called 'pizza'. I dragged her out of that bar, the guy getting really pissed off, almost violent, until we'd escaped in a cab.

She'd slept for fifteen hours and hadn't remembered any of it. God only knows what that piece of shit might have done to her. My blood boiled even now, and the heat fired its way up and down my body.

I yanked on Taylor's arm, and he swam up to standing — that's the only way I could describe his swishing and dipping and staggering. His arm around my shoulders — for support, not for sexy — I led him from the bar and down the street to where Mel had informed me his car was.

We found the orange spaceship.

Yes. *Orange.* The car looked like a rolling penis suffering from a particularly radioactive venereal disease.

We walked around to the passenger side. His gas tank hole door (I don't know what it's called) stood popped, and a line of crusty white trailed down to the ground, where an open bag of sugar had been dropped.

Taylor lost his mind. "Nooooooo! Noooooo, not sugar in my gas tank! God damn it! Fucking shit motherfucker!"

He collapsed over the car and began to weep. *Weep.* My hand clapped over my mouth, I tried my hardest not to laugh, but it was too difficult. Taylor didn't notice me doubled over with mirth, anyhow. He strangled the sugar bag, getting spurts of the white granules all over himself.

Naturally, I snapped a photo. For posterity!

A bubble of pure delight exploded through me. I hadn't been this happy since Yash kissed me.

We hadn't even ruined his gas tank. Mel had just put the sugar on the ground and popped the gas tank hole door.

157. BWAAHAHAHAHAHAHAHAHAAAAA!

Time for Operation Righteous Vagina Dentata Part Two.

Chapter Eight

**F*ck-Ups One-Fifty-Eight through Two-Thirteen
Operation Righteous Vagina Dentata Part Two
Now with More Bite!**

It took me five minutes of promising sex to Taylor to get him peeled off the ground. Apparently true heartbreak can overcome the promise of sex. I'd had to dangle anal before he'd even look at me. So to speak. I assured him that we'd take care of the car tomorrow, and we hopped a cab to his apartment. We had to get to his place, for that was the entire point of the exercise.

158. The pretend sugar in the gas tank was just a bonus evil prank, as well as a way to get out of having him drive in his inebriated state

I texted Mel.

Me: I'm on the way to your place with the chicken noodle soup.
Mel: I'll be here waiting for you.

Taylor grew fifteen hands in the cab, and by the time we arrived, I was about to clock the guy to get him off me.

I paid from his wallet, wrestled him out of the car, and got us into the elevator. Mel, the hoodie pulled up to hide her shining face, had shuffled into the elevator behind us. I pushed Taylor's non-shining face to the wall and pinned him there so he wouldn't see her.

"Do you like it rough, baby?" he asked with copious slurs.

At this point, my internal bile would not allow me to baby talk with him any longer. The hatred swirled through my stomach and brain like a swimming parasite. I rolled my eyes and searched his pants pockets for keys.

What I found first was a tiny, liquid-filled vial, nearly identical to mine. I held it up so Mel could see.

"Fucking piece of shit," she muttered.

"What?" Taylor asked.

I smushed his head to the wall. "Nothing, cutie!"

159. Is murder really so bad?

Mel passed me my pair of black leather gloves. I slid them over my hands before we got to the door.

The elevator dinged. "Let's go," I told the scumbag.

We wove to his apartment and I used the keys I'd found in his front pants pocket to let us inside

160. Shudder, not enough bleach for my hands in the world

I left the door slightly ajar, and Mel would wait in the hall until I gave the all-clear.

Taylor swerved toward the kitchen. I headed him off and asked, "Where's the bedroom?"

He tittered—tittered—and pointed, so I pushed him that direction. Once we arrived, I gave him a solid shove and he fell across the bed face first. Whew.

161. Unfortunately, I now had a view of his flat, frat-boy butt

My skin crawled even to be in here, knowing that likely, if this had been a real situation and not an amazing 'operation,' he would have roofied me by now. I growled my frustration, and ick, and impotent rage.

"Don't be like that," Taylor muttered. "Take off your clothes, don't be a bitch."

162. But being a bitch was my new oeuvre!

That was it. That was fucking it. I took off my stupid shoes and threw them into the living room. "You taking off your clothesh, babbeeeeee?" he asked.

"Oh, yeah." I stomped into his closet. Neck ties. I yanked five off his automatic tie rotator—really?—and sauntered to him once again. The first one I wound around his eyes. He started to lift it, but I jumped on his back and put a knee between his shoulder blades. "I like it rough. Remember?"

"Sh-shouldn't I blindfold you?"

"Sure, of course. I'll go next." I knotted the tie behind his head.

163. No way the silk would recover from this sort of knotting
164. Heh heh

Next, I jumped off him and grabbed a wrist. Thank goodness he had a metal bed with lovely posts at the head and foot.

By this point, my blood pounded in my ears, and a feeling of unholy power coursed through me. I'd never, ever in my life perpetrated anything of this kind. I'd spent my entire existence taking everyone's shit—with a smile. Lest the teacher, boss, parent, friend, bus driver etc, got mad at me. To hell with that. A cackle pealed from my mouth—loud, mean, angry—while my hands clawed like a supervillain's, and suddenly I understood why people went rogue.

165. Misbehaving was fun

"What?" Taylor asked, softly. He was almost out cold at this point. I yanked his arm and tied up his wrist anyway.

I didn't bother to respond to him anymore, but left the bedroom to let Mel into the apartment. As soon as she got inside, I gave her the highest of fives and a hip-bump. "Did you see him flip his shit?" I asked.

She jumped and clapped. "Yes! I can't believe popping that gas tank door…thingie…"

"I don't know what it is, either."

"And throwing a little sugar around would be so satisfying! Is he out?"

"Oh, yeah. Let's go tie him up the rest of the way."

Like two little girls skipping toward Disneyland, we joked our way through incapacitating our very own douchebag. We left one of his hands free, but tied both legs. We also placed his phone near his free hand, so that if he couldn't untie himself, he could at least call for help. Although we'd traipsed into supervillain territory, we yet had mercy.

166. We totally took a picture, though

He didn't even stir, but began snoring.

We regrouped in the living room, chests heaving with breathless excitement. As one, we settled, stared at each other, and said, "What now?"

"Jinx!" I blurted. "You owe me a Coke."

She grinned at her deserved punishment and looked around the room. I did the same, now that I didn't have a horrible man-child to deal with. Ugh. The walls were dark gray dotted with naked woman art. Everywhere. And the place was a gross mess. He was rich, and Mel said she knew he brought in a maid. How did anyone get his place this nasty in the space of…a week? Dirty takeout in piles on the expensive-looking coffee table. Filthy socks piled under it. Ew—was that a pair of underwear hanging off a chair? And gross workout clothes on the kitchen counter, which we could see from the living room.

"Let's get tetanus shots after this," said Mel.

"Perhaps a spa day at the antibiotics factory," I agreed.

Mel said, "I think we should go through his computer. Read emails, find his Reddit username, stuff like that. Dig for transgressions."

We beelined for his desk. "It's hard to type with leather gloves," Mel said.

"That's why I brought latex ones." I fished into my purse and drew them out, two pairs. "I also brought cayenne pepper to put in his aftershave."

Mel slapped me with a look. "Whoa, bad girl."

"I just want to be thorough."

"You've really had it with assholes, haven't you?"

"You have no idea." I snapped on my latex with the evil grin that came more and more naturally to me, and we began exploring the wide, wide world of Taylor online. His emails yielded paydirt almost immediately. He'd stolen several of Mel's authors, just as we suspected. We took screenshots and saved them to a flash drive we'd brought.

Then we began digging a little more into his sent items.

"Bless his heart," Mel whispered.

"To his own uncle!" I followed.

The little shit had been leaking internal meeting notes to a competing editor at another big publisher! Plans for book rollouts, trend data, all sorts of stuff. Seems he was working his way into an elevated role at the new pub—a couple of rungs above where he was at Mel's company. "Screenshot it," Mel said.

"Done and done."

Next, we perpetrated the most wicked of modern breaches of trust—we explored his browser history.

167. We all look at porn. Don't lie

But this... Lucky my stomach was empty, because barf vomit city. The ye old standard sexy sex was there, but then we found all this fetishistic crap with horrific racist names and gross faux-Japanese costumes and the like.

"I may never date again," Mel said, "knowing this is what lurks among us."

More screenshots of this stuff. Mel said, "I think our big boss, Diana, might be interested in this. Me so horny? Him so out of a job."

His Reddit username yielded even more wonderful bounty, including his commentary about how much he hated women (click and save!), minorities (click and save!), non-Americans (click and save!), anyone who wasn't a millionaire, and on and on.

Then... We spotted it. Right on the desktop—a folder simply named *Sluts*. With a look to Mel and a deep breath, I clicked it open. Trophy pictures of women. In his bed. Very graphic activities. During which the women were sleeping.

Grind grind grind. I might file my teeth clean off tonight. "I'm copying all of these. If we recognize anyone, maybe we can tell her."

"Or not!" Mel hung her head. "Maybe they're happier not knowing. He's not dating anyone now—hopefully they're never coming back."

"What if he's posted them online?" A nasty, sick heat crawled over every inch of my body. To know that I would have ended up in his *Slut* file of horrors if I hadn't been actively watching for it… Those poor women.

A giant snort-snore from the other room made us jump and scream, but he was still, blessedly, knocked out cold.

We had more than enough screen grabs to embarrass him into the next millennium, and I copied every single photo in that horrendous file with the offensive name. I erased the previous hour's worth of browser history, the temporary folders, and removed the flash drive.

Mel bounced with agitation, looking as if she'd peel off her skin if we stayed there any longer. But halfway to the door, I stopped.

"What's wrong?" she said.

"Nothing. It's just…" I set my purse down right in front of the door and started for the bedroom. "He has to think he got laid, right? I don't want him really putting it together that my face equals email leak."

I hurried back into the bedroom and turned on the light. He didn't twitch. He wasn't even snoring anymore. I untied his two ankles and wrist and began peeling off his clothes.

168. This might be the grossest fuck-up of them all

"I can't look," Mel chirped from the doorway, sounding as if she'd rather watch Jabba the Hut take a shower.

"I'll take one for the team." With my eyes ninety percent closed, I unbuttoned his shirt and pushed him to and fro until it could be discarded on the floor. Then, wishing I had taken a shot of some liquor with paint-peeling capabilities, I yanked off his pants. I left the boxer briefs on, because I'm only human, and my gag reflex already twitched. Touching this gross excuse for a human being—who'd been pampered and paid for all his life, who drugged women and, yeah, raped them—made my skin want to flee and assemble into another life form far away from this planet.

Finally, I messed up the covers and pulled down a towel or two in the bathroom to make it seem like someone else had spent time there. I left a scrawled note from 'Amanda' about what a good time she'd had.

When it was done, and he lay sprawled across the bed, I

didn't feel like tying him up again. Rage tinged my vision red and I swayed as I stood there, staring at his pathetic ass. So what if we got him off Mel's back, or fired? He'd buy into another job, better than I'd ever have, in a trice. And no doubt his disgusting perv habits would continue unabated. I mean, sure, I'd tried to seduce my almost boss, but when he'd said no, I'd respected it.

But what could we do? If we emailed the files on his computer to the police, we'd admit to the B & E. Well, kind of. He'd let me into the apartment, but I didn't know the murky legal ramifications of rummaging around on his computer. They were probably not in my favor.

Mel touched my shoulder gently and I jumped. "You okay?"

"I'm enraged at this piece of crap."

"Me too." She chewed on her lip, seemingly as at odds with herself as I was.

"Is your boss Charlie—his uncle, right?—is he a good guy?"

"Oh, yeah. The total opposite of this asshole."

The gears clicked in my brain. We didn't need to send any of this to the cops if we could at least send it to Charlie. Then his current job would be gone, the pipeline to another would be damaged—at least through Charlie—and people would know how he was a scumbag.

Then I got the most amazingest idea to have ever idea'd. I whispered to Mel, "We need to send these files to his mother."

She rocked backward. She put her hand to her heart. "Dag. Giselle. Whoever. I think you may have been taken over by the angry spirit of a vengeful Amazon warrior goddess, for this is the most amazingest idea to have ever idea'd."

169. Told you

We dived back into his email and, sure enough, we found his mom. She seemed like a sweet lady who sent him recipes, restaurant reviews, and…a maid over to do his laundry once a week.

"He doesn't even pay the maid himself," I said with an eye roll.

170. My eyes would get stuck staring at my brain if I kept rolling them

Mel took note of his mom's email address. I'd send her the terrible photos from a dummy account. Some of them had his face in them, his body, his hands on the women... so no doubt about their authenticity.

We took a moment to scan the rooms, to make sure we'd left nothing behind. Mel's glove-clad hand had just gripped the front doorknob when I said, "Wait."

"What now?" She gave me a very exasperated pair of eyebrows. "I've created a monster!"

"*I've* created a monster! Bwaahahahahahaaa!" I threw my head back and did my evil villain laugh again, and my BFF leaned away from me.

171. Yes, be afraid

172. Be very afraid

The laughter ripped from some deep, dank part of me, perhaps building up for years—decades. Was this what happened to a goody two-shoes in the end? Maybe I should adopt a weird hair color, or a villainous costume. Where was my catsuit? Where was my spell book!?

I took off for his bathroom and ran some hot water into a glass he had on the counter. Then I fulfilled a ten-year-old me dream—I put his hand in it. Cool girl Adrienne Johnston had done this to me at my very first sleepover. I'd completely pissed myself, and all the girls had laughed. Even my sister. I hadn't even known about such a trick, and would never have done it to someone. After that, I became a nerd pariah and Adrienne, the most popular girl in our class. She dubbed me Kosto*pee*los, and it had stuck.

Well, I wasn't Kosto*pee*los anymore. I was Giselle! Or something! "Fuck Adrienne," I whispered as I kneeled by his bed. In no time at all, it happened. Taylor whizzed all over the bed, and Mel collapsed onto herself on the floor laughing. So did I, spilling the water on his duvet, sheets, and floor. I didn't care, I plopped down next to her, and we had maybe the best laugh of our lives, even better than the time we'd gotten drunk and gone to see a midnight showing of *Twilight*.

I had no idea how long we lay there, faces hurting, eyes weeping uncontrollably. My body seemed to float lighter. As if my soul had been injected with helium, like a Mylar balloon with the words 'I don't give a fuck' emblazoned across it in sparkly pink.

Mel squeezed my hand and sniffed a wet-sounding glob of snot. "I'm glad you're on my side."

"Always."

Our mission accomplished flawlessly —

173. With bonus wee

We left the apartment. *Wee* left? Heh.

A chilly wind hit my still-grinning face on the way out of the building. I departed first, as if I were leaving after a hook-up. Mel followed five minutes later, just to be all sneaky spy about it. We met a couple of blocks down, both shivering and happier than hell. I was in pain from the laughter…but it had replaced any crying I'd been trying not to do. About Blade, or my job. For better or worse, I was actually calling the shots now.

174. And damn, did it make the blood pound in my lady boner.

"I'm fucking up, and I love it!" I screamed to the street, filled with New Year's revelers spilling from bars and restaurants.

This gleeful admission was met with scattered applause, and one offer of, "Wanna fuck up with me?"

New Year's Eve was the perfect fuck-up night. It and me were one. One gorgeous entity dressed in tackiness, filled with frivolity and contemplation both. And covered in sparkles.

We naturally gravitated toward the revelers outside the bars. They had drinks in their hands, even on the sidewalk, but nobody cared. Not tonight. Not at the start of a brand new and shiny year — a happy baby who never exploded into poop.

175. So to speak

176. Of course, many years did, in fact, explode into poop

177. This last year had dumped on me quite a bit

178. Pun intended

Mel grabbed my arm. "It's only ten minutes to midnight."

"Then we must acquire cocktails post haste."

We shook on it and hurried into the nearest bar. The place was a lovely zoo, and while we waited at the bar for literally anything inebriative —

179. Totally a word

— I gave Mel my faux fur so she appeared more festive, and I took her hoodie so I looked less hooker-ey.

180. Less hooker-ey because the hundred I'd just been offered was an insult

181. I had an MBA

182. I was a thousand-dollar-an-hour girl

183. At least!

We barely made it into the street before the collective New York voice began counting. Ten, nine, eight — my heart leaped into my throat — seven, six, five — I was a whole new woman this year — four, three, two —

"This is my year!" I screamed.

One!

Everyone whooped, clapped, hugged. Three different men attempted to grope me, so my first acts of the New Year were an instep smash, a hip check, and a low punch to the groin.

184. Fitting

Mel turned to me after helping me get a very drunk and drooling redhead off my hoodie. "I don't have a boy to kiss," she said.

"Me neither. But it's better!" I took her into my arms and squeezed with all my might. Into her ear, I yelled above the din, "Boys might come and go, but my Mel is forever, and I love you!"

I planted a smackeroo right on her mouth. The quick and

dirty —

185. Wink wink

— Kiss ended with her laughing at me, which was terribly fitting. I'd been getting rather a lot of that lately.

As one, we downed our cocktails and joined in the impromptu dance party now boogeying into the street. Cabs honked for us to get the hell out of their way, but not a one of us paid attention.

We danced. And danced. And *danced*. My feet stung with more blisters than in a Violent Femmes song, but this two square feet of dress was surprisingly comfortable. At least the shoes were good for dropping fuckboys trying to grab my whatnots.

By three a.m., Mel had had enough, so we went back to her place and just passed out, grins on our faces and stamps on our hands.

* * * *

186. Hung over

187. So hung over

188. Had I invented hangovers?

189. No

190. Not even I would fuck up that much

191. Giselle probably had

192. Dagmar's contribution – pleading the fifth

My heaaaaaaaad. My stomaaaaaaach. My haaaaaaaair. Ouch. I rolled over. Ugh, this bed was lumpy.

"Get off me, ass breath," muttered Mel. "And answer your phone."

I got off her, as requested. My tummy lurched, but I kept rolling right off the bed so that I wouldn't barf on her with my ass breath. *Bam!* I landed on my elbow and my face both. "Auuuugh," I moaned while holding my broken face and flailing on the floor for the phone still screaming in my purse. "What," I answered with Kathleen Turner's voice.

"Shut up!" offered my loving friend.

"I'll breathe on you more," I threatened. I couldn't follow through, however. I dropped the phone and crawled to her trash, barely making it before my revelry made its reappearance.

Me and the trashcan had a nice lie down. I'd just worked up the gumption to do something about the acid burning a hole through my esophagus when I remembered my phone. Oh, whoops. Dang it. The phone sat all the way over there.

193. Three whole feet away

I rolled onto my back and stared at the ceiling. A weak noise floated to my ears. "Are you okay?" I heard. Aw! Someone cared about Dagmar on my phone!

Roll. Roll. By the third roll, I'd made it to the thing, still lit up with my call. I rolled on top of it so that I faced up. But then it was underneath me.

194. Why was life so haaaaaard

Okay. Time to woman up. I pulled the phone out from under my ass and said, like a human, "Hi."

"Giselle?"

Someone cared about *Giselle*.

"Yash. Hi. I'm sorry. My hangover is having hangover babies in my head, and those little brats are playing drums."

He chuckled in that low way of his and my body tingled with a new feeling. No, not bile, but lust. "I'm sorry. I hope you had fun at least."

"I did." Taylor, roofie, B & E, bed piss—his, not mine. "I really, really did."

"Good. I was going to ask you out to dinner tonight, but perhaps—"

"Yes."

"Are you sure you feel up to it?"

My tummy threw itself into my ribcage by way of protest. "Quiet, you," I muttered.

"What?" Yash asked.

"Nothing. Uh…Maybe you're right. But I really want to"—bang you, bang you, bang, bang bang bang "—*see* you. I mi—"

I clapped my teeth closed. I'd almost said "I miss you," but that would be disastrous. Both to say…and to admit to myself. Especially after one date!

The only date I had meant to go on.

"Tell you what," he began. The phone rattled, and I heard a smile in his butterscotch voice when he returned. I suddenly understood why Bonnie got so stupid over Clyde…if he'd had a sexy damn voice like Yash's. "Do you enjoy dumb movies?"

"Dumb movies are the best kind."

He exhaled a grin. "Will Ferrell?"

My mouth dropped. "I love Will Ferrell. I would marry anchorman Ron Burgundy even though we all know what it did to Veronica Corningstone."

"I knew you were a keeper, Giselle."

195. Uhhhhhhhhh

I fell onto my back.

He continued being far too marvelous. "Listen, come over tonight. We'll order in greasy food for a hangover and watch every Ferrell movie you can stomach, pun intended."

"I should hope so."

"Although…if you feel more comfortable, I can come to you. I am a man you just met, after all."

196. No no no!

"No, that's okay. I'll give your info to my best girl, and if I'm never seen again, she'll report to the police the person in whose freezer my body is dismembered."

"Excellent. I'll just have to dismember a different lady instead."

I snorted. Wow, my imaginative beau could get very dark.

A pillow landed upside my head, and my best girl said, "If you don't shut up, it'll be *my* freezer."

I managed to crawl into the living room. "Aren't you worried that you might be in danger from me?"

"All the time. Especially when I can't stop thinking about you. You might break my heart."

197. Don't say things like that!

I inhaled to make a witty rejoinder...but this was one piece of bullshit I couldn't bear to blow. "So tonight, what time?"

"Come over around eight. I'll have everything ready. I'll text you the address." He paused. "I wanted to take you with me to the UK for Christmas. Is that a loser thing to confess?"

His adorable earnestness mixed with macabre jokes sucked all free will from my body, and I was no longer a lying mess of dork lying ten feet away from her own hangover, but a wonderful, worthy woman who could make such a man's eyes sparkle.

Seconds ticked by. His silence on the other end became labored. Don't ask me how I knew. My heart knotted. My veins froze. "What is wrong with you?" I blurted.

He gasped.

"No, no." I fell into the couch. Well, my head did. Sitting would have required too much effort. "I mean...what are your flaws? Because I'm a mess, Yash. I'm not great, and — and I'm not great. I'm flailing in life right now. Why are you into me?"

The silence this time turned ponderous. *I think.* I wasn't a psychic, I was Ass-Breath of Loserville, in the Famewhore Blogs District.

"Giselle," he began. "You're funny. And you're hotter than hell. And you're obviously smart and adventurous, no matter what mess you're currently experiencing."

Hot? Adventurous? He should have met me two weeks ago when he'd've died of boredom. Blade almost did.

198. Better not think about that too hard

He blew into the phone and I managed to throw one leg over the couch. I was still on my back, but I'd achieved that much. "Let's see, my faults," he began. "I'll have to think hard because they're so few."

"Uh-huh. I'm going to make you watch a *Dance Moms* marathon with me tonight."

"Christ, no! Okay. I write alone in my apartment in my

underwear."

"Yum," I said.

"Not so much. I write in my underwear and...*the shirt*."

My intestines gurgled. "*The shirt?*"

"It's an old, unbelievably holey rag that used to be white, but is now gray. If it were named in a clothing catalog, it'd be called 'despair gray.' Or perhaps 'disease.'"

I burst into laughter.

"It's got many stains, most of them brown and/or green, as if I took a giant shit on it, and then blew chunks."

"Ugh, you are a writer, aren't you?"

"Yes, I am. It's disgusting. Pit stained. And I think it has a bit of a permanent funk."

"Why? Why do you keep a disease shirt to work in?"

He laughed. "It's lucky! I wrote most of my first book in it—I was pretty single at the time, go figure—and I got the call that my agent wanted to represent me *and also* the call that the book had sold *while I wore it*."

"Aw."

"The second call happened on the toilet."

I covered my mouth so that my guffaws wouldn't wake Mel again. "Wow. Nice detail."

"You wanted the bad. Turns out—I poop."

"Not me, you pervert."

He listed more grievous faults. "I bite my nails. I will leave dishes crusted until they smell. And I will likely have to spend solid time cleaning my bathroom today so you don't faint from horror."

"That's... That's gross."

"You're the mess, not me."

"Don't sass me, stinky shirt."

"Fair enough." The line clicked and echoed for a moment. "Let's see... I put almost everything off until far past the point of being a responsible adult. I had to start letting them take the rent directly from my account. I got many eviction notices because I just forgot."

"Holy shit. That's next-level irresponsibility. I feel a lot better about myself now."

"Excellent."

I threw my other leg up over the couch. "Out with it—more dirt."

"Oh, come now," he said, very British-ly. "I have to save a few terrible habits for the third date."

"Someone's optimistic."

He laughed, the adorable and smarmy sound of a man whose performance on date number two would not be in doubt. I joined in, because I had no doubts, either.

"I'll give you one more," he dangled promisingly. "I write fan fic."

"My best friend does that."

"It's *X-Files*. And I didn't write it in the 90s, I write it now. And it's about Mulder…and alien Scully."

My mouth dropped. "You mean…Scully is an alien?"

"Mmm-hmm."

"And…I'm going to regret asking…what sort of alien is she?"

A great and terrible silence descended through the line, and I began picturing a redheaded FBI agent with three boobs.

The truth was weirder. "She has tentacles," he finally ground out.

I began giggling uncontrollably. Mel yelled from the other room, but she would forgive me once we Googled and read this fan fic.

199. "Oh, my God, I love you!" I blurted into the phone

He gasped. It was a manly gasp, but still very gasp-y in nature.

"I mean…" *Oh fuck shit fucker fuckery fucking fucksticks!* "I didn't mean *love* love, I meant—"

"You mean 'tentacle Scully reaming Mulder' love you."

My leg fell off the couch, I laughed so hard. Every cell in my body had turned into a bubble and I floated away on a sea of Yash. "Yes. Wow. That is a very damning flaw. And also a very damning virtue."

"Thank you."

"You understand I will be reading these immediately."

He sighed. "Yes, I understand. Please be forewarned that I'm not half the lover alien Scully is."

"Neither am I. It's Scully as played by Gillian Anderson. She's the hottest person on earth."

"Or on Saturn Five." He laughed at his own silliness and said, "Until eight, my dear. Enjoy the first day of your New Year."

"January first!" I agreed with enthusiasm. Wait... January first. The first? "Oh, shit, I have to work! What time is it?"

"Noon-ish."

"Aaaah!" I flipped my legs to the ground. I should have been at the coffee shop an hour ago! I'd agreed to work January first before I knew I'd be enacting mighty and glorious revenge the night before. And also drinking.

Yash's voice got higher. "Oh, no. You have a flight? Will you be back by eight?"

I paused on my knees while the world swirled. Shit.

200. Shit

"Uh...yes. I have to... I'm not flying. I'm... I'm... teaching?"

201. Yes. Teaching

"Yes, teaching," I agreed with myself.

"Oh. What do you teach?"

Uh. *Uh.* "Landing."

"Landing? Fuck me, you can land a plane?"

202. Landing?!

Uh. *Uh.* "Yes, of course." I stood, but barely. The hangover babies in my head were having grandchildren, and these crotchlings were real second-generation trust fund assholes. "All flight attendants can land a plane. In case the pilots die."

He groaned. "Does that happen often?" His voice had risen in octave, like Mariah Carey's. "I don't love flying — are pilots constantly dropping dead?"

I stumbled through Mel's room and into her closet. I

could not barista in my Forever 21 jailbait garb. "No, of course not. It's just standard protocol. For safety." I shoved clothes aside until I found a simple button-down. "For us." Jeans. Jeans. Where were her jeans? "Flight attendants. Like when we...uh..." Her shoes were too big, shoot. "Shoot hijackers."

"What?"

Wait—what had I said? My head swam, my stomach swam, and the thread of this stupid conversation had been lost on me at 'tentacles.' "Just kidding?"

"Oh, good. You—you don't carry a gun on the plane, do you?"

203. I really needed to start listening to what came out of my mouth

"Nope. Well, I've got to be getting to Flight Attendant... College...of...Piloting and...Safety Systemic...Systems."

204. I was the best liar ever

"I had no idea it was a college degree that flight attendants got. You learn something new every day, eh?"

205. Apparently

"See you later," I told him before hanging up before I said anything else ridiculous before I ruined my chance of getting laid forever.

I yanked on two pairs of Mel's socks to make her shoes kind of fit. She glared at me while I bent down to give her a kiss on the forehead. "Thanks for a great night, baby."

"Your breath is even worse now. And you can just send that garbage can down the garbage chute if you don't have time to wash it."

Dutifully, I scooped it up and held my nose on the way out. "I'll get you a new one."

A happy grunt was my only reply. I trashed her trash and hopped a cab to work. Thanks be to all that is holy, I found a mint in my purse and sucked on it while spreading into the cab seat like a pool of, well, vomit. The whole world was made of angry molasses, and I swam through it with a headache the size of Alaska. Hopefully, Hunter wouldn't fire me.

Actually... Who the heck cared?

And yet I did actually care that I'd put my fellow retail drones out—

206. Fucking up should not adversely affect the drone underclass

The cab pulled up to JaVaVaVoom. I paid and leaped from the door. And face-planted on the sidewalk. The tumble knocked the wind out of me, not to mention the rest of my stomach contents. On my hands and knees, I panted and spit out the rest of last night. Oh, gross. So, so gross.

Laughter erupted above me and I managed to lift my head just enough to see Hunter guffawing a safe distance away. "Well, Dag," he said. "I see why you're late."

I collapsed onto the sidewalk in the posture adopted by lazy fetuses. The ground could not possibly be dirtier than the satanic rituals happening inside my body. "Ugh," I replied, saying it all.

"Go home. We can handle it."

"I'm sorry," I groaned. Oh, God, I wanted to die. "I tried."

"I hear you, and I appreciate that." I heard a shutter click and I knew what that meant. "But I also reserve the right to mock your sorry ass forever."

I flashed him a weak thumbs-up, and he, still laughing, returned to the coffee shop. My hand dropped to the sidewalk with a smack.

Home. I had to get home somehow. What should I do about the pile of puke? Was it rude to leave it on the sidewalk? But how did I clean it?

207. Ugh, I'd lost my lunch more in a few weeks than I had in a few years

208. That's a sign of high-quality living

Two old ladies stopped beside me. "Oh, dear," said one, a white lady in a leopard-print hat.

"My goodness," said the other, a black lady in a leopard-print hat.

"Help me," I groaned.

White friend said, "Mavis, this silly bitch is hung over.

Ha! Don't get your Keds in her mess."

Black friend said, "She might be still drunk. If she isn't, she should be. You get her other arm, Hazel."

Hazel and Mavis hauled me with all their might to my feet. That is to say, they tugged weakly, and I hauled my hungover ass to my feet. "Thank you," I managed to groan. I shoved my hand into my purse for my sunglasses, which I'd forgotten existed up to now. Aaaaaahhh. Bye, bye, evil sun. Swaying, I said, "I have to get a cab so I can go home. I have to rest because of cute boy."

Hazel sucked on her dentures. "Cute boy?"

Mavis sucked on her dentures. "I haven't had a cute boy in twenty years."

"That's because you don't put out soon enough," Hazel admonished. "At our age, you can't wait three dates. He might be dead by then. It's happened to you already."

"Twice."

I just stood there, rocking and holding my stomach. I could only dream that Mel and I would be discussing senior sex in leopard print one day.

They got me a cab and poured me into it. I asked them if I should do anything about the vomit, and they said no, that New York in the seventies had been puke as far as the eye could see.

Would they let me move in with them?

The two ladies waved as the cab took me away, and I slid all the way to lie in the back seat. The number of germs now swarming my body probably numbered in the gazillion range, but perhaps they'd be killed by the alcohol. Alcohol. I sniffed. I sniffed my arm—I smelled like booze. It oozed from my very pores!

209. Perhaps even…my soul

210. Scumbag achievement unlocked

By some miracle—i.e. the cab—I made it home. The walk to my elevator and into the apartment was a blur, and I just made it into the bedroom before I collapsed.

As I lay on my bed for a while and stared up at the ceiling,

I thought about the pain I was in. The trouble I had caused last night. The excessive partying. The disregard for the laws of man.

211. And I loved every single moment of it

212. It is a far, far better thing to barf from fun times than to barf from sadness

Via crawling, the party girl's method of creeping, I made it into the kitchen, where I grabbed a sports drink from the fridge.

213. Plan ahead to get a-drunk

Sports drink and I crawled into the living room and collapsed onto the couch. No doing my taxes today, no freaking way. Heh heh. I sipped and flipped on the TV, where daytime talk shows would lull me to sleep. Before I conked out, I set three different phone alarms for a few hours from now — neither rain nor snow nor sleet nor hangover would keep me from sexy Yash tonight.

Chapter Nine

F*ck-Ups Two-Fourteen through Two-Sixty-Nine
The Handsome Prince and the Fairy Bookmother

Some number of hours later—reading clocks is hard in that condition—I managed to eat a little soup, down eleven whole crackers without incident, brush my teeth four times, and apply makeup. Yeah, I was superwoman, queen of looking cute after cosplaying garbage.

I nearly broke down and invited Yash over to my place, but there were just too many things there with *Dagmar* written all over them. One was a giant metal 'D' in Times New Roman hanging on the wall of the living room. There used to be an '& B' there as well, but I'd taken a baseball bat to them.

214. Sometimes coping involves baseball bats

Old me would never, ever have done such a violent thing. New me hadn't thought twice about it. Bashing the letters on the front stoop had been a good upper body workout, and amused my neighbors. I'd even gotten to know Lydia in 301 as she'd taken her own turn at the bat. She had an ex named Blake—small world.

I took a baggie of saltines with me in the cab to Yash's place. I'm a classy date—

215. Ready to put out and I bring my own snacks

Arrived, rang the bell, got buzzed in. When the elevator doors opened, there he stood before me, sexy as hell in jeans and soft flannel. He jammed his hands into his pockets and looked such the hot dork I nearly jumped onto him and committed a public act of indecency in the hall. However,

I was too hungover for jumping…and humping would only happen after I'd gotten a meal in me that stayed down successfully.

216. *Oh goddess of hussies, hear my plea*

217. *Or goddess of booze, maybe*

"Hi! Are you feeling okay? How did flight training go?" he asked.

He began to lead me down the hall and I almost asked, "Flight training?" before I remembered the lie I'd told about teaching other flight attendants to land a plane. Wouldn't pilots teach that if it were true?

218. *Please don't think about that too closely, Yash*

"Everything's great," I assured him. As we arrived at his door, my stomach gave a tremendous *gggguuurrrgglee*. He laughed at me and I added, "I haven't eaten very much today."

He opened the door and a wondrous smell of delicious nearly knocked me over. "I can help with that."

Once inside, he liberated me from my purse and led me by the hand to the living room. His soft, warm skin almost distracted me from the plethora of food on his coffee table. Almost. For lo, I beheld a bounty of sweet and sour veggies, noodles, egg rolls, cream cheese wontons, and even more. I sank to my knees beside it and hugged the table.

Grinning from ear to ear, he got on the floor beside me. "I hope this satisfies?"

"Uuuunnnnghhh." I rolled onto my back like a puppy. "Insert here." I pointed into my mouth.

His eyebrows rose.

"Your steaming egg roll."

They got higher.

"Your hot and sour…dumpling?"

He yanked me by the arm until we made our way to the couch. "Dumpling, eh? Have you ever seen a man naked before?"

"Not as many as I should have," I replied honestly. Too honestly, probably.

Didn't seem to bother him, for he smiled anew and handed me a pair of chopsticks. "Pick a carton, any carton."

"I love you."

"No, you don't. You love me for my hot veggie buns." He sniffed indignantly and pretend-sobbed into an egg roll.

I started to giggle, my iffy stomach forgotten in his dorkiness. I pointed to the noodles to start, so he handed them to me.

"Can I get the lady a drink?"

I uttered a squeaking sound that was both embarrassing and stereotypical. But, in embarrassing fashion, I didn't care. "Do you have any ginger ale? It's okay if —"

"I do — I'll be right back."

In a very clever surreptitious manner, I used his absence to investigate the lay of the foreign land. Not bad. His décor was sort of space-age and modern, but not stark or cold. Tons of books, naturally. Books are a must in a boy. And the walls were a lovely sky-blue — happy, bright, and unexpected. And — ha — it totally smelled like cleaning supplies. The man who put this place together would always pleasantly surprise a woman. If only Giselle could move in…

219. But she didn't exist

220. No biggie

221. Definitely not ruining my life

222. I'll just blog about it

223. That would make ruining my love life better

He returned, a cobalt-blue glass in hand, cool and frosty from ice.

"Thank you," I said.

He bowed. "Your next choice is…" He walked to his entertainment center and I noticed for the first time the enormous TV thereon. Like sixty inches or something? Huge! A very *man* TV. Stylish and manly — the ultimate straight girl one-two punch of fabulous.

Not the trifecta, though. The trifecta includes a lumberjack or astronaut.

224. Lumberjack and astronaut is called the Quadruple Almost Clooney.

I'd just popped a piece of bun into my mouth when he presented me with options for my viewing pleasure. "Holy moly. You weren't kidding when you said you dig Will Ferrell."

"Afraid not." He sat beside me, and I flipped through the stack of DVDs. *Anchorman, Blades of Glory, Talladega Nights...*

"*The Ballad of Ricky Bobby!*" I said with a bounce. "That one also has Sacha Baron Cohen. And race cars."

A slow smile spread across his face, and I could tell I'd chosen well. His eyes sparkled as he said, "And John C. Reilly," which might have seemed weird, except that I knew they were shining for me. *And a little for Mr. Reilly, who, come on, is funny as hell.*

"Oh, yeah." I held up my hand and he high-fived me. The small gesture almost turned me on as much as any kiss.

Almost.

Bonding over silly movies is an excellent sign in a boyfriend. I mean...one-night stand.

225. How badly was I fucking up this one-night stand?

226. Pretty boyfriend badly

He pressed buttons and adjusted settings, munching on an egg roll while he did so, and I nearly died. I nearly died of feelings right there in his tasteful, (newly) clean, interesting living room.

227. Why?

228. Why had I met this marvelous man on a night full of lies?

229. Why had I not just come clean the first time he called me?

230. Why was Giselle here instead of Dagmar?

231. And why was my boob so itchy tonight?

I scratched my boob with my arm and knew there was no going back now. I was doomed. I shoved rice into my mouth. Sooner or later my secrets would burst forth. They had to. Unless I just legally changed my name to Giselle, abandoned every person who ever knew me before, and ran away with Yash to live in a hut in Bora Bora.

232. And also with that blond guy who played Thor

Yes. That was the solution to all my problems.

233. Why hadn't I considered this before?

He settled in beside me, his remote-clicking completed. Except for one thing. He flashed his whiz-bang universal remote so I could see and clicked a button.

The room lights dimmed.

I laughed so hard I spat out a little rice. He didn't seem to care, but grinned. "That's another of my secrets. I'm a huge geek."

"That's a secret? Besides, I don't know if that was geeky or Austin Powers-ey."

"The couch rotates."

"And vibrates too, I should hope."

"For her pleasure."

He said it so low that he vibrated *me*, the wicked man. I pushed a wonton into my mouth instead of jumping him. I needed the sustenance or I'd faint during hour four of sex.

234. Optimism

235. Numbered because looking forward to anything positive was probably a mistake

Talladega Nights began, and he slid in next to me, our thighs snuggling like new best friends, our mouths full of delivered happiness. We laughed in the same spots, and soon, my belly burst with fullness and so did my heart.

236. Oh, no, that was poetic

237. Poetic!

Enough of this girlfriend shit. I wasn't Dagmar anymore. Not in any way. I would not be that woman who trusted and went along with and supported people who hid and dissembled and took. Giselle was independent—the only way to keep a girl safe from the vagaries of others.

238. My own vagaries were enough to deal with

I set my carton on the table, wiped my mouth of sauce, and plucked the chopsticks from his hands. His eyebrows raised and a little pulse in his neck jumped. My mouth split into a giggle—that tiny sign of his excitement nearly made me want to sing with joy.

I bit my lip as I'd seen Britney Spears do in many a sexy music video. What next? The last time I'd attempted to be aggressive with a guy, it ended with a printer up my butt.

Here goes nothing.

I crawled into his lap to straddle him. He smiled and didn't throw me to the floor. Splendid. His hands slid up my jean-clad legs to cup my ass, his eyes locked onto mine the whole time. We sat there, gazes held, anticipating what we both hoped would happen next. The old me would never have made bold moves like these.

239. To be honest, it was probably good that Yash was bedding Giselle instead of me

He yanked me closer and kissed me. Respectfully, at first, his mouth soft. A warmth suffused my chest. My hands clutched at his T-shirt, and his arms wrapped all the way around. Oh, God. My breasts pressed against him, my thighs caressed his waist. I hadn't sat on a man this way in…in a while. And I hadn't wanted to drown in it for a lot longer than that.

The sound of race cars zoomed around us. It was a strangely hot soundtrack to make out to. Maybe this was why NASCAR was so popular.

He lifted me up. My arms locked around his neck as he swung me onto my back on the couch. I'd been about to suggest we adjourn to the bedroom, but—

240. Lying hussies can't be choosers

I'd always enjoyed sex, but a shiver raced through me this time. A huge realization had come to me during the last couple of weeks—about my previous relationship, about how little he'd respected me. Blade had, more than once, said something to the effect of, "What do I say to get you to stop talking and take off your clothes?"

Even if Yash and I only experienced this one night together, I didn't feel as if he was using me, or merely saying the right things until I agreed to shut up and put out.

241. Although…was I doing that to him?

242. Better not think about that too hard

Surely part of being a fuck-up, like all horrible people who succeeded in life, was not being the nicest Mary Sue who ever lived. Right?

Yash jerked his T-shirt over his head to reveal… Holy hunk. Angels sang. Kittens frolicked. The sun shone through the heavens even though it was nine o'clock at night! Bless the new breed of cool dude, New York writers — they spent as much time in the gym as they did at the keyboard. Sometimes more.

Morals? What morals!?

243. Abs

244. Abs were what mattered

245. Also

246. Abs

I licked my lips and actually caught a bit of drool. Like a femme fatale, I beckoned him with my little finger, and my literary hunk dutifully crawled over my body.

He blinked, slow, sultry. I ached for him in places I couldn't remember the name of at the moment. He leaned toward me, his mouth parted, ready to… "Shit, I need to get a condom." Making a face, he leaned away a few inches. "Sorry — romantic, eh? I have a clean bill of health. I can prove it, I have the paper around here. I got it to attra — " He cut himself off and sat up.

I cocked my head and leaned on my elbows. "To what?"

Bashfully, he shook his head. "Later. But let me get the…" He smiled and left the room.

"I'm on the pill," I called. "And I just got a test too. All clean!"

He returned quickly. "I have no doubt. But I like a double protection against pregnancy. Rug rats." He pulled a face and shuddered. "Shit, probably shouldn't have said that, either. Are kids a deal breaker for you? Shit, I'm bringing this up on the second date."

"And saying 'shit' a lot."

He groaned.

I giggled and reached for him. "Music to my ears on all counts. Now..." I took the condom from him and tore it open. "Let me help you with that."

This was it! I was going to casual the sex! My heart leaped into spasms in my chest—hell, in my feet. Every inch of my skin wanted to rear up to greet his hands, his mouth. And so it did. Again and again his lips roamed across my skin. Then he flipped me over and perpetrated all manner of filthy greetings to the skin on my backside...

247. So to speak

248. Hi, hello, bonjour, ciao, and nǐ hǎo

He did everything right. Everything, and several new things I hadn't heard of. One of them might have been 'orgasm' in Croatian for all I knew. And judging by this lovely man's smiles, laughter, and general, er, *tumescence*, I made him just as happy as he made me.

When we'd exhausted ourselves, and our foreign vocabularies, on his surprisingly comfy couch, he said, "Relax."

He smoothed my hair over my forehead and kissed the spot. I shivered, filled to brimming with happiness, joy, bewilderment, relaxation.

"I'll clean up dinner," he assured me. "We can watch the rest of the movie in the bedroom? If you'd like. Then you can fall asleep whenever you want after your long day."

My brain swam in a sex haze. That was the best I'd had since...since my first fella. Yash definitely outscored Blade in both the freestyle and dismount categories. A ten out of ten, even from the Russian judge.

But what now? I watched Yash's gorgeous butt as he ran food into his kitchen.

Shouldn't I be leaving?

But I was so sleepy.

Shouldn't I be leaving?

But watching movies while snuggled in bed.

Shouldn't I be leaving?

249. But but but…

250. Butt butt butt

I needed to get out of here. He couldn't think this was anything more than a spectacular booty call. I sat up and searched for my clothes. They'd gone a-flying some time ago.

Yash returned with a bowl of ice cream.

Ice cream.

Nope, *non, nein* I should stay, I should definitely stay with the hot naked guy bringing me ice cream.

He waved the bowl in front of me and drew me to the bedroom, both of us laughing as I licked my lips and followed my nose. Soon, I snuggled against a cushy pillow, and he started the movie for me in the darkened room. His bed was king-size and featured a snuggly duvet cover dusted with the galaxy and stars.

I was lying in heaven.

He soon joined me, and he dipped a spoon into the bowl of shared ice cream. The warm and the cold, the funny and the serene — they drugged me, lulled me. I fought it so hard, his…his…Yash-ness. Why couldn't he have been a hot asshole like Blade? I knew what to do with that kind of man now. A Yash, however… The guy who stays must be navigated.

Was I assuming he would stay? But a nice man is still able to be bored.

With a cold tongue, I licked my ice cream spoon clean and rested my head back.

I opened my eyes to bright sunlight in a strange room. Yash's room. I started to sit up, and he came through the door, head peeking first with an adorable grin. "Hi," he said, all sleepy-like, and I melted back into the covers. He held two steaming mugs aloft. "I hope you're a coffee person?"

251. Of course — I served coffee all the time at my 'airplane' job

I nodded, and he sat beside me. "I have one cream and sugar, one black." He raised his eyebrows in the question.

"Black," I replied.

"Good! That stuff is vile."

He handed me the vile stuff and I groped for my phone… which must be in the other room with my clothing. Heh heh.

252. *I'd just lounge in bed*

253. *Naked*

254. *Drinking the coffee*

255. *My naked hookup brought me*

"So…" I began. "What or whom did you hope to attract with your clean bill of health. From last night?"

He laughed. "Before last night, it had been about…seven and a half months since I'd had sex. Around month three, I got a full STD panel in the hope that—"

I returned his laugh with a giggle of my own. "If you test it, she will come?"

"Something like that."

"It didn't work in a very timely manner." I ran a finger down his gorgeous thigh. "How can it be that hard for you to get booty?"

He took a long sip of coffee. "I'm not that into casual sex. I like relationships. The sex can be amazing, and there are layers of comfort and trust because you're not strangers. After my last breakup, a year ago, I went on first date after first date, and a few seconds. Awful. Stilted. Some terrible people, some lovely women, but we just didn't click. I went on thirty dates or so—matches from the Internet, friends, enemies, paper airplanes thrown in my general direction— and, after they all came to naught, I just quit. I couldn't do another painful, boring dinner wherein I told the same bloody stories about myself. They're not interesting enough to recount that many times."

He paused and looked down at me. "That was much too much information, wasn't it? I should say something manly about banging women with abandon."

I shook my head. "No. No, you shouldn't. You shouldn't be anyone other than who you are, because that guy is way too awesome."

He gave me a long, slow kiss that curled my hair and eyeballs, then went to make breakfast.

Breakfast? No way. My insides roiled. This kind, sweet man had trusted me enough to take the next step. I flailed in the bed until I couldn't stand it anymore and got up. I was closing tonight, and I had to show up for my coffee drones. Maybe I'd bring the crew donuts to apologize.

256. You can get away with more shit at work when the drones love you

But it was haaaaaard to get moving. Because his bedroom was made of warmth and sunshine. My skin felt like a dance, and my heart beat lighter than it had in...in...wow, far too long.

And the sex. Wow. Sweet. *Nasty.* I'd achieved nasty sex! And, God, I wanted it to happen again *immediately*.

I had to get moving because I knew I must say goodbye to Yash forever. I couldn't keep up a lie this enormous. I mean, a girl could lie about her weight, or her number of lovers, or about how often she changed her future cat's litter box... but her *name*...and *occupation*...

Her identity?

I managed to get on my clothing —

257. While he offered to make me breakfast

258. While he stayed naked and impossibly hot

259. While he smiled as his hair flopped over his brow

260. While he told me what a good time he'd had

At the door, he promised to call me. I nodded and bit my lip to avoid saying...anything. He kissed me, his mouth warm and sweet like coffee. I felt that kiss in my toes. In my pleasantly sore lady business. In my soul *oh, God, no, no soul talk, was I trying to kill myself with feelings after one bang?*

Well, two bangs in one night.

Go me.

I squeezed him tight and nearly ran down the hall to the elevator. I could still smell his skin on mine — the faint aroma of his cologne and his him-ness. No showers for a week, until the reek of me outlasted him.

I stepped onto the sidewalk and tied my scarf tighter. A cold walk would do me good. Four hours until I had to get to work—throwing winter on my tender feelings would be smart.

This entire life exercise was designed to force me to expand my horizons. I'd done good things, bad things, and good-bad things.

And before my fuck-up-a-palooza, I'd spent my entire adult life going from one serial boyfriend to the next. Two, exactly. Unconsciously hunting for a husband, just as my dad expected of me. My sister had found hers in college—the proverbial MRS degree—just as expected of her. But I hadn't. I probably could have, though. Shit, I'd still be with Blade even now if he hadn't gotten a job in L.A.

I shivered against a blast of cold air, both the internal and the external kind. Would I really have married that guy?

Ugh, my head jumbled like a Boggle board. Things I should do. Things I shouldn't. And whose opinions were they, anyway? Mine? Dad's? Society's? Oprah's?

The honest truth—I was a lying liar who lied. I could not see Yash again. Better that he thought well of one night instead of getting hurt weeks down the line, right?

Right.

I popped into a bakery to get myself a donut to make my deep thoughts more palatable. Mmmmmmm, chocolate-glazed regret.

Yash should be chalked up to a beautiful one-night stand. A reminder that there are fabulous men out there who are kind, have good taste in goofy movies, and screw like sex demons. These 666 mistakes were about new experiences, and should be embraced as such. My mistakes shouldn't drag on and on, like a trip to the DMV. They should flame out fast and wild, a match in the darkness.

Thoughts of screwing sex demons kept a spring in my step the rest of the way home, and as soon as I got in the house, I put my Yash feelings into a blog post. I didn't call him

Yash, of course. I had called him Writer Guy — WG — before last night. But, as of this morning, he would be elevated to Sexy Sex Writer Guy — SSWG.

This silly little project of mine had begun to go viral. Thousands of blog followers. I was close to one hundred thousand Twitter followers. I wasn't just me and my brilliance — I think a lot of people were stuck in situations they didn't like and dreamed of saying 'fuck off' to everyone and everything. People were living vicariously through me.

261. I was living the nightmare

Strangers had started telling me how they'd been bold at work, or stood up for themselves with their own jerky partner. All these people taking inspiration from me ruining my life... It was magical. Maybe some other mousy woman would read my misadventures and realize there was more to life than blending into the wall.

262. There was having some motherfucking fun, too

I threw on comfy work clothes and, on the way to JaVaVaVoom, texted Mel to get together after my shift to sew destruction upon Taylor via his mother. We agreed to meet at an all-night Internet café in Brooklyn for maximum anonymity.

263. Anticipation of getting some small form of justice for all the women that scum had abused...

264. Priceless

My bones, they were a-chilled by the time I got into work. I pushed open the door and swept inside, a whole fifteen minutes early —

265. Sorry for my punctuality, fuck-up list

— When I heard scattered applause. I looked up to see if we'd been visited by a celebrity when I realized the staff cheered for me. Hunter pointed to a photocopy behind the bar, and there I lay, on the sidewalk, next to my own vomit. Every one of my fellow drones began whooping.

I bowed, my face wide with the most embarrassed grin of my life.

266. My dad would be so ashamed

267. No decent man would marry a sidewalk drunkard!
268. Good

"I have so many people to thank," I said. I came around the bar and addressed my adoring public. "My friend Mel, who insisted on the keg stands. The two twin guys who bravely bought us Martinis despite the fact that we could not even remember the fake names we gave them." Lacey giggled at this one. "My dignity, for being on vacation in the Bahamas. Thank you for the warm tribute. And fuck you all."

The entire coffee shop began applauding then, and I gave a Queen Elizabeth wave on the way to the back. I searched my heart for some sense of regret. But I didn't care. Not even a little. What was I going to do about it now, anyway? I deserved the ribbing and, truth be told, a glow warmed me to know that I'd behaved like a twenty-something for once instead of a biddy.

Had I well and truly thrown the old Dagmar out with the bathwater?

I tied an apron around my person and Hunter pointed me toward the register. "Have at it, loser," he said by way of welcome. "Later on, I'm going to teach you about the different beans of Asia."

A woman approached the register. She wore a scarlet suit and black fedora over a glorious mane of purple afro. The white baby hairs at her temples were the only indication she might not be my contemporary—her deep brown, almost onyx skin was flawless. I said, "You look snazzy as hell! What can I get you today?"

She quirked an eyebrow and leaned forward to peer at my name tag. "Dagmar. Dagmar, that's a rare name. Did you, by any chance, work for Carmichael Burns?"

My eyes widened. "Who's asking? You can't be his new girlfriend—you're wearing too many clothes."

She snorted. "And I'm about seven decades too old for him. Marlene Hodgkins, Hysterical Books."

I took her proffered shake and nearly yanked her over

the counter with the force of my enthusiasm. My stomach leaped into my throat, but not from alcohol poisoning for once. "Dagmar Kostopoulos. Yes, I was his right hand. Until it wandered, so to speak."

Marlene nodded. "Damn shame. That Kardashian salad book has shockingly tasty recipes, and is hilarious. Was the humor you? Khandye seems bland as toast."

My mouth dropped to be remembered, and by a woman who was so amazing in the field. Hysterical Books promoted women writers and released some of the boldest, most fun writing by women for women out there. They took chances on voices that the big five ordinarily wouldn't, usually to great success. And Marlene was their queen, a.k.a. editor in chief. As such, my hands fluttered nervously. "I'm flattered beyond belief. I've been a huge fan of your press for a long, long time."

"I never forget a name, or a piece of literary gossip." She glanced around, but nobody was queueing up behind her. "And thank you. Have you decided to quit books completely? Or is this temporary?"

I shrugged. My every instinct screamed to lie to make myself appear less terrible, but that was the old Dagmar. Giselle told the truth. Kind of. "I'm having a life crisis. So I'm… I'm fucking up."

Her eyebrows shot up again. She had such an expressive face! I bet she wasn't much of a liar with a countenance like that. She leaned against the counter to peer at me closer. "Fucking up how?"

"Well…" This time, I leaned closer. "I decided that being the dutiful assistant editor had gotten me nowhere, so I wanted to try living like a boss. My old one, to be specific. I tried to bang my new boss" —I pointed with my head in Hunter's direction—"during my job interview. I got rubber burn from the dress I wore, and he said no anyway."

She blinked once, twice, her speckled brown eyes alighting with palpable curiosity. "Too bad — brother is fine as hell."

"Right?"

"Why, though? To see why Carmichael did it? Or just for fun?"

I cocked one hip and contemplated this. "I— It was the latter, really. But maybe it was the former, too. Holy shit, could that have really been the reason?"

"Dagmar, I love it. When I was thirty-one, I took a year abroad in Italy to, eh, 'fuck up,' as you so perfectly put it." She'd said 'fuck' like a society matron tasting the word—a strange, but enjoyable, canapé. "They kicked me out, and then I wrote a book about it. My passport was barred for ten years."

I clapped my hands and laughed and laughed. "You're a level up. I'm not worthy!"

She graced me with an adorable single shoulder shrug and ordered her coffee. I jumped off the register to make it myself. Even if I never touched a book again, it was nice to know there were people out there fighting the good fight for talented authors, and not being scumbags about it. Unless in Italy, where apparently all bets were off.

When I handed her latte over, I said, "Please come by again."

"I will. Keep fucking up. Women don't allow themselves to do that nearly enough."

I actually had to take a step back and turn—tears had sprung to my eyes. Was this woman my fairy bookmother? I'd never in my life been given permission to make mistakes by an authority figure. And, even though I was practically living a performance art piece at the moment, I still hadn't thought of it as the right thing to do *per se*. Dudes called it 'finding themselves' then they went to Thailand for a month to pay for sex and drunkenly barf words on a typewriter.

Marlene made me feel proud of my ridiculousness. No hookers needed.

"Hey, Dag," Hunter called. "How about you do your fucking up in the bathroom? Some kid yakked in there, and I think you're the perfect person to handle it."

269. Dagmar Kostopoulos, professional barf expert

While I mopped up vomit, I naturally considered Taylor. We would screw that Taylor good right after work. Well, not screw. *Ew.*

Chapter Ten

F*ck-Ups Two-Seventy through Two-Ninety-Nine
Going Full Austen

It was midnight in the city that never sleeps. So, naturally, Mel and I were not asleep.

I didn't have to work the next day, and her office was closed until next week. Publishing doesn't work over the holidays — or, in general, a lot of the time. *Rimshot.*

We met at the Internet café, and I handed her a glass of rosé the moment she walked in the door. "Hair of the dog," I said.

She examined the pink liquid. "Hair of the poodle might be more specific." She set her purse down and sat at our desk. "Your post about lying to SSWG got picked up by Buzzfeed."

I nearly dropped the wine bottle I was using for a top-off. "What?"

After taking a huge swallow of pink, she said, "Yeah. Some writer there included you in a list of the top five new funny women of the Internet. Our readership has quadrupled just today."

"Wow!"

While we toasted my dubious blog's success, my stomach squirmed like a fibbing fibber who fibs. Wow for me, but not Yash. *Yash.* He was way too sweet to be the butt of lies uttered by a deceiving deceiver and celebrated by a million strangers.

But I buried that guilt way, way deep down. Guilt did not get a girl onto Buzzfeed. My whole life had a bright yellow

Win badge on it now, and if fake Internet recognition wasn't a sign of *Win*-ning, then I didn't know what was.

270. Really

271. I had no idea

Besides, I thought while swallowing more guilt—it tasted like rosé—I would never speak with Yash again. He might be hurt, but how sad could he really be after a one-night stand?

My phone buzzed. Mel intercepted it and said, "Yash says you were the best first night of sex in his life, and he's counting the minutes until he can see you again."

272. Shove that feeling way…way down

273. Past my heart

274. Which was currently experiencing a burning sensation

275. Like an STD

276. Of emotion

"That's…fine," I said. She crooked an eyebrow. "Love 'Em and Leave 'Em Giselle, that's what they call me."

"Who calls you?"

"The one I loved and left. I mean, the one I indifferent-ed and left." I shrugged indifferent-ed-ly. "A lady's imagination is very rapid—it jumps from admiration to love, from love to matrimony in a moment."

My best friend blinked at me. "O-kay."

I cleared my throat. "Do you see how I'm super good at sex stuff, though?"

"That's my Giselle."

I changed the subject. Expertly. "Now let's ruin an asshole's relationship with his mother."

Mel cracked her knuckles and went to work. Soon we had a dummy email account called TaylorRoofiesWomen. We figured that would get Mom's attention.

"Poor Mom," I said.

"Poor *roofied women*," she replied.

I raised my glass to her point.

Like Amelia Earhart, we bravely took off for unknown parts. The parts in smutty pictures.

Mel typed 'Dear Mrs. Walters—'

"Very good," I commended. "Be sure to blind copy Charlie."

We started to compose the email, but something nagged at my brain. "Do you really think," I asked, "that he'll stop? Maybe we should send these to the cops."

"I don't want to get arrested for breaking and entering."

"Well, what if I just did it myself? I could always say that…that I switched our drinks, so that *he* got the roofie he tried to give to me. That's a pretty smart way to not get roofied when you're out with a dude you don't know."

"That is clever, if you order the same drink he does. But still… Wait." She smiled, slow and sneaky, and got that sparkly, wicked look that inspired me to stretch my evil imagination. "What if we sent them to DirtyLinens.com? That site will go to court to keep sources private—they've done it before. A story on a site that huge would force the cops to investigate…hopefully keeping us out of it."

"The poor girls. They'd be in the newspaper, too."

"Yeah, I can't imagine the site would show their faces, though."

I shook my head. "No."

Mel sat up on her leg. "We can't just let him keep doing this! I know there's a thousand guys out there doing the same thing every night, but maybe exposing one will help people everywhere to stop scumbags."

"And I could blog about doing that after the story comes out."

"Yes!"

"So…" I leaned back in my chair. "So we just send them to DirtyLinens.com? I can't really believe they'd have a hard time finding a girl drugged by him for corroboration."

She nodded. "Yes, I think we have an obligation to womanity. Mom can read about her precious boy online."

We toasted again and drafted a note to the gossip site, included all the photos—even number five, the most vomitus photo ever created—and told the whole story of how he operated.

Mel began drinking straight from the wine bottle. I felt that I was becoming a good influence on her.

277. Shaping the drunken future leaders of tomorrow

I searched DirtyLinens for stories about the Walters family. One reporter in particular seemed to hate them, including cousin Archie, who routinely got arrested with hookers and blow. This reporter was a woman, so we concluded that she was the ideal recipient for this particular mail bomb.

My cursor hovering over the Send button, I said, "I hope you can do the right thing, Abby Anderson of DirtyLinens."

Mel saluted the screen. "God speed."

"Or maybe Satan speed. The morality of what we're doing is vague."

My BFF shook her head. "Nope. We're taking down a piece of shit."

I hit Send and we saluted each other with a drink. Again.

"Hey," I said after swallowing, "wanna plaster his neighborhood with these pictures so everyone knows he's a drugging piece of crap?"

Her eyes got wide. "Uh…no. Not a good idea."

"We'd blur the ladies' faces."

"Nope."

"Key his car?" I bounced in my seat. "Set fire to it?"

A guy at the computer across from us flicked his gaze up in alarm. "Mind your own business," I spat at him, and he returned to his porn or whatever.

278. Damn it feels good to be a gangster

"You're a little scary as Giselle, you know that, right?"

I cackled and cackled, my heart feeling light as a feather, vengeful as a demon.

My phone buzzed and Mel glanced at it again. "You're going to have to tell this guy it's over. He's begging to see you again tomorrow…er, tonight. It's already tomorrow."

I shrugged and logged off the computer completely, erasing the browsing history as well. As I grabbed my purse, I said, "A girl likes to be crossed a little in love now and then."

Mel practically shoved me out of the door. The cold air smelled like snow. "It's happening again, Dag. You need to dump this guy—for the good of both of you."

"What's happening? I'm totally going to dump him. I mean…like…after one more date. Just to get him out of my system, you know?"

We took off toward her place and she muttered, "It's Greg from sophomore year all over again."

I stopped on the sidewalk, and a guy nearly plowed me over from behind. When we'd untangled, I spun on Mel. "That's not true."

"You're going—"

"Don't say it!"

"Full Austen. You are already Full Austen for him! After *two dates*. It took two months with Greg."

I began walking again. Okay, stomping. *No. No Austen!* I shook my head when Mel caught up to me. I assured her, "I am in control of this situation. I will be calm. I will be mistress of myself."

She ran in front and shoved her pointy finger in my face. "Again!"

"Shut up! I may have lost my heart, but not my self-control."

"Then end it, *Emma*. Now." She shoved her hand in my back pocket and handed me my phone. "Do you remember what you did with Greg?"

I shook my head. To all of it. I snatched my phone. "I will dump Yash…tomorrow. I can't dump him at one a.m.! He won't be able to sleep. He needs his sleep to write." I gritted my teeth. "And Greg was a misunderstanding."

"You showed up at his house party dressed as Elizabeth Bennett and asked him to dance because 'To be fond of dancing was a certain step toward falling in love.' Thank God the Internet wasn't such a thing then, or else that photo would be the first thing in your Google search results for all time."

I started to crumple. "But he was so nice in poetry class." I took off walking again. "Besides, this is completely different. Yash actually likes me. And knows my name. Kind of."

Mel fell into step beside me, her air slightly less hostile. "You have a tendency to go too far. You're kinda scary with this Taylor thing. It's weird, really—you're either super beige or every color in the rainbow with bonus firecrackers."

I stopped short, my formerly light heart plummeting like an anvil. Oh, hell. She was right. She pulled me in for a hug and I squeezed her back. You couldn't get mad at a friend good enough to call you on your shit.

My phone buzzed again, but, instead of a text this time, Yash was calling.

"Don't panic," Mel said.

"Eeeeeeeeeeeeeee," I keened. Oh, God, I was going to vomit my own heart onto my shoes. I slid the answer button. "Hi, Yash," I whispered.

"Hi, I hope it's not too late to call?"

I shook my head. "No. I never mind when you call."

Mel stomped her foot beside me and slid her finger across her throat. It was the most adorable threat I'd ever gotten.

I began the terrible speech, "Uh...listen—"

"I just called to say that I cannot stop thinking about you. And wishing you were here." He laughed. "Reminds me of 'to wish was to hope, and to hope was to expect.' Can I expect you soon, sexy Giselle?"

My breath caught. My eyes went wide. He'd just *Sense and Sensibility*'d me! "And how do you expect me?" I asked.

Mel began having some sort of anger fit. I passed her and sped into my own delusion.

Yash said, "I expect you to come over right this minute. I want to taste you again."

I clapped my hand over my mouth, and I really, really could not breathe then.

279. Or ever again

280. All the oxygen on planet Earth had fled

281. For Yash was so hot, he'd burned it away

"Yes," I replied, breathlessly, like a proper heroine.

282. How could I decline such an offer?

283. Giselle was only human

284. Dagmar was the demon

"I'll be there in less than an hour," I assured him.

"Good." He paused and chuckled, and my panties suddenly got wet. "Mmmm, I can't wait."

Mel caught up to me then, and I flicked off the phone.

"You didn't do it," she said.

I remained noncommittal and drew up the hood to my jacket. I yanked on the little strings, and the hood closed over my weak, dissembling face. Faux fur caught in my lip gloss, yet still I ran from her.

She stomp-chased me. "Come back here! We're picking a different guy for you!"

"No!" I yelled into the wind.

"It will never work, Dagmar."

"Yes, it will!"

"How?"

I stopped at a busy intersection and her determined little nay-saying self plowed into me, nearly knocking us both into oncoming traffic. She grabbed me by the shoulders. "Snap out of it! For his sake, if not your own."

"But he wants sex. Shouldn't I give the nice man sex?"

"You're going to do it no matter what I say, aren't you?"

"Well, I *am* a professional fuck-up."

"You're a loony."

I sniffed and began crossing the street. "I'm either a daring modern woman or Trash Whore McGhee, depending on the blog commenter."

285. Either way

286. Sex sex sex

We arrived at Mel's place and I gave her a hug at her door. She shook her head and said, "You're going to get hurt."

"Yeah, well... At least I'm the one doing the hurting this time. I'm not twiddling my good-girl thumbs while my boyfriend plans an exit strategy in L.A. and fucks Amy." I kissed my bestie on the cheek. "Excellent job tonight, bestie. One of us should check the dummy email, right? In case the journalist writes back?"

"Let's meet tomorrow and go to the café again. You owe me a movie or something for abandoning me tonight for a *man*."

287. Ditching your girl to meet a guy? Definitely a fuck-up

I started toward the street to hail a cab to Yash's and waved back at her. "My courage always rises at every attempt to intimidate me."

"Full Austen, you loony!"

The whole cab ride to Yash's, Mel's words rang in my head. How did the jerks of this world deal with the guilt? They probably didn't have any. They were out for themselves, and, therefore, they succeeded.

288. They wanted

289. They took

290. They enjoyed

291. Profit!

Ugh, Dag, just shut up, already! This was fun sex, for goodness' sake. Leave it to me to make a chart of it in my brain with a pro-con list and highlighted Post-it notes. I was the worst modern woman ever. The whore of Sodom got this stuff right two thousand years ago, and we had the benefit of birth control now.

The cab stopped. I paid, rang the bell, and waited in the elevator.

The doors slid open, and Yash stuck his head out of his door and waved me in with a huge, adorable grin...and a suggestive lick of the lips.

My mouth fell open and the gears in my brain stopped. The sun seemed to shine from around him, from inside him. There was no tomorrow. There was no guilt. There existed only that smile, and the promise of what it meant for my immediate future. There was no Dagmar, only Giselle.

And Giselle's fuck buddy wanted to taste her. I giggled and closed his door behind me.

* * * *

"What are you smiling about?" a heavy-lidded Yash asked the next morning.

I pressed my lips together and shrugged.

For that bit of coquetry, I got a tickle on my backside. I jerked away, laughing, and he repeated, "I demand you tell me. You can't smile for no reason—what do you think is going on here?"

Even first thing in the morning, he could make me laugh. "Remembering last night. When this terrible man I know did terrible things to me."

He nodded and tucked my head into his shoulder. I snuggled into his warmth gladly. Yash was my personal drug, and I wanted all the high-flying hallucination I could get. Before the inevitable come-down.

"I see," he rumbled. "And what awful things did this degenerate do to you? So I know to never do them myself."

"Well... First he fed me wine."

He gasped. "Shocking. Plied you with drink?"

"Mmm-hmm. And then he took my clothes off!"

"*No.*" This time the tickle to my backside turned into a rub. No—a caress. Definitely a backside caress.

I wiggled my bum in appreciation. "And then he... He..." I couldn't say it out loud.

"He what?"

"He..." I got up on my elbow and whispered in his ear. "He went down on me."

Yash flipped me over. It was my turn to gasp. Holy hell, he looked like the devil himself—too handsome by half, stubble on his chiseled jaw, unruly hair falling over his forehead. What was a girl to do?

292. I had to let him do it again

Wouldn't Jane Austen want it that way?

In the hazy afterglow of a class A orgasm, Yash went to make coffee, leaving me to my brain's hijinks. Yash was so giving that he inevitably invited comparisons with Blade, who rarely performed that particular lovely task. But he'd always wanted me to suck the sausage. Slurp the salami? *I am very bad at slang.* I didn't mind *per se*, but a lot of the time he'd just grab my head and start pushing it down—in the middle of watching TV, or once when I was making dinner.

I grimaced and buried my face in a pillow. It's just not polite to shove your girlfriend to her knees when she's got a carrot in one hand and a peeler in the other. Potentially dangerous for one's dick too.

Blech.

293. Better not think about that too hard

Not thinking was quickly becoming my mantra.

I decided not to be selfish, so I got up, slipped on a soft plaid robe of Yash's, and joined him in the kitchen. Yash had busied himself with the coffee pot in nothing but boxers, and I had to stop myself from shoving him to his knees. Ahem.

"More smirks on that face," he said. "Do I need to come over there?"

I sat on one of the stools at the counter and held up my hands. "No, no, I'll behave. You'll get dehydrated or something."

"One of us will," he countered with a wicked smirk of his own.

Oh, Momma.

"Can I help? I make pretty good toast."

He poured me coffee and passed a mug over. "Toast? Did the pilots teach you that?"

Pilots?

Shit! I kept forgetting I was a flight attendant!

"Yes," I said. "I know how to make toast when marooned on a desert island and/or while wearing an oxygen mask."

"Very hot."

He pulled a stool to sit across from me at the narrow counter. "So what do you have going on today?"

"I'm going to meet a friend later tonight, but, today, I was thinking of beginning my descent into crazy cat lady."

"Do — do what?"

"I'm going to adopt a cat. Or four."

His face slid into a mask of horror. "Christ, why?"

I gasped. "You don't like cats? That is a far more egregious sin than what tentacle Scully did to the Lone Gunmen, which gave me a nightmare, FYI."

For real — Yash's fan fic was funny, weird-ass stuff.

"Hey, they enjoyed it." He came around the corner. "Just — not four, okay? I can deal with one, if I must. But they're so...so..." No words completed this sentence, but his expression conveyed every thesaurus synonym for 'ick.'

I poked my hand into his chest. "You can't tell me how many pets to have."

He took a noncommittal sip of his coffee.

"Yeah, I see you." I stood and drained my mug. "I'm going to rescue a helpless animal, like Mother Theresa would, you jerk."

I sashayed my way to the bedroom, where he met me. "Okay," he said, waving the virtual white flag. "You're worth putting up with a cat. How about a dog, though?"

I stomped on his foot.

He hopped away. "Hey! Not nice."

I hissed.

Ever determined, he got in my face — adorably, but also obstinately. "Who will look after the cat when you take off for exotic locales like Cleveland?"

Shit. I *kept kept kept* forgetting I was a flight attendant!

"Um...my roommate. She wants one, too. So, bye, then, I guess." I stuck out my tongue and started getting dressed.

"Stop, stop, " he begged. That half-smile tugged at his lips. "Want some company?"

I pulled on my jeans. "I don't know. You've been rude. You don't deserve to see me play with my pussy."

He burst into laughter and fell back onto the bed. "If I'm nice, might you change your mind?"

"I'll have to consult her and see. But you'll have to buy us muffins."

"A discerning puss. Fine." He sighed. Then he did it again, with extra groan-y-ness. I hit him with his own robe. "Fine, I'll come look at these stupid cats with you. If only to choose the most puppy-like one."

The puppy-like look he hit me with then could have melted the heart of a woman made of ice buried in a glacier on the planet Jupiter after she'd sworn off men for a thousand years.

I was not a woman made of ice — I was a floozy made of... flooz. And my flooz was oozing like a raging river.

294. No!

295. No flooz ooze!

A short time later, I made him buy me the biggest muffin we could find on the way to the cats. Munching and laughing and holding hands, we made our way to a no-kill shelter nearby.

296. Munching

297. Laughing

298. Holding

All of the above — giant mistakes. Especially munching and laughing. That's a good way to choke and spit out muffin in front of your one-night stand. Or two-night stand. With bonus sex puns.

We arrived at Purr-fect Pals, and I had to stop myself from running through the place squealing like a five-year-old.

Then I thought... Why the hell shouldn't I?

"Oh maaaaah gawd!" I squealed. I tap-danced by the tabbies. I curtseyed to the calicos. I shook my butt at the black and white ones, whatever they're called. The two ladies working the counter rolled their eyes at me, but Yash laughed at my antics, even as he ducked away from any feline attention. A flash of memory flitted through my mind — every adorable pet my father had never allowed me to own. Pets were a pain and distracted a girl from homework.

Not even a gerbil.

Or a goldfish.

Although I had owned a pet spider in high school. My father and sister hadn't known about him, or else they would've torn my room apart to kill him. Daddy Medium Legs and I had co-existed for years under the agreement that I didn't stomp him, and he didn't crawl into my mouth or ear as I slept. I'd kept my end of the bargain. Hopefully, he had, too. When I left for college, he'd disappeared. I always dreamed that he'd kept another overworked girl company through her lonely, nerdy high school years.

A touch on the shoulder brought me back to reality, and the *four*-legged pets to be had.

"Since you forced me here, want to tour the kitties?" Yash asked.

I nodded, because how could one say no to a man who used the word 'kitties?' Even if it had come out a little like he'd said 'broccoli farm.'

Hand in hand, we wandered the world's most purr-fect place. The generic pun should have irritated my elevated literary sensibilities, but it didn't even give me paws.

The kitties frolicked in the meowting room, which is, naturally, a meeting room for cats.

My heart. My heart was going to explode. Yash tiptoed through cats young and old, avoiding them. But they wound around his long legs the more he tried to escape. He kept looking at me with despair and frustration in his eyes, every so often pointing to a particularly offensive one as if to say *Look at the horrors I'm experiencing so I can fuck you. Look!* His hatred was…hilarious.

And also the kitties were adorable and stuff.

"Mewr," I heard from below me. I looked down…into a pair of endless amber eyes. The cat's gray little ears flopped forward, and she frowned so forcefully that she reminded me of me in high school.

I heard more sounds, like, "OhmahgahIloveyousomuch!" and "Ggggagaggrrrbbbrbrbrbrbbayay!" Suddenly, I fell to my knees, and the sad cat was in my arms, and the noises… They were coming from me!

The call of the wild is coming from inside the house.

"Wha is… Wha is… Wha is?" I kept saying it over and over again.

"Scottish fold," supplied a helpful shelter volunteer. "So adorable, right?"

The cat began licking my face. I nuzzled the top of her head with my nose, and more of those ridiculous noises fell from my mouth.

Yash gave a very loud, "Christ," and sat on a nearby bench, his head in his hands.

The volunteer, sensing an easy touch (heh), went in for the kill. Or no-kill, per the shelter rules. "She's six weeks old, one of a litter that came in from the street in Brooklyn a couple of weeks ago. Already spayed and has her shots."

"Poor street kitty. Forced to sell her wares to a stranger." She head-butted me and started purring. "She's so sweet." The cat meowed a mournful cry, clearly vouching for her tender nature. "I'll take her," I told the volunteer. "I probably need to sign something?"

He smiled through his patchy beard. "Yes, you'll need to be screened by two of our staff."

Yash said, "Do you think your roommate will like her? She might not, so maybe you shouldn't —"

"Roommate?" The volunteer, name tag reading *Achilles* — really? — looked from one to the other of us. "Oh, we'll need to meet you both."

I laughed. Achilles did not. "What?" I asked.

"We have to make sure both of you are suitable. I hope one of you, at least, works at home?"

"What?"

"So that the cat will have constant cerebral stimulation and learning time."

"Giselle is a flight attendant," Yash offered helpfully. "She knows how to land planes."

"Flight attendant?" Achilles gasped as if Yash had said I made cat pies for a living. He clutched his hemp necklace. "No. No, no. You'll be away from home much too much!

135

And a plane is no place for a cat!"

What? "I—" I cleared my throat. "Yes, my roommate works from home. So, it's fine. For the cat's...mental acuity." My frowning cat mewed and started pawing at my cleavage.

Yash had begun laughing. Not politely.

Achilles' brows drew together. "We must meet this" — he literally air quoted — "'roommate.' Until then…" He yanked the purring furball from my boobs. "No cat for you!"

A sear of pain. Yash's jaw dropped. I looked down where three longs scratches erupted into blood across my cleavage.

Yash pointed. "See? She hurt your b—" He'd been about to say 'boobs' in the cat shelter, but settled for making a vague hand gesture around his own chest. Much better.

"You're not helping," I ground out.

Achilles said, "Call the roommate if you want the cat today." He stomped away without offering to help me with my bleeding tits. But they weren't my biggest problem, although Yash might beg to differ, for he'd procured a tissue and had started to dab at them, his face full of worry.

Worry more for the girls than me, I thought.

299. How the hell would I manufacture a nonexistent 'roommate'?

Wait—

Several moms were frowning my way, so I slapped his hand away from its graphic doctoring of my boobies. I whipped out my phone. "Mel! Roomie! What are you up to?"

"Oh, no," she replied less than enthusiastically. "Are you in jail? Did you sneak onto a flight in a stolen flight attendant uniform?"

I laughed less than enthusiastically. "So very funny. No, I need you to come to the cat adoption place so they can meet you, my roommate, who works from home, so that they understand that my job as a flight attendant won't put the cat's...learning potential at risk."

A pause. "Was that a sentence that made sense to you?

Because it sounded like a jumble of insanity to me."

I smiled at Yash, who still fixated on my chest, and at Achilles, who bared his teeth at me from across the room. I took several steps away and whispered directly into the mic of my phone. "Please? Please? I'm in love with a cat but they want me to have a 'roommate' — "

"Nice air quotes."

"Because of my fake job. Also, you need to call me my fake name."

A sigh sounded through the line. Another. By the third one, I knew I had her.

"I want your DVD of *Bridesmaids*."

"Done."

"*And* the DVD of the all-woman *Ghostbusters*. And you have to clean my bathroom. I really hate scrubbing my bathtub."

Aw, heck. I didn't even clean my own bathtub until it gained sentience. I shot a tight-teethed smile to Yash. "Yes, fine."

Mel whooped. "Okay! Let's grift a cat."

Chapter Eleven

F*ck-Ups Three Hundred through Three-Hundred-Seven
Lying to Cats, Yash, Achilles, Brooklyn and McKatee

While we waited for Mel to arrive, Yash retreated to the corner to hide from the beasties. A pretty little calico followed him. He backed up. She followed. He slid down to sit in the corner. She lay down right in front of him. He frowned up at me while I laughed. Served him right.

Achilles vacillated between glaring at me from afar and sending smitten smiles to Yash. Yash's job of being a writer had been well received, as had his bulging biceps.

After five minutes or so, the calico placed one paw on Yash's knee. His big brown eyes widened. He stared pointedly at his phone, but didn't move the cat. She jumped into his lap, and my heart grew three seizes. Sizes.

300. Heart seizing

His shoulders at his ears, his elbows pointing straight out, he didn't touch her for five solid minutes while I just watched. Ever so slowly, he lowered his phone and deigned to look at the bundle of adorable in his lap. Finally, he gave her a slow head pet and she started purring.

301. So did I

He turned his eyes to mine and said, "Oh, sod off."

Mel kicked me in the leg. "Hello, Giselle! It's me, your roommate who is real and who works from home at my unspecified job and who has come to adopt a cat with you."

The calico bolted at Mel's loud outburst. Yash's shoulders fell. Achilles swayed as if he were about to faint.

I forced a laugh and stood. "Oh, Mel, you're so funny. Of

course you're real."

"You're *really* scaring the cats," Achilles hissed.

I yanked on her arm and drew her to the side, Achilles at our...heels. Before we could collaborate stories even a little bit, he said, "You will be interviewed now. This way."

He led us down a side hallway with several doors to the right. We were taken into the third interrogation room. Interrogation because it sat windowless and dark, save one sad light bulb in the ceiling. A cold metal table and chairs were set out for our comfort.

We sat on one side of the table, and two other women came in and shut the door behind them.

"Should I call my lawyer?" Mel joked.

Neither woman laughed. One of them narrowed her eyes at Mel and wrote something down in her notebook.

I flashed a look to Mel that said 'shut up.'

She rolled her eyes so hard they click-clacked.

Lady with Narrowed Eyes, a Latina woman in her forties, spoke. "I am Brooklyn, this is McKatee." McKatee, a tall Asian lady, was Brooklyn's sister by another mister—they were the same height, weight, identical droopy ponytails and disapproving expressions.

I kicked Mel to silence her.

302. We had a running joke about bad names

303. You could call them our...Achilles' heels

304. I'll stop now

Brooklyn said, "I understand that you, Giselle, are a flight attendant?"

I smiled my most responsible cat mom face. "Yes."

"Airline?"

Uh. Ugh. Ugk? Why hadn't I prepped this before now? Um...what were some airline names? My brain wiped itself clean, like a dry erase board.

I turned panicked eyes to Mel, who broke into a slow smile.

She said, "Giselle flies with Lufthansa."

McKatee's nostrils flared. "Lufthansa? Is that Swiss?"

I nodded. "Yes."

Mel's head dropped to her hand. "No."

Brooklyn narrowed her eyes, of course, and said, "Which one?"

I cleared my throat. What the hell had she said? What the hell had *I* said? Holy crap, when I lied, my whole head went fuzzy! My cat scratches began to sting anew. I said, "Lufthansa is German."

Mel slowly turned her head to stare daggers in my direction, but I bit my lip and stared at the interrogation table.

"Really? You fly with a German airline?" asked McKatee.

Better to double down—Lufthansa had to have at least one American flight attendant, right? It was a big, wide world. "Yes. Why not? *Guten tag*."

Their mouths dropped, but apparently neither one could figure out how to elaborate about why not, so I won that point. Pretty sure the poor airline lost, though…

"How often are you traveling away from the apartment?"

"I-I spend about forty percent of nights away." Was that the correct amount? "Right, Mel?"

"Yeah. I—"

"Mel's a stay-at-home writer, like my guy Yash," I blurted. They liked writers. "So she can definitely teach the cat her ABCs." I laughed at my joke. Brooklyn and McKatee did not. Brooklyn made another note.

I turned to Mel. Mel blinked, started an eye roll, aborted the eye roll when I kicked her, and said, "Yes. I'll be home to spend lots and lots of time with the cat."

"The cat?" McKatee sneered. "This 'cat,' as you so snidely put it, will be your *child*!" She punched the table and we both jumped. "Now…how many hours a day will you two spend with the cat—nurturing her, teaching her, ensuring that she has high self-esteem in her pouncing and hunting?"

Mel put her hand over her mouth and I knew she struggled not to laugh.

"We will devote every day and night to the ca—our new

child's developmental goals," I said. I kicked Mel for good measure.

"You won't!" Brooklyn yelled. "You have a job *outside the home*! You might as well feed the cat *meat*!"

"Cats are carnivorous," Mel said.

The two interrogators stood as one. I kicked out to find Mel's legs, but she quickly moved away with a snotty glare.

McKatee huffed and puffed. "They are not meat killers! Cats are gentle, loving creatures who would never hurt a living being unless they had to, because some trampy air whore neglected them!"

My mouth dropped, and I, shocked, clutched my bosom, and the gentle, loving cat scratches located thereon.

I closed my eyes and pictured the little Scottish fold's mournful face — sad, no doubt, because of a protein deficiency. Biting my tongue was one hundred percent against my new oeuvre, but I'd never rescue that cat unless I played nice with the Feline Fanatics here.

I opened my air whore mouth. "Brooklyn. McKatee. I will quit my job to take care of our new daughter. I haven't named her yet because I believe that children should name themselves when they've developed their own personalities and...and feline dreams."

Mel piped up, "And I'm magic with salmon-flavored tofu." I reached out to her and squeezed her knee. She grunted. I suspected that I would receive a great deal of kicking in my future.

Brooklyn sat back down. "Quitting your job would be a good start. You swear you won't feed the cat meat?"

"Of course," I lied. Those poor cats... Maybe I could adopt them all? But how would I feed them once I quit my fake job with Lufthansa?

Brooklyn and McKatee retired to the corner to whisper.

Mel leaned over to me and whispered, "You are cleaning my bathroom four times for dragging me here to listen to the rantings of Dumb and Dumber. In addition, we need to figure out a way to rescue every cat in this building. Maybe a midnight raid."

"There's no way that illegally herding cats could go wrong," I said.

Brooklyn returned to the table. "We have decided to give you a trial run. You may have the cat for a month during which time we will make random home visits. I'll just need both of your driver's licenses, Giselle and Mel."

Mel whipped her head to me.

My mouth fell open, unable to concoct a story...anything... Oh, hell, the cat of my dreams was slipping from my grasp!

I stood. "Okay, look. You remember that guy out there I came in with?"

"The super hot one?" McKatee asked.

"That's the one. When I met him, I was at a club, and I was just having fun for the night pretending to be a flight attendant named Giselle. In reality, I'm a barista named Dagmar, and I know the truth will come out eventually, but he is seriously the best lay of my life, and I was recently dumped by my family, my boyfriend, and got fired all in the same day. My boyfriend cheated on me and got a job in L.A. without telling me."

McKatee gasped. "That piece of crap."

"I need to climb Yash like a tree, okay? And I need a cat to love. I will take such amazing care of her, I swear it. I'm going to be a crazy cat lady!"

McKatee placed a hand on my arm. "You won't regret it. It's really working for me."

305. Not the recommendation I wanted to hear

"I'll help too, of course," Mel piped up. I figured there was no reason for her to stop pretending. She had come all the way down here.

"So," Brooklyn said, "you're not out of town forty percent of the time?"

I shook my head no.

"And you're just pretending on the name thing to keep that dude in your bed?"

I nodded yes.

Brooklyn looked at McKatee. McKatee looked at Brooklyn.

"You can have the cat," McKatee said. "I'd eat meat to eat that man."

We shook on it.

"We'll bring your paperwork in here, *Giselle*."

Those two women were as different from me as could be, but the call of quality dick is universal to hetero ladies.

I jumped for joy. "I'm getting a cat! She's so sweet, Mel. You're going to love her!"

"How do we explain the fact that the address on my license doesn't match yours?"

"Nobody goes to the DMV to get their address updated. Mine is from two apartments ago."

We filled out the paperwork. I didn't know what to think about the surprise home visits, but Mel was over there all the time, anyway. Heck, maybe she should just move in...

It took an hour and three more lectures about talk-therapy discipline for the cat, the non-patriarchal home rules we'd need to abide by for her benefit (my house was a brand new matriarchy, thank you very much), and the acceptable brand of vegan foods and toys she'd be allowed to play with.

Mel and I ran out to grab a litter box and supplies, brought them to my place, and went back to pick up the cat. Yash tagged along, but stayed in the cab when we got to my place. Whew.

"I guess I need to get this little girl home," I said. I cradled the cardboard carrier she was in, nearly crying with happiness and excitement. I'd always wanted a cat!

306. Remember, kids:

307. Lying does work!

"You're so lovely." Yash gazed at me with velvet eyes and tucked a strand of hair behind my ear.

"Oh, brother," muttered Mel.

He continued, "I guess I could come over to help with this thing... Have you named wee Lady Scot here?"

I pondered this uber-important question. "I think I'm

going to call her—"

"No!" Mel kicked me in the calf and I nearly dropped the cat. Argh, it stung! Perhaps Mel was harboring some attitude about the interrogation room.

"No, what?" I asked.

Clearly not wanting to say goodbye, even with a cat involved, Yash dangled in his sexiest voice, "I'll buy a pizza for lunch." He hit me with a panty-melting stare, the kind that would cause me to let him do whatever he wanted with that pizza.

The cat in my arms mewed, and I said, "Moaning Myrtle agrees."

Yash broke into a laugh. "That's a clever name, even if it is for a cat."

I blinked my eyes most innocently. "Do you not like cats, Yash?"

"Why would you think that?" He swallowed a smile.

"Mmm-hmm. The name is an homage to kitty's roots— J.K. Rowling created Harry Potter in Scotland. Plus, she's gray like a ghost."

Mel yanked on my arm. "I really think we ought to do this ourselves, *Giselle*." She sank her claws into my wrist and I yelped in pain.

Oh.

Oh!

No, Yash couldn't come to my place! But he was already out of the door, calling a cab!

"Shit!" I said.

"Don't swear in front of the cats!" Achilles yelled across the room.

"Blow it out ya ass, honey." Mel peered out of the glass door. Yash hadn't gotten a cab yet. "Giselle, my roommate, you are a very smart woman."

I'd never heard so many lies in one sentence. I clutched Myrtle to my bosom. "That's it. The jig is up, right?"

My bestie kicked me. I leaped away from her. She advised, "When we get there, you distract him with...fondling or

144

something, and I'll make a sweep and try to clear anything incriminating."

I turned to see Yash waving us toward an awaiting cab, so I nodded and pushed through the door. Mel stepped on the back of my shoe and I wiped out across the sidewalk, having saved the cat from being smashed at the expense of my knees. Gah—they throbbed and screamed even worse than my tit scratches.

Yash ran to help me up while Mel got in the cab. "Now your legs will match mine for bruises," she called.

Chapter Twelve

F*ck-Ups Three-Hundred-Eight through Three-Fifty-Six Lying to Yash, Ethel and Some Patchouli-Stinking Scumbag

Mel, Yash and I pulled up to my apartment building. Oh, excuse me —

308. My and Mel's apartment building

Mel jumped from the cab and sprinted to the door. I followed with my eyes, puzzled and anxious, until I realized that she now stood squarely in front of the buzzers, which listed me as D. Kostopoulos.

309. Good thing I had an accomplice

310. Who was smarter than I

I shoved Moaning Myrtle into Yash's arms to distract him while I paid for the cab. I hurried after him just in time to hear him ask, "Do you not have keys?" to Mel.

"She's always forgetting them or losing them," I offered.

I let us in and we proceeded to the elevator.

"Yes, I'm a total idiot," Mel agreed. "I can't even clean a bathroom, so Giselle has to do it. Forever."

Yash laughed and stood before us, facing the doors, holding the cat a foot in front of him. I clutched my stomach. Mel kicked me. I was going to get an ulcer and a clot from this adventure. And dishpan hands afterward. Today had already been such a carnival of emotions, I think I left my lungs on the Ferris wheel and my kidney in the fun house.

311. Life had become a clown car, and I was driving Bozo off a cliff

We piled into my place. The moment we got in, Mel ran

to confiscate the 'me' in the apartment. After she kicked me in the butt. Literally.

I rubbed the smarting area in question and grabbed Yash's arm as he began to walk by. He handed Myrtle's box back to me with obvious relief. I said, "Let's—let's start her out in the kitchen."

Without explaining why—

312. Less evidence in there

—I pushed Yash that direction. We went through the swinging door and I set her box down and sat next to it. I tapped the floor, and Yash sank straight into sitting cross-legged. I opened Myrtle's prison to release her into her new home!

I opened the box and waited. And waited. We stared at the box, but no kitty head appeared over the lip. We stared. Yash sighed. We stared. Maybe she'd gotten too used to life on the inside.

I took her moment of reticence to clean up my cat scratches. I was gaining new burns, marks, and scars at an alarming rate. The fast lane was rife with dangers.

When I'd finished, Yash started to rise. "I could use a—"

"No!" I yanked him to the floor, a lot harder than I'd intended. He yelped in pain—guess everyone would have an ass clot by the end of the day. "I'm sorry, I didn't mean to be so rough."

He cocked an eyebrow. "If you want to be rough with me, at least ask if I prefer to be blindfolded first."

I smiled, then I thought about that...

"Uh," I gasped, out of breath, "you stay with the cat. I'm going to get the litter box and stuff."

"What? No! I—"

"Would *you* like to set up the poop box?"

His face fell as he contemplated these horrific options. He sported the most disgruntled eyebrows I'd ever seen, even from Mel. "I'll stay," he finally offered. Clearly, only the promise of one kind of pussy kept him in the presence of the other.

"Thank you, you wonderful, giving, *handsome* man."

He grunted.

"Here—" I grabbed him a beer from the fridge. "Here's a better thank you. I'll do everything. Just sit tight." I backed away. "Sit. Right there. Just…"

Mel peeked her head in and gave me a *look*.

"Sit!" I ordered Yash.

"Woof," he replied with another *look*.

313. Oh, quit judging me

314. Like you never lied to everyone about everything all the time

I laughed it off with a charming head toss and ran through the swinging door.

Mel met me in the living room, where my ancient landlady, Ethel, stood. Oh sh—

"Dagmar," she said in entirely too loud a voice. "What was that I saw going up in the elevator?"

"My two friends," I said. "They're with me—I vouch for them." I tossed my head again, but it didn't seem to appeal to her the way it did Yash.

"There was an animal carrier, Dagmar."

Holy hell. Every time she said my name, it seemed to get louder. This lady couldn't walk past three doors in the building without wheezing—how did she have the stage projection of Meryl Streep?

"Yes, I got a cat," I whispered. I drew Ethel away from the kitchen. "It was a spontaneous decision today—isn't it wonderful when we rescue helpless animals from being butchered and murdered?"

Her lips tightened.

Guess *not*.

Ethel said, "Dagmar." Why. Must. She. Keep. Saying. It? "You need to pay a pet deposit and fill out the necessary forms."

"I'm so, so happy to," I assured her. I wound my arm around her shoulders and started us toward the front door. "I have cash on hand. I'll bring it down to your apartment in no time and sign those papers."

She nodded and finally smiled. "It's five hundred, and I'll be waiting."

"Five hundred dollars?" That was all my emergency cash. This Myrtle had better bring the purring and unconditional love shit ASAP. "Uh, yes, of course."

Yash pushed through the kitchen door. "What's five hundred?"

I gasped. Mel gasped. Ethel gave him a lusty once-over.

Words blurted from my mouth. "The pet deposit. I'm taking care of it. You please look after Moan—"

Ethel made a rickety beeline for Yash. "Who is this? A new boyfriend?"

Yash smiled a wide, winning, landladies-love-me grin. "Uh, just a new friend of the roommates here."

Ethel turned slowly toward me. "Roommate?"

315. No!

316. Noooooooooooooo!

I burst into laughter, the kind they ship you to Bellevue for. "Why…the cat, of course! New kitty roommate!"

Ethel laughed because Yash was laughing. I was laughing because I'd jump out of the window otherwise. I took Ethel firmly by the shoulders and opened the front door. "I'll be by with that money."

I grinned when I closed the door on her.

317. Which totally made it better

Mel whooshed out a long breath—her face had become a horrible shade of purple. I had a feeling I resembled a distraught blueberry myself.

I clutched my racing heart and turned back to Yash. "I have to deal with the pet deposit. How's Moaning Myrtle?"

"She's peeking up over the edge of the box."

"Progress!"

He shrugged. "Why don't you come in and be with her? Maybe Mel can take the money to your landlady."

Yes, that would be a great plan, if Mel lived here. She couldn't sign my lease addendum.

I shot a panicked gaze to Mel. She said, her voice full of venom, "Uh... I... I...hate that bitch Ethel!"

Yash's eyes went big.

Mel licked her lips. "Yes. That horrible gold-digging, homewrecker lured my...uncle out of his happy marriage and then ruined his life! I'd own this building myself if it weren't for that hussy." Mel turned away, her hands clutched around her stomach. Her shoulders shook. Obviously, she was overwhelmed with the emotion that came with telling such a tale.

That emotion being laughter, of course.

My beau backed away from the both of us, which was the only sensible thing for him to do, really. "I'll... I'll just..." He licked his lips. "Beer." He exited into the kitchen.

I let out a huge breath and Mel flopped onto the wooden chair near the door.

Mel grinned and whispered, "And the award for best performance by a fake roommate goes to..."

"Thank you," I replied.

"You will now be scrubbing my oven. I have never cleaned it, and a burning smell happens every time I use it."

I put a hitch in my voice. "But I'll be at your house so much that Moaning Myrtle is going to be a latch key kitty."

"You made your cat bed, now lie in it. Get it? *Lie*?" She slapped her knee.

I gave her comedy routine a C-minus at best. I asked, "So — how's the apartment cleansing going?"

She nodded. "The mail is hidden in your closet — you should open your mail more often."

"Thank you. Thank you so much. Okay, will you please go and watch Yash while I sign the cat papers?"

"My floors need a serious mopping."

"Argh! Okay! You know, the next time you lie horrifically to your boyfriend and expect me to participate in an elaborate, time-wasting ruse, I'm going to charge you cash."

"*Cash*. What a good idea!" She grinned wickedly. "I have a five-hundred-dollar deposit for future shenanigans."

"I'm ruined." I yanked my emergency cash out of the hollow book in my bookcase.

She sauntered over to me, a maddening smirk on her kisser. "And…boyfriend?"

Before I could digest that Freudian slip, Yash stuck his head through the door. "Did I hear the word boyfriend? Do you have a secret, Giselle?"

I froze.

"Do you have a secret boyfriend?" he continued with a cheeky grin.

Whew. I grasped at my chest again. This day was going to give me a heart attack.

318. I had hoped that today I might die of orgasm overload

"Maybe I do, and maybe I don't," I said.

"All right." He came slowly toward me, that *look* in his eyes. No, not *that* one, the *good* one. The very, very good one.

319. The one that ended up with me ass over head

His perfectly executed panther stalk ended right next to me. "Any other secrets, mysterious Giselle?" he whispered into my ear.

I shivered.

Mel said, "Oh, barf. I'd rather watch the kitten poop." She grabbed the litter box and huffed into the kitchen.

Yash yanked me into his arms. "I thought these people would never leave." He planted a hot, dirty kiss to my open lips and…and…grrfflsh ajdjdhdhha unnffffff.

320. Maybe I could write a literary erotic novel

321. The hero threw the hussy onto the couch and grrfflsh ajdjdhdhha unnffffff-ed her

When he let my dizzy body up for air, he said against my mouth. "Can I at least be in the running for the boyfriend position? My résumé special skills section is most excellent."

Let's make something perfectly clear:

322. What I said next wasn't my fault

323. It was the hormones released from such good kissing

324. Such sexy, nasty, sweet kissing

325. The kind of kissing that kills everyone in a Shakespearean tragedy

326. It was his perfect butt's fault

327. It was the economy's fault

328. It was caused by the big bang billions of years ago!

329. It just plain was not my fault when I said…

"Yes, please be my boyfriend."

A crash sounded from the general area of the kitchen, and I knew Mel had heard. Or maybe God had heard, and he was breaking my collection of Beyoncé coffee mugs to teach me a lesson.

330. A lesson I'd soon forget

"Giselle," Yash said, "you are really starting to drive me crazy." He picked me clear off the ground and held me to him. I clung to those giant shoulders like a life raft in the *Waterworld* my life had become.

331. My life had a forty-two percent rotten rating at rottentomatoes.com

Mel stuck her head into the room. "You'd better take that cash to Ethel, Giselle. She's a lying Jezebel getting in over her head, you know."

Yash was really starting to regard Mel as if she had a few screws loose.

332. Ironic, for it was my loose screwing that had gotten us into this situation

"Yes," I chirped. "You two play nice," I told her and only her.

It took about fifteen minutes to give Ethel the pet deposit, sign the lease addendum, and dodge her highly invasive questions about Yash. Look, I appreciated the fact that she was old and didn't give a crap about anyone's opinion, but I still think there's no age at which "How big is his cock?" is an appropriate question.

I raced back up to the apartment as fast as the elevator would climb. When I pushed into the kitchen, Moaning Myrtle sat in Mel's lap swiping at a catnip mouse dangling from two of Yash's fingers.

Relieved as all get out, I fell against the kitchen door. And crashed through it straight onto my behind. "Ow!" I yelled, pain jarring from my tailbone through my skull. I rolled onto my side and clutched my butt with my free hand, certain I'd never sit pooperly again. Or properly. Aaaaagh ooohhhhh.

"Are you okay?" my people asked in unison on either side of me.

I burst into laughter. "Yes. Oh, hell, that hurts."

"Your ass is going to be as black and blue as my shins," Mel said, rubbing my affected area.

"Thanks, bestie. It takes a real woman to rub her friend's butt."

"Any time, Jezebel. Whoops, I mispronounced 'Giselle.'"

I felt a scratchy, wet spot on my forehead, and I opened my eyes to see Myrtle sitting right in front of my face. Her soft, gray fur fluffed every which way—she looked too adorable to really exist. Kind of like Yash. She licked my forehead again and I giggled. "Thanks, Myrtle, darling."

Yash took my hand and helped me to sit up. It hurt, but was bearable. I held out my palm to Myrtle, who sniffed at me and began to lick my fingers.

Two adult humans in the room said, "Awwwwwwwww." The third abstained.

Myrtle allowed me to pick her up, so I collected her into my lap. Her purr was a hoarse, wee motor boat and made us all laugh. My entire being seemed to want to burst with happiness. My best friend at my side. An adorable new companion. And a boyfriend so hot he melted my butter.

Butter-melter fixed a butter-melting stare on me. He smiled. I smiled. He asked, "What does the 'D' stand for?"

"What?" I asked.

He pointed to the wall. Where my giant 'D' hung.

I whipped my head to Mel—Dagmar elimination had been her job!

Mel whipped her gaze to the cat, and ignored me to pet her, the traitor.

I said… I said… "It's Mel's." Ha! Take that!

Yash smiled while he awaited a no doubt colorful explanation.

My best friend lifted her head and gave me a death stare. At this rate, I would be Mel's indentured maidservant for the rest of time, and in the grave, I'd have to polish her bones.

Mel took a long, deep breath. "It stands for…" she said, "for…d-d-d-d…dddd*dd*…Daniel Craig! Yeah, Daniel Craig. Because he's so hot—he inspires all my fanfic. Which is what I write. Because I'm a writer. Like Giselle told the cat people."

"Yup!" I blurted.

Myrtle leaped from my arms and bolted behind Yash.

"Help!" Yash blurted while dancing away.

"Be brave, Yash, and she might not eat you." Oh, who was I kidding? I wanted to run at Yash too.

And lick him, like Myrtle was now doing to his shoe.

333. But I didn't

Yash turned to Mel. "I'm a writer too. Have you been published?"

Mel looked askance at me and picked up Myrtle, who was a little storm cloud of loving fluffy wuffy widdle biddle adorableness!

334. I am killing this crazy cat lady thing

"Nope, not published," Mel said. "But I'll get there someday. I have a popular blog, see…" She took the cat back into the kitchen while loudly hinting that anyone who wanted to grope another person in the house should stay out of the kitchen to do so.

Yash slid his arms around me from behind. "She couldn't have possibly meant us?"

"Of course not. Everyone wants to watch us kiss."

He spun me around and pulled me into his hips. He began slowly pumping them against mine, and my brain began to slide out of my ears.

"Hey, Giselle?" he started.

"That's definitely my name."

"Will you do me a favor?"

He brushed his lips across the nape of my neck. I shivered from head to humping hips. "I will do you all the favors."

His laugh tickled my collarbone and I died, the end.

He asked, "Will you put on your air hostess outfit for me? I need to rip it off you."

335. "Sure, baby"

A loud cackling sounded from the kitchen door, and I wondered why Mel was making that obnoxious sound and *oh, God, what the hell had I just agreed to do?*

I yanked my head up, knocking my forehead into Yash's.

"Fuck!" He stumbled backward into the wall, where a framed picture nearly clocked him on its downward path to the floor. It crashed, Yash crashed, and Mel's laughter crashed like triumphal cymbals.

Yash mumbled, "I bit my tonbue." Now he clutched his forehead and mouth.

At least he wasn't thinking sexy thoughts about fake air hostesses anymore.

"Let's sit down." I drew him to the couch and deposited him thereon. "I'll get you a cold drink — that will help your poor tongue. We can't have that thing sprained."

He flashed me a lopsided grin and I ran to fetch him a soda with ice.

As soon as the kitchen door swung closed, Mel said, "So when are we going to the Internet café?"

"Ugh! I forgot all about that. I was too busy —"

"Lying?"

"No! I was adopting an unloved pet, like a literal saint."

I sat down on the floor next to her and Myrtle. I collected the storm cloud into my lap, where she mewed and purred as long as I stroked her head. My shoulders fell — wow, cats really did help you relax.

336. No wonder pussies are so popular

337. These jokes never get old

"I have to get Yash a cold drink. He bit his tongue."

"I thought he was biting your tongue."

"He had been until Lady Laughs-a-Lot put in her two cents." I made a face at her and rose with Myrtle. I put the cat on the counter and got Yash a Coke with ice in it. Myrtle seemed amazed at this new firmament she could explore. I let her pad around while I swigged the rest of Yash's beer.

Mel grinned and said, "You'd better get into the living room to babysit your boyfriend."

"Yes, I will. But I need to set up the litter box so my apartment—"

"Our apartment. I'm living here rent-free from now on."

"Doesn't smell like cat piss. I guess I'll do it in the bathroom off the living room. If I put it in here, she might not be strong enough to push the kitchen door open yet."

"I am not setting up the shit box for you, honey."

I let out a desperate laugh. "Yeah, I know. Can you take this drink to Yash?" I handed her the Coke and whacked her on the backside to get her going.

"I'm sending you my hospital bill," she muttered.

I followed her into the living room with the litter box in my arms. I'd have to do some major ass-kissing to make up for all this nonsense I was putting Mel through. And we still had to go to the Internet café to check on our other clandestine caper.

I bit my lip to suppress a giggle—it was kind of fun, really. All this…scheming. I'd gone from the kid who cleaned erasers for extra credit to a roofie-ing strumpet who strung along men. I knew it was wrong—boy, I knew—but it was as if my brain had just snapped. The teenage years I'd spent being a responsible adult had caught up with me. But being an irresponsible rebel when you're an adult is so much better. There was sex! And booze! My giggle became full-fledged as I carried the plastic poop house into the bathroom.

My grin still plastered to my face, I returned to the living room to grab Myrtle and show her where to do her business. I found a puzzled-looking Yash, a panicking Mel…

338. And a Netflix account on the TV that said 'Dagmar' in bright white letters

"Shit!" I said.

"Nice," Mel assured me with a thumbs-up. She petted Myrtle, sitting in her lap, and awaited the fallout.

"Uh, I can explain," I told Yash.

His eyebrows rose, and I started breathing so hard, the room started to spin. "It's...uh... That name... It's mine."

He stood, confusion thundering across his face, chased by the first hint of anger. No. Noooooooo. It couldn't be over yet! He was the perfect man and oh, God, what was wrong with me? I wasn't smart enough to be this devious! *Giselle*? What had I been thinking, creating an alter-ego—

"That's it!" I blurted. "That's it"—I pointed to the screen—"that's my alter-ego, Dagmar. Dag. That's my pet name for myself. It's like...my sexy name. Sometimes I use it on flights with creepy guys, so they don't know who I really am. Yeah. It's an inside joke between me and Mel." I whipped my head to her. "Right, Mel?"

She started laughing. The cat bolted to the arm of the couch. "Alrightey, Dagmar."

Her acting skills were shit.

339. Mine, however, were amazeballs

340. Maybe I should be an actress?

Maybe I should pay attention to Yash, whose mouth hung open. "But," he said, "Giselle is a pretty sexy name already, yah?"

I smiled. "Thanks."

"Much sexier than Dagmar."

My smile drooped. "Thanks."

"I understand why you'd fib to strange men, though. There can be some really crazy people out there in the dating world."

Mel fell off the couch, but she covered it super well by playing with the cat.

I cleared my throat. "It... It started a long time ago, when I was a teenager. It's just a silly thing now, but it explains why you'd never see the name Dagmar around me."

He lit up. "Like the 'D' on the wall! It could mean 'Dagmar'."

"Five points for Yash!" Mel said, helpfully. "I'm going to use the big girl litter box." She sauntered off into the bedroom.

I'd just begun to breathe normally again when Yash came up to me, a photo of my family in his hand.

What new fresh hell was this?

He said, "Is this your dad? You look just like him."

"Yes. That's me, my twin Vanessa, and Dad."

"Twin?"

He'd said it the way everyone always had. Incredulous, with a hint of 'Why don't you look like *her*?'

My teeth gritted, the way they always did. "Yes, she's the golden child—beautiful, blonde, perfect—and I'm the one they didn't count on." I snatched the photo and started walking it back to the bookcase where it lived. Usually face down.

"What?" Yash fell into step with me. "What does that mean—the one they didn't count on?"

I shook my head. "Nothing. Doesn't matter. They both live in Connecticut, so—"

"No, no." He gently turned me around. "I've upset you, and I'm sorry. I don't see why she's the *beautiful* one. You're the more interesting looking of the two of you, and far prettier."

I laughed. He appeared confused. I laughed again.

"Giselle, you are a lovely woman. Vibrant, sexy. Petite and sumptuous." He tucked a strand of hair behind my ear. "With mesmerizing, mysterious brown eyes that haunt me. Seriously, I had a dream about your sparkling eyes."

"Uh…" A stifling wave of heat overcame me, and I backed away. I didn't know what to say.

Yash blinked helplessly at me, awaiting my saying something. "Your family…was not kind to you?"

I shook my head, my mouth dry. "My parents had only

wanted one kid, but they got two. They struggled to make ends meet. My dad told me they resented me as the...the interloper. That the blonde, blue-eyed kid with the small nose like Mom was better than the Greek-looking one."

His mouth had fallen completely open. "What the fuck? What the... What the fuck? That's horrifying! Why would he even tell you that?"

"When he was tipsy at my sister's wedding, I asked him why he'd treated us differently our whole lives. He just spilled it all." I stared at the floor and shrugged. "Dad always took pride in his tall, golden daughter, especially after Mom died. Vanessa could do no wrong, and I—"

"Could do no right."

He grabbed my shoulders, and I managed to pick up my head to look at him, tears in my lashes. I swiped at them— really, I should be over this by now, right?

"Baby, you do not deserve being treated like... Fuck, I don't even know what to say. Hating one child because of eye color? It's...like a dystopian novel. I've seen this sort of thing in Desi families—the light-skinned kids being preferred to the dark ones. But I'm a dark one, and I'm great the way I am. So are you."

I squeezed my eyes shut. "I'm not trying to say... I mean, I'm still a white girl. I don't experience racism or anything."

"I understand what you're saying. But you have suffered, in your family, for not being some stupid ideal. For what it's worth, I'm crazy for pocket-sized girls with dark, flashing eyes and weird senses of humor."

He actually managed to make me laugh. It was worth a lot.

His hand under my chin, he said, "Fuck them if they can't see that you're a wonderful, beautiful person. Are you close to your sister, at least?

I laughed again—this one, short and unsweet. "No. She took on her role as the good one like a duck to water."

"Then none of them deserve you."

I searched his eyes for a sign of a trick. If any friend had come to me saying she was lesser than for being unlike Western beauty standards, I would have told her she didn't need to conform, that she deserved love and was perfect as is. Intellectually, I knew I was fine the way God made me. I would say such out loud to anyone who asked. But deep down...

Deep down it's hard to undo twenty years of Dad programming me to believe I was a big-nosed, olive-skinned, brown-eyed, short-statured bug on the windshield of his shiny life car, and if I just tried harder, maybe I could make up for my undesired presence on this earth.

Mel's voice cut through my self-loathing. "Well, Dagmar... Giselle... Whatever, right?... We need to get going. We have to get pedicures or something. Out of the apartment."

Yash swept me into a powerful hug, and I clung to him far longer than was polite. "Yes, we're getting pedicures," I agreed over his shoulder.

He took a step back from me. "In the winter while it's snowing?" He shook his head with a smile. "Being a woman is very difficult, especially with horrible fathers."

"You have no idea," I assured him.

Mel said, "Oh, yeah, her dad is a total piece of shit. Sexist, racist—"

"Okay." I stopped her with a loving grimace while I swiped the tears from my eyes. "Enough thinking about my family."

"Bless their hearts," Mel agreed most savagely.

Yash's hand lingered in mine. "Can I come over later on? I am dying to see your flight attendant uniform. On your short body with its sun-kissed skin." He lowered himself until we saw brown eyes to brown eyes. "Please?"

The room began swaying again. "Hopefully I have one clean," I hedged.

He picked me up into a hug and planted a rather chaste kiss to my lips.

"Thank you for not exploring her tonsils," Mel said.

He left, and I collapsed onto the carpet. Myrtle came

running over and mewed at me. I scooped her up, and she lay on my chest to purr and knead at my boobs. *Aw.* I would never hate Myrtle for being gray. She was the perfect kitty daughter just as she was.

Mel got down next to me. "I haven't seen tap dancing like that since *Singin' in the Rain*."

"Thank you. I appreciated your Ode to Homewrecker Ethel. I wonder if she was ever half that interesting in real life?" I hugged Myrtle. "Although, she did ask a lot of cock questions about Yash, so…"

She sat up. "Shall we visit the Internet café to see about the home *we* wrecked?"

"He wrecked himself. But yes. And after that, I have to try to find a Lufthansa flight attendant uniform."

She wrapped her arms around her eyes. "Why? Why did you say that airline?"

"*You* said that airline, jerk bag!"

Without acknowledging her contribution to my mess, she continued, "And then we have to get pedicures. In January. And then go home in flip-flops."

I hauled her to her feet. "The pedicure thing is your fault too. And we can probably get away with getting manicures. Or nothing. He's a man, he won't know."

"Okay, but you know what?"

"Yes, yes. I'll be paying. I'll probably be paying for a long, long time."

341. In more ways than one

* * * *

On the train ride to the Internet café, I typed a post for Craigslist asking for a flight attendant uniform. Said it was for a play. As soon as my cell service returned, I hit Send and hoped for the best.

It was nearly dinner time, and my stomach rumbled in anger. The only person I'd fed recently was the cat. Hopefully, she wouldn't fill my handbag with poop.

I peeked into my bowling bag, and she booped me on the nose with hers. My squealing noise turned heads on the sidewalk, and Mel laughed at me. Myrtle hadn't seemed to mind the subway, and I couldn't bear to leave her at home. She needed affection from her captor after her ordeal of being kidnapped by strange women and the people to whom they lie.

342. *I would need the cat to love me after my boyfriend eventually dumped me*

343. *I knew I wouldn't get a happily ever after*

344. *Maybe a restraining order, though*

I told Myrtle she must stay in the bag while we were in the café. She nodded and told me, "Of course, beautiful Mother Dagmar."

345. *Crazy cat lady step one: Hear it when they talk to you*

We got to the café and found a spot at a corner computer. My heart began thumping, wondering what, if any, response we'd get. Soon we logged into the account and... there was a message!

"Oh em gee," I said.

Mel turned green. "I'm afraid to open it."

"Me too. Let's make Myrtle do it."

But Myrtle said no, loudly, and denizens of the café gawked at us.

Her hand shaking, Mel clicked on the email from Abby.

I want to meet in person to hear about the origin of these photos. I checked with my resident geek, and they don't appear to be Photoshopped. When and where? I always protect my sources.

I jumped in my seat. "Yes!"

"We can't meet her," Mel protested.

"We have to. For womanity, Mel." I took a breath. "I'll do it myself. You don't have to come, it's totally okay."

"No way. We're in this together." She scooted closer to me. "I didn't even tell you about his car, did I? It cost him a few hundred to get the fuel drained and stuff, and then they figured out that there was no sugar, so he knows it was a totally wasted expense."

"Ha!" We shook hands and Myrtle lifted her paw out through the bag in my lap to swipe at us with her talons of solidarity. I disentangled myself and rubbed away the blood on my smarting wrist.

I checked my phone, and lo and behold, someone had responded to my Craigslist ad! God bless this city. A guy in Brooklyn said he had just such a uniform for two hundred dollars.

Mel read the phone upside down and whistled. "I'm not letting you go there alone. For all we know, he sells duplicitous young women into Greek slavery."

"Doesn't bode well for me." I decided to meet him at a coffee shop a block from his apartment in an hour. I wasn't such a fuck-up that I'd meet a weird dude at his sex dungeon.

346. Only non-weird sex dungeons for me

This expensive task completed—ugh, I'd be eating ramen for two weeks straight—we turned back to Abby, the intrepid journalist who would help us deal a blow against sleazebags everywhere.

Or at least one.

I slid the keyboard toward me, wishing I'd brought hand sanitizer.

347. What was that brown, crusty thing on the side of the 9 key?

I began:

Dear Abby,
We wish to remain anonymous, but will make ourselves available to answer questions.

I turned to Mel. "Let's Deep Throat it."

"The porn or the parking garage?"

"I love you, Mel, but I'll keep my passion for you above the waistline."

"Butt pats notwithstanding."

I shrugged and returned to my important missive.

Let's meet Sunday morning, 1am, at —

"Which parking garage?" I asked.

"There's one near my place open all night."

"How do you know?"

Mel blinked. "Because it has a big sign that says *Open All Night*."

"You're a genius."

She set her head in her palm and let out a puppy whine. "One a.m., though? I have to work the next day."

"After two weeks off, ya lazy bum. Adventure knows no sleep! Once more unto the breach! And/or parking garage."

"Yeah, yeah."

She looked up the address on her phone, and I finished the note to Abby.

Mel reached into the bag in my lap to pet the vicious adorable contained therein. "You're feeding me a hot dog on the way. I'm starving."

"We can't have that."

Hot dogs in hand, and one for Myrtle—my purse was a goner—we proceeded to the subway, then the coffee shop. Except...

I referred back to my phone, and yes, I had the address right. Oh, wow. This would be a new experience for me.

"Sexpresso?" Mel read the pink and black neon sign, accompanied by a photo of a hot blonde woman dripping coffee on her bikini-clad boobs.

I recoiled. "That's how you scald the girls. How is that sexy?"

Mel crossed her arms over her chest. "This whole day is a mystery. Earlier, I helped you steal a cat. I told a heinous lie about an old lady. And now I'm going to assist you obtain a uniform for a job you don't have to keep a man who doesn't know your name...all while in a coffee shop strip club.

Emily Post just doesn't cover days like today."

"Probably a very good thing. Come on." We opened the heavy, wooden door and descended into a pink nightmare of darkness.

Everything looked...

348. Sticky

That's the most positive word coming to mind. We proceeded through a black hallway (not touching anything, obviously) and soon found ourselves in a giant, warehouse-type room. Men of all sizes, shapes, and ick-levels sat around the stage, upon which two lovely ladies danced for definitely not enough money.

I leaned to whisper in Mel's ear. "I wonder how much they make?"

She punched me in the arm. "I'm not dogging strippers, but you are not becoming a stripper."

"Of course not. I'm not that talented a dancer."

She nodded. "That's true. You'd probably twirl off the stage and stab a scumbag in the eye with your stiletto. Speaking of... How do we know which one he is?"

We took a survey. Two fifty-something twins in tracksuits were harassing a very unhappy-looking waitress. Mob, probably, according to television. Another stick-skinny white fellow was clearly masturbating under his table, so... no. We passed a man muttering in Russian while playing with a switchblade. Mel nearly retreated then, but my lust motivated me. I intrepidly kept exploring. I was the Amelia Earhart of sleaze.

I met the eyes of the grossest man in the place—a handy achievement. It had to be him. If I Googled the word 'weirdo,' his be-speckled, long-ponytailed, lime-green plaid jumpsuit-ed mug would be pictured there. In his lap sat a plastic bag from a popular teeny-bopper clothing store.

"We're going to be culted into the Manson family," Mel said.

"We shower too much for them," I assured her. "I have to meet him. I have to get that uniform."

"And what after that? You'll get you and Yash free standby seats to London so you can take your fiction on the road? And we have not even begun to discuss the 'please be my boyfriend' crap. You're gonna bust his heart wide open, honey."

Tracksuit Number One sidled up and rubbed his belly on me. I nearly screamed, but I was rescued by a blonde in a thong, who pulled him aside for a lap dance, bless her.

"I'm just a random hookup for Yash," I assured Mel. "I'll—I'll end it by kissing his best friend soon, and then he'll be happily rid of me."

"Oh, did I say *his* heart? Because I meant you—"

"La la la!" I passed her and made a beeline for Weirdo. I didn't want to consider breaking my heart or Yash's heart. Especially after he'd been so amazingly perceptive and wonderful about my family situation. Blade had never told me I shouldn't feel inferior to my sister—he'd actually once confessed that he'd hit that if he could.

But enough with assholes and on to weirdos. Up close, the guy reeked of patchouli and armpit stench. His feet stuffed into gold-spray-painted loafers and his hair was dyed gray over older purple dye.

I girded my loins—

349. And my nostrils—

And said, "Hi. You have a uniform for me?"

He twitched. "What's your name?" His high-pitched voice barely sounded over the 80s hair metal pounding through the place. British accent, but not a real one. A Madonna-in-the-country terrible accent. He twirled the grease at the end of his handlebar mustache, and I fought back a barf.

Myrtle peeked her head above my bag, fixed on him, and hid again.

Smart girl.

I said, "My name doesn't matter. Let's see the uniform."

He leaned forward. "How do I know you're not the feds?"

Holy hell. "A fed? Here to arrest you for what, assaulting everyone's eyes?"

"Wouldn't be the first time!"

Mel and I exchanged a glance. Not a happy or hopeful glance.

I leaned down and grabbed the dirty plastic bag at his feet. Yup, it was the right uniform, current even, according to the airline's website. It was a size too small for me, but that would probably be okay since it was a sex fantasy and not a job requirement I might need to wear on a deserted island after a crash.

I fished a wad of twenties from under Myrtle and held them out to Gross Guy.

He yanked them from my hand and counted them before stuffing them into a pocket on the chest of his horrifying polyester jumpsuit. His red-rimmed gaze flicked up to mine. "I want four hundred now."

Mel groaned behind me.

"I'm not paying you more than two hundred," I said. I stuffed the uniform in my bag. A smothered "Mewr?" sounded in protest. "And I'm leaving now."

I turned to go. He grabbed the back of my jeans to hold me there. The waistband cut into my abdomen, knocking the wind from me. Panic gripped my whole body, and I melted into jelly. He wrapped his hand around my upper arm and twirled me around. "Give it back," he said into my face, and I died of strip club buffet breath.

The disgusting man reached into my bag for the uniform. Oh, hell no. I gritted against my fear and stomped on his foot. He yelped and snatched back his hand just as Myrtle hissed after him — good cat! I backed up, gripping the bag with all my strength. His fingers dug into my arm and I couldn't shake him off.

Mel bashed him over the head with her purse. "Let her go! Hark, a vagrant! You, sir, are no gentleman!"

People were noticing now. The tracksuit guys started toward us, their cigars dangling from their lips. "Help me," I screamed to any and all denizens who felt chivalrous. Gross Guy would not let up — he started to shake me, hard, my head bouncing from shoulder to shoulder.

The two guys arrived to help and one of them immediately shoved against Gross' shoulder. He finally let go of my surely bruised arm.

One final yank and I clutched the uniform to my bosom. Mine!

Mel said, "Run!" She pulled on my coat. "Come on."

In a split second, I decided that his act of skullduggery should cost him.

350. I lunged for his chest pocket and tore out my wad of cash

Just before Tracksuit Number Two shoved him to the floor.

One of the waitresses poured a carafe of coffee onto his crotch, and his yells chased Mel and me from the place. We ran and ran, not daring to glance behind.

We stopped, breathless, a few blocks away. I gestured Mel into another coffee shop, this one with no naked people in it, and we took our drinks at a table in the back away from their doors and windows.

I opened my fist, and the cash scattered across the table.

Mel's jaw dropped. "You took back the money?"

I grinned.

"You stole that uniform!" she gasped.

"I liberated it from a vomitus hustler who assaulted me."

She burst into laughter. "Holy shit, Dag! I can't believe you did that!"

I put my bag in my lap and peeked in to make sure poor Myrtle was okay. A surreptitious look around the coffee shop told me that nobody working was paying attention to us, so I liberated her from her leather prison and set her in my lap. She snapped at my finger, but quickly came around and accepted my love. "What a good kitty you are, Moaning Myrtle. You defended me against that horrible man! At least your life isn't boring, cat."

She bit my finger harder this time. Mel kept laughing and laughing. I yanked my digits away from my adorable hellion and returned to my coffee, which never bit me.

"You—" Mel sobered for a moment and peered deep into my soul with her clear green eyes. "You really have changed, you know that?"

I spread out the skirt of the ensemble across the table. "I have. I-I understand I'm not being Mother Theresa or anything, but it feels amazing to talk back against the bullshit that I used to just take."

She picked up the stack of cash and fanned herself with it. "Maybe you *should* change your name to Giselle."

My heart missed a beat, and the thump jolted me. I looked up, and she met my eye after she paused rubbing the cash on her face. She flashed a smile and put it back on the table.

I said, "I… Can I do that? Maybe instead of the inevitable horrible breakup scene with Yash—"

"Which was entirely preventable."

"Shut up. Instead of that, I could just change my name to Giselle, get a job at the airline, and never see my family again!"

Mel sipped her latte. "I like that last part."

We slumped in our seats and drank the restorative caffeine. After a couple of quiet minutes, Mel sniffed into the air. "What is that smell?"

I lifted up the skirt and took a whiff. Oh, hell. "Patchouli and…unknown. Ack, it's so gross."

"You have to rinse that whole thing out with vinegar and then dry it."

"I guess I'll be going home then. He'd better be very appreciative of this uniform. I'd better not have to wear it long." I winked.

She groaned. "I feel obligated to warn you, Dag—"

I plugged my fingers into my ears like an actual child. "Nope. I don't want to hear it. My life is made of lies and denial, and that's the way I enjoy it."

Myrtle meowed, and I took that as agreement. Two in favor of horrid living, one against.

The ayes had it.

Mel gave me a look tinged with sadness. I couldn't take

her pity. *Pity?* After all the fantastic changes I'd been making in my life? We were outing a serial rapist. I'd stood up for myself against multiple scumbags and had gotten a new job on my own terms. Heck, I even had a new cat and a boyfriend! I was no Kardashian, but I was pretty happy at the moment, even if some parts of my life had taken an... odd turn.

I scooped Myrtle back into her bag and stood. "I'm gonna go and wash this thing."

"I don't want you to get hurt," Mel said, rising also. "Or Yash. He's really nice, Dag."

My stomach dropped. "I know he's nice. Nobody minds having what is too good for them."

"He's not too good for you, so shut up, Jane Austen."

I pretend gasped and she broke into a smile.

I said, "We're not...serious, okay? And I've already been hurt, Mel. At least I'm the one in charge of it now and not a pathetic loser chasing after crumbs from the people running the show. I'll see you Sunday night—I have to work tomorrow." I swooped her into my arms for a hug to diminish the razor in my words and left the shop.

The air had become frigid and steam shot up from the subway grates, turning the night as murky as my thoughts. Mel's words rang in my head, swirling and whirling on my walk to the train, on the train, on the way up to my apartment. I gathered my laundry stuff and nearly ran down the stairs to the basement.

No. *No.* I wouldn't backslide. I'd overcome too many of my mousey, pathetic ways.

I plunged the uniform into the warm water of the laundry room's washing machine and poured vinegar after. I slept better now than I had in years—decades even—because I didn't lie awake worrying about my father's approval, or my job, or if I needed to go to the gym more because I'd caught Blade ogling a model-waitress-nurse. I didn't cry anymore when my sister tagged me in nasty jabs on Facebook. I didn't spend half my weekend ironing ugly khaki clothing to make me look like an efficiency beast.

I had fun now. I *was* fun now. And I'd be damned if I'd return to that sad sack Dagmar. The very thought made hot sweats break out across my skin.

Maybe I really would change my name to Giselle.

I took the stairs back up to my apartment two at a time, and I didn't set a timer for the wash. It took me twenty minutes, but I managed a French twist, then I set the jaunty pillbox uniform hat on my head and took a picture for Yash. He replied that my hair was going to get way too mussed to keep it on. My giggles filled the whole apartment.

Mussed.

Nope — no going back.

A couple of hours later, I informed Yash that his flight was ready to board. Yes, yes — eye-roll worthy, but I didn't care. I ordered Indian food and hoped that it was good Indian food since he was, well, Indian.

The uniform fit tightly — very — but I did manage to get it on if I didn't button the skirt. And the horrible smell had fled. I'd quickly used hem tape to hitch the skirt to a mini, and I slipped on black heels to complete the ensemble. No doubt the conservative button-down wasn't meant to open so far over my cleavage. In my defense, however, it wouldn't close over my not-so-massive girls.

All in all, I thought while posing in front of my mirror, not bad. And we wouldn't even have to bang in a disgusting airplane lavatory.

I even put a black ribbon around Myrtle's neck — it turned her into a French ingénue from the 1960s. Until she chewed on one end and covered it in drool. "He doesn't like you as it is," I told her, "so be pretty." She licked her butt, which was the equivalent of a cat shrug in the face of unrealistic feline beauty standards.

While I waited for Yash, I blogged and prepped a few Twitter updates to time out over the next few days. It was fun to talk about getting the cat and the uniform, although I didn't call it a flight attendant pretend job. I said I was pretending to be a nurse a.k.a. sexy scrubs. The instant validation that the Internet offered made me feel powerful. Yes, some condemned me, but many people, women especially, said they wished they had the guts to do what I was doing.

My intercom buzzed and I jumped in my chair. I closed the laptop and ran to the panel to let Yash up. Happiness nearly melted my bones to know he was on the way, in my building, in my apartment. In my bed.

351. But I didn't really have feelings for Yash

352. Just overwhelming joy whenever he was around

353. And the feeling that I might die if I never saw him again

354. Whoops that was a feeling

355. But not feelings with an 'S'

356. Better not think about that too hard

This logical flight of denial burst like a bubble when he knocked. I made a ridiculous girl sound, raced to the door, took a deep breath to calm myself, and opened it.

I swept the door wide and gave a curtsey. "Welcome aboard, sir. If you'll follow me to the first-class cabin?"

He braced himself on one side of the threshold and fixed a hard gaze on me. "We have a problem, *Dagmar*."

Chapter Thirteen

**F*ck-Ups Three-Fifty-Seven through Three-Sixty-Seven
In Preparation for Takeoff, Please Ensure that Your Seat
Is in the Uh-Oh Position**

The world went black. Then red. Then kind of stripy. Breath would not fill my lungs, and I started to flounder. I wanted to say something, anything to make it better. Oh, shit—why hadn't I prepared a speech for this inevitable moment?

He licked his lips. He took a step forward to loom over me, his beautiful brown eyes full of censure.

I floundered backward. "Yash, I—"

"I only have a coach ticket, madam air hostess. I'm afraid I'm just a poor writer."

Yash grinned, and now it was me bracing myself on the door frame so I didn't fall over. Holy hell. Sweet Beyoncé. Blessed Nicki Minaj! Wondrous relief turned my innards to sand. Thank you, God!

Or maybe... Thank you, Satan?

357. The fact that I may have switched deity teams was concerning

I giggled and ran my hand down his arm. He wore a soft, V-neck cashmere sweater in royal blue, his heavy coat slung over an arm, and looked good enough to eat and lick and eat some more. His collarbone. His long, strong neck. The tiny peep of chest hair at the depth of the vee.

Thank you, Satan!

He kept up the bashful writer act as I led him into the living room and closed the door. "Well, I can see if perhaps

I could bump you to first class. I mean" — I ran my fingers along the very deep opening of my blouse — "you do want me to serve you for the entire, long flight, right?"

"Yes, Miss Dagmar." It came out quite breathy, and my pulse leaped to know that I was making him as breathless as he'd made me. For slightly different reasons — my heart still beat a thousand miles an hour from leftover fear and adrenaline.

358. Wow, it felt so good for him to use my real name, though!

359. It had never, ever sounded sexy to me...until now

I shrugged one shoulder like a proper coquette. "Oh, my. An opening has just been found for you."

"Really? That's incredible. I've always been very happy with the openings you've presented to me."

You could not have wiped off the red that heated my cheeks right then for anything. We were both giggling at our dirty jokes when I gestured to his seat — number 1A, of course.

"I can't sit there," he said, pointing. "An interloper is already in my chair."

I peeked around his shoulder to see Moaning Myrtle sitting smack in the middle of the couch. She started with that raspy, squeaking meow of hers and only stopped when Yash approached.

He flicked his hands to try to shoo her away.

She stared at him.

He turned back to me helplessly.

She stared at him.

I stared at him.

He crossed his arms. "I guess I'll have to go back to coach. Across town."

I rushed forward and removed the cat, her protestations notwithstanding. "Not at all, sir, here's your seat."

Myrtle frowned at me as if to say, "You chose a man over our family."

I stuck my tongue out at her as if to say, "I chose a man *and his cock* over our family. Don't make it seem petty."

As he sat, Yash asked, "Where's Mel?"

I almost said 'At her apartment,' but I remembered just in time. The thing I actually said was, "She's visiting a first-class passenger of her own tonight."

"Good for her."

With a fresh smile, I bustled to place a napkin over his lap. It took me a moment or two to get it in just the right position, smoothed over his…his…

He yanked me into that lap, with its growing erection, and tipped me back for a kiss. My body lit up with wanting him, his hands, his everything everywhere. One of his hands slid up my skirt to cup my ass, and I pulled away to come up for air. "Sir, your dinner service will get cold."

"Let it."

I yelped as he stood, me in his arms, and carried me to the bedroom.

360. I should've been a fake air hostess years ago

361. All of the benefits, none of the rude passengers or turbulence

Obviously, I'd had sexual partners before. But I'd never had the experience Yash gave to me. He made love to me as if I were the only woman in the world. As if my skin were made of magic. As if my touch was the greatest thing ever to happen to him. He wasn't merely a good lover—he was an amazing partner. My body had never responded as it did with him. I was a sex goddess, a muse, a siren all at once.

And I'd never felt such blind, wanton lust in my life. Yash had awoken Sleeping Beauty. Well, the super dirty version written by Anne Rice. At one point in the last hour, I'd literally seen through space and time, and yes, I was using 'literally' correctly.

After he'd had his way with me, he lay me back down on my bed and chuckled. "What's that face?" he asked. "Have I not made your Mile High Club dreams come true? By the by, that was a dirty 'come' joke."

"You're a lofty writer, after all," I offered, slightly out of breath. "I didn't mean to make a face. I'm very happy with my work shift this evening." I nuzzled his chest. Gah, he smelled of sex and man and unicorns.

"Okay." He tucked me into his shoulder and played with my hair, which had, indeed, not survived his manly onslaught. The hat was long gone, although I still wore the crumpled remains of the skirt. Heh heh. "When I first got here, you gave me a very odd look, so I was worried you were upset."

My stomach twisted and my bliss ruptured. I sat up and clutched my rumpled sheet to my bosom. "No, nothing." I turned to the side and looked down at him. His hair had flopped over his forehead and I smoothed it over his brow. "You're wonderful." He seemed to want to pursue the conversation, so I was tremendously grateful for Myrtle for mewing to be let on the bed right then. She was too small for the jump, so I helped her into Yash's lap to distract him.

It worked.

"I think my dinner service is a bit cold," I said, subject change-ingly.

He sat up and tipped my chin to him. "I bet it was perfect, too. Dessert was certainly perfect."

A wave of guilt shot through me at being called 'perfect'. I wasn't perfect. I'd never be perfect. I'd tried, and it had been pointless, anyway.

I plastered on a smile and stood. In the most authoritative way I could with bare breasts and a too-small skirt, I said, "Would you like dinner in the first-class cabin or the sleeper compartment?" Did airplanes even have sleeper compartments? Or was I pretending to be a train steward?

My perfect beau ran a hand through all that amazing, wavy hair. "Wow, what a choice. And what a professional you are."

I shrugged. "I do get many, many tips."

"I bet. Let's take dinner in the sleeper compartment?"

I curtseyed, and his eyes followed my breasts, which made me blush anew.

362. Really, if I was going to act like an immoral strumpet, I should stop blushing

In my best sashay, I came around the bed and fluffed a pillow behind his back. It necessitated shoving my boobs in his face. Then, I grabbed a DVD from the living room and popped it into the player in the bedroom. At least Blade had left me with some good electronics (for which I'd paid half). I sat beside Yash on the bed and pushed buttons, and he took the opportunity to push some of mine. It was hard to get a DVD to play while he tickled my neck and lightly pinched my nipples.

After a few minutes of naked kissing, during which I may have blacked out from overzealous whoremones, he finally deigned to let me feed him.

Before I left, I played the movie. "*Airplane!*" he exclaimed. "You are too good to me, Giselle. Oops, I mean sexy Dagmar."

I laughed entirely too loud, like a machine gun of fakery, and bolted from the room.

In the kitchen, I tamped down on my emotions—all of them, the good, bad, and guilty—and set about reheating our meal. How did truly bad people do it? I knew sociopaths had no conscience...but what about your run of the mill Wall Streeter, or those people who run over your feet with their SUV strollers even though there's plenty of room, then scream that you tried to injure their baby. Yes, Vanessa had done that to me. And my feet.

My ruminations screeched to a halt as Yash's arms stole around me from behind. "Mmm, it's starting to smell good. I'm sorry I let the food go cold."

"I'm not."

He pumped his hips forward—his naked hips—and we hit the counter. I did not mind hitting the counter. "Don't do that sexy low voice thing you do," he begged. "I'm starving, but I will carry you back to the bed like an animal."

"I'm sorry," I said in the apparently sexy low voice thing I did. I swatted his hand from the very naughty place it had discovered. "Behave, you."

"Never." With a great, heaving sigh that was absolutely on purpose, he unwound from me and leaned against the counter. He tore off a corner of naan bread and munched on it. Even that I denied him—I popped it in the oven to warm.

"May I ask a question?" he asked.

"You just did."

"Yes, so clever."

I got a pop to the backside for my insolence. "Sir, that is very inappropriate and against regulations. Do you want me to call the air marshal?"

He held up his hands. "Don't arrest me, please. I'm too brown, they'll send me to Guantanamo."

I started to laugh, but the truth of that statement was just too depressing. Guantanamo might not exist as Guantanamo, but one existed somewhere. I gave him a kiss on the cheek, because that made up for state-sanctioned institutional racism, right?

Time to get back to the subject. "Ask away," I said with only a little trepidation.

Fifteen percent trepidation.

Eighty at most.

"You asked me to outline my flaws." He ran a finger down my arm, and I nearly dropped the bowl of malai kofta I held. "So fess up. Tell me *your* darkest secrets."

My brows knit. "I-I… My flaws are…flaw-ier than yours."

"Everyone thinks that. Everyone with a good heart, anyway."

Bllllllleeeeeerrrrrgggggggg. Now was it. Now was the time to come clean, right? Only three dates and six orgasms in… I should do this.

"I… I—"

363. "I'm a recovering perfectionist"

He cocked his head. "Explain."

I stirred the food in my hand and set it aside to busy myself in the oven to check on the naan that had only been in there a minute. "'Recovering perfectionist' sounds like a humblebrag, but it's not. It was a disease. I used to be…

very driven, people-pleasing. Always the best grades, the longest hours, first in, last out. I bowed to every boyfriend's whim, my father's whim, and tried to make myself the perfect woman for *them*...but not for *me*. I think... I think I told myself that those were the same thing."

"They're not."

The oven door slammed closed, although I hadn't meant to do that. I squeezed my eyes shut — I'd actually started to tear up. "I know that now. Anyway, I lost an important job, my boyfriend dumped me and moved to L.A. the next day, and my father thinks I'm useless. So I stopped the ride and got off." A nervous laugh escaped me. "So to speak."

"Is that when you became a flight attendant? What was your career before?"

I took a deep breath. "I was..." The word 'editor' almost spurted from my mouth, but I couldn't. The publishing community was too small, and I'd be found out far too quickly. "In advertising. A copywriter."

364. If you squinted through rose-colored glasses, it was kinda sorta with a fib on top true

"You wrote?" His entire face lit up. "That's amazing! Don't get me wrong, nobody should be in an environment that makes them unhappy, but it's lovely to hear you may have a little understanding of where I come from."

He was so beautiful in his joy that I threw my arms around him. "You're an amazing writer, Yash. That is absolutely my educated opinion."

The way I got squeezed back, I almost suffocated. From happiness.

I unwound and said, "So yes, that's when I started my new...career."

365. Of professional deceit

"I'm also lazy with the laundry, get jealous of Mel when the cat is cuddling with her more, and flip other drivers off."

I put the spicy potato curry in the microwave and zapped it.

He perused the food. "You have a nice selection here."

"Really? I was so worried. I'm totally clueless, except about what I think is tasty."

"Then I shall have to cook for you. My mother had no daughters, so all four of her sons know how to cook. I'm the best one."

"Really?"

He nibbled on his lip. "Third best."

"Third?" I clapped. "So you're really second worst."

"Yet another flaw for me. That's fifteen for me and two for you."

366. If I only had two, then they were the size of Long Island

I bit my lip. "So…do you think your mom would like me?"

"No."

It was the way he said it—like no freaking way, you piece of gum under my mother's shoe. "Oh?"

His eyes went soft and apologetic. "I'm sorry, but she will never like any non-Desi girl I bring home. It's not personal." Suddenly, a sheepish cloud passed over him, and he crossed to the fridge to grab a beer. "Would you… Would you beta read my new book?"

I dropped the plate I held. It crashed to the floor, making both of us jump backward. My heart spiked into life *yet again*, but, thankfully, the plate had been clean. "Are you okay?" I asked him.

He faux-cowered against the cabinets across from me. "Yes, I'm very nimble."

"As I've learned. Sorry, I was just shocked at what you asked." And at how fast he'd changed the mother subject. Oh, well. My own parents hadn't liked me—one more source of disapproval wasn't a big deal.

I removed my oven mitts and took his hands over the shattered plate. "I'd be so honored to read it, you have no idea. But I'm very intimidated."

"No, no." He squeezed me back. "I don't write lofty screeds examining the inside of my navel. Or at least, I try not to. There are enough people doing that. It's commercial fiction, and you are more than woman enough to handle it."

My smile was real and grateful. "Thank you."

OMG OMG OMG gimme gimme gimme book book book!

The microwave beeped just as I'd gotten on my knees to collect plate pieces. Yash said, "I'll get your broom, if you have one?"

He made as if to seek out the closets and crannies of my apartment, and ha ha ha no, that could not be allowed. He might wonder where Mel's bedroom was. And I'd been the most anal person in the world — half the items in my bathroom sported my name for organizational purposes. Blade had been very particular about his items only being for use by him.

Asshole.

I said, "I'll grab a broom. Why don't you watch dinner, mister third best cook?"

He shot me a very rude gesture, which I returned, and I sought out my dustpan and broom while laughing. I swept up my mess in my miniskirt, my tits swinging in the breeze. It was actually kind of fun having a sweet domestic scene with Yash while I was half naked, and he, wholly.

That last part especially.

I leaned a hip against the counter after I'd finished cleaning. "I'm a piss-poor flight attendant, making you heat up your own food."

"Don't make me fly the plane, and we'll call it even."

Our dinner service reheated, I insisted he return to the bedroom so that I could perform my job. I cleaned off the kitchen cart so I had something to roll and loaded the food, plus a bottle of wine.

I'd fetched my hat, so I added that to my ensemble of skirt. I wheeled my cart to the bedroom. He laughed and applauded when I entered.

With a curtsey, I asked, "You ordered the Indian sampler?"

"That's the name of the last thing I did in bed."

FYI: It had been delicious.

After he'd put his pants back on—hot food plus naked laps equals boner-killing emergency room trip—I loaded up a plate for him, heaped naan on top, and poured him a glass of wine.

I climbed into bed after having shucked my skirt and donned a long button-down opened to a scandalous level. We toasted wine and shared the goofiest smiles ever. The word 'besotted' flashed through my mind. Such an excellent word. An old-fashioned-sounding word. It wasn't 'enraptured,' which had an air of too-pure loftiness. It wasn't 'dumbstruck,' which implied a disparity of interest levels.

I was besotted with him. And he with me.

The certainty made me sway. I hadn't been looked at this way in such a long time. Maybe not quite ever. It was the kind of look that people started wars to keep fixed upon them. I had to close my eyes, the emotions overwhelmed me so.

His lips brushed my forehead, his hands gently twining into my hair. And in that moment, my besotted state fled. I landed in the middle before I understood what had begun.

367. I was in love

Chapter Fourteen

F*ck-Ups Three-Sixty-Eight through Three-Eighty-Seven
Love Is a Many Stupid Thing

368. I was in love
369. I was in love
370. I was in love
371. I was in love
372. I was in love
373. I was in love
374. I was in love
375. I was in love
376. I was in love
377. I was in love
378. I was in love
379. I was in love
380. I was in love
381. I was in love
382. I was in love
383. Oh, damn it all to hell
384. I was in love

* * * *

My chest started to ache from so many mistakes all at once. Like heartburn caused by drinking lava.

I shoved a samosa into my mouth to cover what was surely yet another odd expression on my face. Who the hell fell in love in what — three weeks? Four?

Ruination! Despair! Havoc! Splat.

God—I couldn't draw breath. I floundered among the covers to find the remote control—*Save me,* Airplane!

Yash captured my hand. "I want to watch the wonderful and theme-appropriate movie you've chosen, but I was wondering..."

"Yesh?" I said, a crumble of potato shooting from my mouth.

"I want to know what it's like to be a flight attendant. It seems quite a brave job." He grinned, taking an interest in my occupation. It was so sweet, I hate-loved him for it.

385. Just imagine how perfect he'd think 'editor me' was for him

At least I could give my brain something to consider other than *love love love* blerg. The cogs in my head turned to remember the flight attendant learning I'd done via the University of Google. "Well, it's a fun job, most of the time, but a lot of hard work. We're not only the face of the airline, but the safety crew as well." Everything I'd read from the point of view of flight attendants had made me respect the hell out of them. All customer service jobs are tough—gaze in wonderment at the burn scar on my shoulder—but to do it at thirty thousand feet while constantly remembering emergency procedures, smiling, and controlling entitled passengers...or the worst kind, the violent kind.

"First-class service is more involved than coach, actually, because there are fewer passengers, so it's more intimate. Sometimes I'll have to facilitate a fine against a smoker who thought they'd get away with it, or I'll accidentally spill a drink on someone, which is the worst."

"What do you do then?"

I fed him a bite of samosa because he was ignoring his meal to concentrate on me. "I grovel and hope they aren't mean. The airline will reimburse dry cleaning."

He chewed the food and smiled, so I fed him another bite. This time he licked the tip of my fingers, and I melted. "I— Anyway, it's an interesting job."

"Do you have to sleep on the jump seats?"

"No. We have tiny crew rooms tucked here and there.

Low ceilings, multiple beds crammed together. Usually, we sleep right next to another crew member, separated by a curtain, so you have to lie pretty still and not mind bumps here and there."

He laughed. "You toss and turn so much, though! Maybe you're only comfortable sleeping with miles of air beneath you."

"Maybe I should get an air mattress."

My dumb joke made him grin, and he finally turned on the movie, thereby ending my interrogation, thank goodness.

It hit me again, a sucker punch to the heart.

386. I love him

Ugh noooooooo. Emotions were so stupid! No way, wasn't love, just something else that felt exactly like it.

I hardly enjoyed the brilliance of *Airplane!* because I now wondered why I apparently tossed and turned in my sleep. Well…not *why* — I was a double agent in the spy mission engineered needlessly by me. No wonder I churned — my conscience had pricked my sleep bubble. Insert deflated air mattress metaphor here.

I managed to swallow a few bites of the excellent food before putting it aside and settling onto Yash's shoulder. My eyes closed, I simply allowed myself to enjoy being here with him. Maybe that was the worst part of the whole thing — the fact that I hadn't been myself with the best man I'd ever met.

387. I mean, I had, but the truth of my heart was buried in bits and pieces between land mines

Or maybe…I was becoming a new person, and the land mines were now a part of me, too. I needed a little explosive in my life. I'd been far too submissive, even if it had been buried under a layer of ambition and intellect.

Maybe my lies were actually redeeming me. I hadn't been a whole person before — I'd been every bit as much of an act as now. Only now, I orchestrated the act. I was the leading lady instead of the comic relief servant, bustling from room to room, from order to order, never starring in her own story.

I sat up and turned to this beautiful man, who'd surely faced his own challenges of being a minority in this part of the world. We all wore masks of necessity.

Suddenly, I wanted to tell him. I wanted to be real for the first time…maybe ever. I'd played the dutiful daughter, the dutiful employee, the dutiful girlfriend.

It ended now. I wanted to love as me. I wanted to be loved for me.

Chapter Fifteen

F*ck-Ups Three-Eighty-Eight through Four-Hundred-Six
The Order of the Scum-Defeating Amazonians

Yash turned to me and paused the movie. "Are you okay?"

Now was the time.

Now was the time. Come on, Dagmar. You'd said you would stand up for yourself. So do it.

I opened my mouth, dry and harsh as a gin martini. Wished I had one of those right about now. "Yash, I need to tell you something."

"May I go first?"

No! Now was the time. But that face... Mother Theresa couldn't say no to that face. "Yes, of course."

"Giselle. Sexy, fun, intelligent, interesting Giselle. Friend to the cats..." Myrtle had been pouncing his feet under the covers for a while now, much to his chagrin. "I think I'm falling for you."

I burst into tears.

His whole face fell. His shoulders fell. I think his skin fell. "Oh, no. That was not the reaction I wanted."

Between sobs, I managed to get out, "I — am — falling — f-f-for — you — too."

"Really?" He swiped at my wet cheeks with gentle hands and gazed at me as if the sun shone out of my eyes.

388. I couldn't tell him now

389. Not now

390. Now?

391. No-w

"Yes, I adore you, Yash," I told him, more than honestly. "You're the most amazing man I've ever met. I know it's crazy because it's early days for us, but...you make me very happy."

He beamed and wound his big hand around the back of my neck. He pulled me into a kiss that lit up my soul. And lit up everything south of it. And north, and east and west and up and down and into the fourth dimension. In only a few moments, he'd ripped off the last vestiges of my clothing and made me forget every lie, every truth, every fleeting moment of good sense I'd ever had and replaced it with his body and heart.

392. It was the best mistake so far

* * * *

Yash was a good influence on me. For the next two weeks, I yanked open the door of JaVaVaVoom a full ten to fifteen minutes early, and I hadn't come to work drunk in all that time. Tipsy cappuccino-making had been fun, but I'd been there, buzzed that.

Today, I passed through the tables and spotted a familiar face. "Ms. Hodgkins, how lovely to see you again!" Today my Fairy Bookmother wore a stark-white skinny pant suit with hot-pink patent leather pumps and a matching wool fedora. The hair underneath the screaming hat? Aqua. "My goodness, you look amazing yet again today. You should create a coffee table book about yourself and your dynamic style. And feature other women of a certain age to show that looking fabulous doesn't end at any decade."

Her eyebrows shot up.

I said, "Shit! That was so presumptuous. I'm Dagmar, we've met a couple of times when you've been here. And I obviously don't need to tell you how to do your job."

393. I curtseyed

394. I admonished myself for curtseying

395. In my defense, she was publishing royalty

I flustered and babbled and nearly tripped over myself while apologizing when the queen reached out to touch my arm. "Of course I remember you. Please sit. Do you have a moment?"

"I have about ten, sure, thank you."

I sat and slung my purse over the back of my chair. I smiled and froze, but managed to squeeze out, "I started reading *Mambo Italiano*. What a decadent adventure. And so funny! I think you're a comedienne at heart." Her book had made me spend hours researching trips to Italy and planning wild times with gorgeous, curly-haired Italian men who all looked, in my imagination, like Yash.

Thankfully, Marlene possessed the grace I lacked. "And you're an editor. A coffee table book about fashionable women in their fifties, sixties, and as old as we can find them would be an amazing idea." She took a sip of her coffee and closed her laptop. "So... Did you try to get another publishing job after Carmichael?"

"No."

"Why not?"

I took a deep breath and sighed it out. "I've been brutally honest with you thus far — might as well continue."

She leaned back. "This had better be good."

I laughed. "I don't know if I'm terribly profound. I lost the job and my douchey live-in boyfriend on the same day, and I realized...I'd been living for these men. For their approval, even as I deluded myself that my excelling was for me. But it wasn't, not nearly enough, anyway. I'd swallowed a thousand insults and demeaning comments, and told myself I must pay my dues. And in the end...it had all been for naught." I tilted my head and stared at the table — her regard was too intense, like a heat lamp made of awesome. "Then a switch flipped. And I knew I had to stop trying. Completely. Instead, I decided to do all the things I'd never allowed myself to do, lest some authority figure think badly of me."

She licked her hot-pink lips. "So...you got a job you didn't have to care about long term and tried to bang the boss?"

"That's about it. Among other things." I knew I was blushing, thinking about Taylor, and Deep Throat, and Giselle the flight attendant.

"And how has this served you?"

I leaned closer. "I'm much happier, honestly, although I miss making books. I really do. But day to day? I'm finally…me. Or, at least, I'm finally discovering who I want to be. I've gotten inappropriately drunk, I've taken down evil, I've begun being very honest about some things while learning how to bullshit about others. I guess — I've learned that being a doormat sucks, and that being the opposite is not the end of the world. Less goody-goody and more baddy-baddy."

Marlene sipped her coffee, the wheels in her head rotating through her shining gaze. I held it this time, because I could be a badass, too. Not 'stealing a police car in Roma' badass, but hey —

396. I'd get there

She asked, "Have you heard of a blog called *Six-Hundred-Sixty-Six Ways to Screw Up My Life*?"

I put on my most innocent face. "Nope. Not at all. Never. And it's 'fuck' up, not 'screw' up."

Finally, I made her laugh. "Pretty entertaining. It's got a nice wit, and it says a lot about society's expectations of women."

"I grew up being force-fed those expectations."

"I never had a lot of use for them. Husbands, kids." She made an 'ick' face. "When some idiot says, 'But who will take care of you when you're old?' I reply, 'My boyfriend who is twenty years younger than I am.'"

Wow.

She slammed her hand on the table. I jumped. She smirked. I think she was starting to like me. "What number mistake are you on?"

My shaky jig was up. "Four hundred-ish."

"Best one?"

I gnawed on my lip. "I'm in the midst of bringing public justice down on a roofie-ing rapist."

Her eyes nearly bugged out. "Damn, girl. And worst?"

"That's easy." I released a breathy laugh. "The man I'm in love with thinks I'm a flight attendant named Giselle."

She set her coffee down with her mouth in an O. "You go whole hog."

"Apparently. It's not going to end well."

"Why are you being so honest with me?"

This answer came easily to me for some reason. "Because I'm tired of faking it."

The queen nodded, a slow, regal head bow that made me want to curtsey again.

Finally, she continued my interrogation. "I made a few calls—I was curious about you. You're hard-working, smart but not arrogant, driven but honest. Maybe too honest. Your former colleagues told me you tried to give Carmichael Burns a conscience. I liked what I heard."

"Uh…bbu…flim…drack…"

"Are those good noises?"

I began to laugh. "Yes! Yes. Losing my job broke my heart. To know that people are saying nice things…well, it makes me feel like I wasn't as huge a drip as previously thought."

"A drip? Does a drip get a new job over a five-minute coffee?" She stood and handed me her card. As she packed up her things, she said, "If you want to be an editor for Hysterical, give your notice to coffeeland here and give me a call. Hand me research on comps for the fashionable women book when you walk in on your first day, as well as a few other ideas about subjects you feel passionate about. Oh, and I think a sequel to Khandye Kardashian's book is in order—her sales have been steady. My sources tell me she's in talks with your former publisher, so we need to swoop in with a better offer. She might not realize it, but she needs you. We should just go ahead and credit you as co-author this time. That blog you have no idea about is hilarious."

I gaped like a guppy and fought valiantly to stop the tears

springing to my eyes. Marlene didn't wait for a reply, for she was a queen who must tend to her court. The rest of her court, because I'd just joined it!

After she left, I jumped to my feet and yelled, "Yes!"

Yes yes yes yes yes yes yes yes yes yes yes yes yes yes yes yes yes yes yes yes yes yes yes yes yes yes yes yes yes yes yes yes yes yes yes yes yes yes yes yes holy shit yes yes yes yes yes yes yes yes yes yes yes yes yes OMG yes yes yes yes yes!

I turned to Hunter and beamed. "I quit!"

"What? Lacey is out sick today."

"Then I'll stay for another week!"

397. A week's notice wasn't exactly proper, but I was a fuck-up, not the director of the C.I.A.

Once in the back room, I threw my apron on and called Mel.

She picked up, saying, "We making plans for Deep Throat Part Two, Even Deepier Throating?"

I snorted. "Hell, yes, but I have news. You are talking to the new editor at Hysterical Books!"

"What? Holy shitnuts!"

I jumped up and down while we squealed together, and I knew she was leaping like a frog, too, because I'm psychic. And also because she'd dropped her phone and stomped on it.

Once she dusted off her footprint, she said, "Dag, that's amazing! How? How?"

My head spun, but for a good reason, finally. "I have to go make a thousand cups of coffee, but I'll dish about everything tonight. I get out at seven, and I'll come over then. Cool?"

"Dagmar rides again!"

"And I totally have fucking up to thank!"

We hung up, and I spent the rest of the day in a delirious haze. A teenager shoved an entire large tea at me because she said the chai was too chai-ey. A dad with three daughters under the age of six screamed misogynist obscenities at me until he broke into a sweat because we'd accidentally toasted his bagel. The guy after him, however, had left me a ten-dollar tip just to spite the asshole. And a lady had tried to play the switching-change grift on me, but I'd demanded a count of the register to prove myself, and the woman had beat feet out of there.

But in the end— Who cared? I'd gotten an amazing new job! I swear, me telling Marlene that I'd hit on Hunter had helped her remember me, ask about me. And I'd have to send a basket of muffins to Carmichael's department thanking all of them for talking me up so I got the new job. Maybe I'd send strawberry ones. Carmichael is allergic to strawberries.

That should piss him the hell off—no mistake about that.

Yet I wondered... How to explain the change to Yash? My schedule would be much more nine-to-six now. Eh, I squished that thought down to be dealt with another day. Because today was made of magic. I gave everyone extra whipped cream and chose the largest pastries from the case. I sang aloud to the muzak wailing from the sound system. My mood infected everyone around me, even Hunter, who said he was sad to see me go after teaching me only half of the Coffee Code.

He'd also heavily implied that once I was no longer his employee, he'd love to see that pleather dress again. Heh heh. I let him down easy.

398. But yes! I had made him want me!

399. Respectful sluttiness works every time

400. Take note, classy bitches

My shift flew by, and soon I'd stopped at home to cuddle and feed my fur monster, and to change into an all-black ensemble topped with a trench coat to prepare for our nefarious assignation. When I got to Mel's, she whipped the door open and said, "A pink trench coat? Very subtle."

I sashayed inside and did a turn for her. "It's the only trench I own, and this is its inaugural appearance. I bought it three or four years ago, but then decided it was too flashy, so it's been hidden."

She shook her head at me, even as she cracked a half smile. "Dag, I always knew there was a pink trench coat hidden inside you. For better or worse, honey, I'm happy you've let her out. Now!" She clapped her hands. "I've got pizza on the way. We shall discuss your new job and then our plan. We do have a plan?"

I shrugged.

"That's what I like to hear."

Over pepperoni and extra cheese in Mel's living room, I told her about the goddess Marlene Hodgkins. Mel knew her by reputation, of course, and we scoured the Hysterical website for their latest news and staffing info. They put out about one hundred books a year in a variety of genres. The common ground was that Hysterical emphasized women's and minority voices.

After the sexist barf bag that had been Carmichael's group, my new home sounded like heaven.

"Should I call her tonight?" I asked.

Mel said, "It's already eight. Send her an email tomorrow that you're very interested and set up a formal time to talk. Have you discussed salary or anything?"

"No. Hopefully she doesn't realize the peanuts she'd need to pay me to jump the coffee express."

"Well, I wouldn't *lead* with desperation."

We munched and sighed over the website for a while longer, then we got down to the task at hand. With our 'serious business' faces on, we made a plan.

I said, "I wish we had a car. We could shine the lights bright against a wall and stand in the dark to talk to her."

"She'll think she's getting kidnapped. We'll just stay in the shadows."

"Or…" I rooted around in the supplies I'd brought with me and pulled one of them over my head.

Mel spit out her soda and fell across her couch.

"What's wrong?" I demanded through the rubbery confines of my white unicorn mask. The thing covered my entire head and neck, and I yanked it off quickly.

"Why do you own that abomination?"

"Don't talk that way about my unicorn, Xanadu! She was my costume last Halloween. I wore her with a pink prom dress I got at Goodwill." I reached into my satchel. "This one is yours."

She whipped it from my hands and peered at the empty rubber face. "I get the horse? But I want to be the unicorn."

"Then you should have bought the unicorn. Don't worry, I de-Bladed the horse before I brought it."

"Good thing. No telling what ick that guy had."

I shot her a baleful look. "I got tested. If he has a dread disease, he didn't pass it to me."

"I hope he has one all the same, though."

"Like dick rot."

"Or scrotum scabies."

Now it was my turn to spit my drink. We were too witty for her light-colored carpet.

"Maybe she'll be too afraid to talk to us in these masks?" I pondered.

Mel pshawed. "Nah. I'd definitely talk to a vengeful unicorn in a pink coat. That's just good manners, honey."

I yanked her in for a hug, and we polished off another slice of pizza. While we waited to go, nerves jangling as if we'd fed them coffee, we Googled DirtyLinens.com's history of not revealing their sources. They definitely went to bat to protect them, even fighting in court and settling lawsuits rather than expose anyone. Gossip about the rich and powerful was their bread and butter.

I pulled my legs under me and flopped back against the couch. "Say the worst case happens, and the cops find me. He roofied himself, basically. All I did was go through his computer."

Mel nodded. "True. I think you could get a deal with the cops in exchange for cooperation."

"Me too. If not, I'd take my case to the public and be a heroine for the ages!"

"Uh-huh. You and Norma Rae."

It was still hours before we were to meet Abby, so we settled in to watch a silly movie and have a cocktail.

401. Because why undertake a spy mission unless you're a little buzzed?

402. It was medicinal

And, boy, it made me feel a lot more confident about all these stupid decisions. Besides, I had a new job to celebrate.

My brain barely kept track of the movie plot, so jazzed was it to have a new literary adventure to mull over. I'd be working at a much smaller press, but one that was likely a better fit for me. And I knew that I'd never get passed over for promotion — or fired, for fuck's sake — because Marlene got horny.

The awesome older ladies fashion book also made my heart race with glee. Women of all creeds, colors, nationalities with fabulous fashion in common, living dynamic lives no matter their ages. What an inspiration! It could feature stories about fashion and life lessons intertwining.

Midnight rolled around, and Mel elbowed me out of my reverie. I'd begun a blog about getting a new job in publishing, but I hadn't pushed it live yet. I needed time to collect my jumbled thoughts, but first:

403. Operation Even Deeper Throating

We dressed in trench coats. Mel's was plaid. Whatever — we were fashion-savvy undercover operatives. We threw our masks into cross-body bags and topped our heads with scarves. I tucked away sunglasses just in case, as well as a few other items we might need.

With a quick prayer to the gods of Lady Justice, we set off on foot to the parking garage. We strolled right in via the pedestrian entrance, our scarves pulled tight over the bulk of our faces. Few cars were in evidence. We stuck to the walls, circling down to the darkest part. Security cameras monitored us from high on the ceiling, but we kept our scarves over our mouths and heads, like chilly Jawas.

Mel and I found a corner and sat down on the cleanest-looking and least-uriney-smelling place. "We're so early," she said. "I hope the security guards don't roust us out."

"Yeah, I didn't consider that. There aren't any cars in this part. Maybe they think we're just banging or something."

"They'll get mad when we don't."

I laughed. It echoed everywhere in the giant concrete box. I clapped my hand over my mouth as Mel shot me a dirty look.

"Sorry," I whispered.

"Maybe you should put your unicorn head on."

"My horn of shame."

She giggled this time, and it echoed, which made me laugh. We'd be easy for Abby to find at least.

"Here—" I said, pulling a flask from my bag. "We need to chill. I feel like I'm going to barf everywhere."

I took a pull of vodka and handed it to her. She swigged as well. Was 'swigged' a word?

404. Shouldn't an editor know that?

405. The kind of editor who helped concoct names for dildo salads could make up any cromulent word she wanted

See Mel and Dagmar. See Mel swig. See Dagmar swig. Swig swig swig. She swigged and she swigged. They swig-swagged together.

See Mel stand. See Mel laugh and fall over. Uh-oh!

See Dagmar stand. See Dagmar grab onto Mel. See them both swiggety swaggety sway.

"Shit," I said. "We vodka'd too much."

"Swuggety schwing," she agreed.

Footsteps echoed through the chamber.

"Shh shhh shhhhhh," we swig-slurred. We did manage to yank on our masks just as Abby turned the corner to our floor.

"I can hear you," she said. "You're not very good at this clandestine thing."

I said, "This is Operation Even Deepier Throating, thank you very much."

She cracked up and came closer. "Am I... Am I talking to a unicorn?"

"Yo."

"Okay."

"Want a drink? We don't have diseases."

"Yeah," Mel agreed. "We didn't sleep with the roofie asshole."

Wow, being pleasantly buzzed was making this meeting easy! We were brilliant at this. We wore masks and everything.

Abby stopped about ten feet from us. "A unicorn and a horse. How on earth did the two of you get those pictures? They're seriously gross."

"Yeah," said the unicorn. "He's a piece of shit. Are you recording this meeting? Because we don't consent to that."

She reached into the pocket of her jacket and pulled out her phone. She showed us the audio recorder and switched it off.

"Great, thanks," said the horse with a graceful burp. "So, if, theoretically, we may have done a slightly dodgy thing to get them, what then?"

She began to take notes the old-fashioned way. "Well, it seems to me that you were in imminent fear of this man, a rapist, right?"

"Yes!" said the horse and the unicorn.

"And is he aware that the pictures have been...shared?"

"Nope." Geez, this mask stifled my face. I now remembered that I'd only kept it on for about ninety seconds at the Halloween party.

Abby continued, "And are you two the only ones besides himself who possibly had access to them? As in, will he put A and B together and get Kooky Animal Chicks?"

We laughed, hard, which made steam inside my mask.

Mel said, "Nope, tons of women in that apartment. Computer not password protected. And we got rid of any fingerprints."

"Besides," I said, "I was invited in."

Abby grinned. "This is all very good. And the answer is no, DirtyLinens will never, ever give you up. My editor is practically drooling over this story. We'll go to bat for you. Not that I have any idea who you are."

The unicorn and the horse clapped their hooves in glee. Then the unicorn got down to business with the story we'd decided on. "I was at a bar with Horsey here."

"Whinney," said Horsey.

Abby's eyebrows drew together.

406. We were not the most reliable witnesses at the moment

"She's just enthusiastic," I said, wishing I had a strong cup of JaVaVaVoom. I put my thinking cap over my mask. "Anyway, this guy, Taylor, started hitting on me. He offered to buy me a drink and I said yes. I told him I'd have what he was having, the reason being I always switch drinks with any guy I don't know in case they try to roofie me."

Abby's jaw dropped. "That's a good idea."

"Yeah. You can also insist they have the same drink as you. Feel free to steal it. So we got the drinks, I distracted him and switched the cocktails. Sure enough, not ten minutes later, this asshole starts acting loopy. I enlisted her" — I pointed at Mel — "to help get him home. We went up to his apartment, and, even in his drugged state, he got really forceful with me. He seemed to be confused as to why I wasn't falling into bed with him. So we decided to go into his computer to inform his mother of his behavior."

"Ha! I've heard of ladies calling Mom, I get it. So that's when you found the photos?"

"Yes. A folder right on his desktop called 'sluts'."

"Ew."

"Whinney," agreed Horsey.

I clutched my fluttering stomach. The booze was starting to war with my nerves. "That's when we Googled him, discovered his identity, and decided to out him. We copied the photos to a thumb drive and left him there to stew in his, er, juices."

"Ew," said Abby, again, saying it all. "Okay, wow. I can run with this. Those photos don't lie, and to know they came from one of the almost-victims is fantastic. I don't suppose you kept any of the tainted drink or anything?"

I shook my head.

"Yeah, that was too much to dream of. I don't know that any actual charges will come of this. His family will threaten us to take the piece down, but once it's up, the Internet will take over. Our plan is to redact the faces of the women, but to ask them to contact us if they recognize themselves. The stories should come rolling in then. Hopefully, he won't be able to buy a drink for a woman in this town for the rest of his life. Oh, do you mind if I print that tip about ordering the same drink?"

"Of course not. Let's stop these scumbags."

She examined us one more time and laughed again. "Well, I couldn't ID the two of you if my life depended on it, so I think you're safe there. Thanks for the story, ladies, and watch your email in case I have more questions." With that, she started making the trek out of the parking garage.

We hung back and, once a few minutes had passed, we followed her direction of travel. A quick peek around a corner told us she wasn't in the building anymore.

A security guard, however, was. "Hey!" he called. "Get outta here, you freaks!"

Hear Mel whinny. Hear Dag whinny. See Mel and Dag run away from the yelling security guard. Run, freaks, run!

There was one item in my arsenal I hadn't gotten to use, so I grabbed it now. I yanked the object from my bag, pulled the wire, and deployed it.

"Oh, my God!" yelled Mel as all three of us were engulfed in bright blue smoke.

I took her arm and pulled her up the ramp toward the early morning air. The security guard hollered to save the band, but our escape was shrouded in blue haze, so we got away clean. Once outside, we kept running in the masks.

Nobody on the sidewalk gave a hoot.

We actually ran past Mel's building. Around the corner from it, we pulled off our sweaty headgear. The night air kissed my head, and it seemed that I'd never felt anything so refreshing, like being engulfed in an Icelandic lake.

Mel pointed at me. "You are a disgusting mess!"

"You too!" We hugged, despite being gross. "We did it! Hopefully, enough women will see that DirtyLinens post that none of them will ever give that scumbag the time of day again."

"And it'll be a good reminder about the state of assholes out there." She took my hand, and we started back toward her place. "I wish the glorious matriarchy would take over already. We'd be given medals. I hereby anoint us members of The Order of the Scum-Defeating Amazonians!"

"Hooray!"

Our breaths came labored on the ride up in the elevator. Once in Mel's apartment, she said, "I love you, fellow Amazonian, but get the hell out. I have work in seven hours."

"Gotcha. I have work in fourteen hours, so I feel your pain."

"Shut up. Love you."

We hugged, long and hard. I felt like a superheroine with her partner in justice.

Mel said, "Congratulations on the new job. I'm so, so happy for you. You're going to be fantastic, sug'."

I started to tear up, as it was finally hitting me. "Thank you. I can't believe how much has changed in such a short period of time."

"What are you gonna tell Yash?"

We stopped at her door and I leaned a hip on it. "I don't know. My schedule is going to be much more corporate."

"Dag, I've kept pretty quiet about this whole thing. I think your soul searching has been good for you — exploring new possibilities, not taking shit anymore. It's been inspiring, honestly." She looked me square in the eye. "But the way you're treating him is wrong. He will find out, and the only way you possibly have of salvaging things is for you to be the bearer of strange news."

I broke away from her gaze, because...well, because she

told the truth. There was a difference between empowerment and being an asshole.

"I know. I know. I'll... I've got to figure the best way to do this." I opened the door and escaped into the hall.

She smiled to lessen the stern talk. "No matter what—hos before bros. I'll always support you. I won't chop up the body, but I will help dig the grave."

"Let's rob a bank next. Murder is above our pay grade."

Mel's nosy neighbor, who'd stuck her head into the hall, gasped, retreated back into her apartment, and turned the bolt. Loudly.

I walked home, the cold air performing wonders for my drunken state. My head wobbled, but hadn't fallen clean off yet. That is...unless I anticipated the conversation I must have with Yash tomorrow. Then the whole damn melon smashed into the gutter.

Chapter Sixteen

F*ck-Ups Four-Hundred-Seven through Four-Thirty-Five
Full Wickham

The next evening, Yash answered his door in boxers and nothing else.

407. Yash answered his door in boxers and nothing else

Not *my* mistake, but I'd suffer all the same.

He pulled me into his arms and planted such a passionate whopper on me that it made my head dizzy. Not to mention my heart.

I wrenched myself away and proceeded into his apartment. The confusion from him hit me like a ton of lies. "I have to tell you something," I said.

Good. I'd gotten that much out.

He closed the door softly. "Uh-oh. That sentence ranks up there with 'we need to talk.' Should I put more clothes on?"

I didn't reply, and he pulled on a T-shirt that had been draped over the arm of his couch.

Heat washed over me, and I sank onto said couch because I couldn't remain upright. God, I might pass out. I just had to do it. Rip the Band-Aid off the bullet hole he didn't know he had.

"Damn, what is it?" He sat beside me and took my hand. "Do you not want to see me anymore?"

"No."

"Oh, shit. You're dumping me."

"No!"

"What?"

I put my head between my knees. "No, I don't want to

dump you."

He whooshed out a huge breath. "Good. So what is it? Are you a secret agent and not an air hostess?"

This was the best lead-up I'd ever get.

He took my hands and looked me in the eye with his soft, strong, melting, sexy, forever eyes.

408. "I'm going away for a month!"

The words shot from my mouth unbidden. Where had they come from? Had a demon invaded me?

409. Probably weeks ago…

"Oh." Yash leaned back onto his couch like a puppet let down from its strings. "Oh! That's okay. A month is nothing in the age of Skype, and there are these things called jet planes. You've perhaps ridden on one?"

I managed a weak smile. What had I done? Was I such a mistake now that I was incapable of telling the truth?

"Where are you going?" Yash asked. "Is it for work?"

410. "Yes."

411. "I'm taking over for another flight attendant."

412. "She's my friend and put me in for her Southeast Asia route."

413. Was that even a thing that flight attendants did?

414. I continued, "It'll be a fun, working vacation."

Yash grinned. "How exciting. I should have the funds for a visit. Can you get me a flight? Does it work that way?"

Uh…

415. "Sure."

"Ah, the perks of dating a jet setter." He wrapped his big hand around the back of my neck and leaned down to brush soft lips across my collarbone.

I bolted to my feet. He fell backward with an open mouth. "Sorry," I said. "I could spend the next week in bed with you, but I-I have to get on a plane in two hours. I'm sorry it's so fast."

His whole face fell even as he smiled. "It's all right. I'm a big boy." He rose and held me close for a long moment. Not kissing me, not groping me, just…cherishing me.

I squeezed him back, knowing this might be the last time. I needed just one more moment to remember his smell, his heat, his body pressed to mine. "I'll miss you so much," I said. I'd never been more honest in my life.

"Me too." He did kiss me then, gently and with overwhelming sweetness. "Be safe, and I'll be counting the minutes until I can visit you."

I tore myself away and left before I could fuck this thing up any more than I already had.

But no biggie, right? I'd just start my new job in publishing. The same field he worked in. In the same city. All while pretending to be in Thailand or Singapore.

* * * *

A week later, I walked into the offices of Hysterical looking like a million books. No more beige and navy for me. I wore skinny jeans, a screaming red blazer bedecked with silver zippers, and sky-high silver platform heels. Every head turned when I walked in the room.

Oooh, this was an *excellent* feeling.

I'd Skyped twice with Yash in this time. I'd bought three different kinds of curtains to talk to him in front of, the most hotel-looking ones I could find.

416. Even my ugly draperies were a lie

But none of the evils of my nature would diminish my triumph on this day. A sweet assistant named Maria showed me to my office, to be shared with another editor, Latisha. Everyone around me radiated sunshine, and it was obvious they were genuinely happy to be at work. None of them wore the furtive, rats-running-from-a-predator glances that Carmichael's staff had.

I met with Marlene to report on the research I'd done — comps on coffee table books about fashion, women, etc. We discussed many angles for the book, as well as several journalist photographers to approach. In just an hour, my soul felt alive again. I wanted to inspire women never to give up, no matter how many lemons they'd been forced to stomp into lemonade.

We batted around a few other book ideas, and the whole meeting made my head swim with possibilities, purpose. It even overshadowed how much I missed Yash.

I gathered my stuff and stood to leave when Marlene placed a hand on my arm. "Close the door," she said.

Dutifully, I shut the small conference room door and returned to my seat, thinking she wanted to talk HR or benefits with me. "What's up?"

"I saw your last post. I'm glad you didn't disclose your new employer or the start date so that it wouldn't be completely obvious where your new job was. You were the watercooler talk around here all last week. Lot of fans in this office."

"I'm glad you thought it was okay."

She nodded. "Did you really tell the guy that you'd be across the world for a month?"

I started to sweat under my fabulous pink bra. "Yes. That's a real mess, but hopefully I can—can concentrate on being here and building a new start for myself."

"I also saw that you have passed two hundred thousand Twitter followers. So, do you intend to keep reporting from the inside?"

"I— Honestly, I have no idea. But I can assure you— This job is my priority."

"Good! It should be. However... I have a proposal for you."

I sat up straighter.

"I want *Six-hundred-sixty-six* to be a book. Published by us, of course." She set her own laptop aside and leaned on the table. "If you don't want that, please know that it will in no way affect your job here. Even if you shopped it around and took it to a different publisher."

You'd need a squeegee to scrape my jaw off the floor.

Her eyebrows rose. I gaped. She started to laugh. I gaped. She slammed her hand on the table. I jumped!

"Uh… Oh, my God, Marlene. That's… That's amazing. Yes. Maybe? I have to talk to my partner. Oh, wow. Can we think about it?"

My Fairy Bookmother waved her hands. "Get an agent, which should be easy with your connections and an offer on the table. Take me for all you can get. Or whomever — you should look after yourself. This is a business."

"Yes, ma'am."

"For my part, I thought it could be a series of essays and stories about the pros and cons of living as a good girl in a bad world. About standing up for oneself and not being afraid to get dirty to get ahead." She slid her laptop back and started typing. "But that's just me. You ultimately have to decide what you want. Personally? I think you could be very, very big. I'm picturing you on *The View* right now…"

She gave me a polite 'go away' look, and I beat feet back to my office.

Latisha, a striking black woman around my age with long, blonde Nicki Minaj hair, laughed when I stumbled into our shared space. "You have the same face everyone gets after a meeting with the diva. You good?"

I giggled and sat down. "Yes, I'm okay. It went really well."

"We're excited to have you. I know Melanie…Mason, you two are tight?"

"Yes, since college."

"Yeah, it was awful the way Burns treated you." She smiled, wide and friendly. "Hopefully, you'll find us a friendlier bunch."

I sat at my desk. "Well, nobody's tried to grab my ass yet, so it's superior to my first day there."

I got a text — Hunter wishing me good luck today. Aw. Ha ha. After Yash dumped me, maybe I could…

417. Better not think about that too hard

To work! I read and typed and made notes…but I could hardly concentrate on the fashion book.

I had *my own book* to consider.

My own book. My own book! Advice for other women?

418. Ha ha ha ha ha ha haaaaaa!

Oh, boy. What to do? Mel would know. Suddenly, my excitement doubled. Both of us could get a massive boost from this! We'd share this grand adventure together.

Of course, Yash would be the smartest person to get advice from. I only knew the business from the other side of the desk—he was a bona fide author.

My phone buzzed.

Mel: HOLY SHIT READ DIRTYLINENS RIGHT THIS FUCKING MINUTE!

I clutched my chest. Maybe my book should be about twenty-something women giving themselves heart attacks.

A thousand scenarios flashed through my mind.

419. They were going to get me

420. Taylor's powerful family would have me murdered

421. My father would release a statement saying that my murder didn't matter

422. Because have you met my better daughter?

I told myself I wouldn't type the URL even as I typed the URL. Bam! Top story. *'Have You Been Roofied by Taylor Choate?'*

No telling what sound I'd just made, but Latisha bent sideways to peer at me around her monitor. "You okay?"

"Yes, thanks." I ducked back behind my own and started to read.

Holy. Balls.

The Order of the Scum-Defeating Amazonians was not the only source that DirtyLinens had found on the Taylor Choate scandal. Stories of his scummy behavior in the office. Accounts of attempted roofie-ing. But we of the Order were the crown jewel of their exposé...for we'd given them pictures.

They'd fuzzed the heads and nudity of the women, but there they were, in all their horrible glory. Some with Taylor giving himself the thumbs-up over the clearly passed out body of an unclothed woman. Some with his body parts on theirs—again, when they were clearly sleeping. Shit, one of them was drooling into his duvet.

The story had only been up sixteen minutes. One hundred and twelve comments…and counting.

I texted Mel back.

Me: Wow. It relieves me to know we're not the only source.

Mel: Me too. I know they won't be able to use our stuff in any legal way, but maybe it will prompt an investigation?

Me: Yes. I need to get back to work now, but I actually have even bigger news. Dinner tonight?

Mel: Of course. I have to take you out on your first day!

I put my phone aside and read more of the article comments. Several women were starting to come forward to talk about Taylor and adding their bad experiences. They read exactly like what had happened to me. The site encouraged them to email Abby to tell their stories, which meant at least one follow-up, no doubt.

Perhaps my ridiculous antics of the last weeks had actually produced a positive result. There would be no shoving this genie back into the bottle. Maybe his family had known what a scumbag he was and maybe they hadn't, but I had a feeling they enabled him often, so I just couldn't find it in my heart to experience guilt.

Not when he'd intended to roofie me…and much worse.

The rest of the day passed in a haze of paperwork and learning and meeting amazing new people. Latisha was super nice and patient with all my ignorant questions, and her taste in office music was fantastic, so we were well matched. She too edited nonfic.

Several of the gals wanted to take me for drinks, so I invited Mel along. We had a wonderful time, and I kept pinching myself that *this* was, in fact, the dream job I hadn't even realized I needed. A community strong in women, together in purpose. Funny how you think the thing you lost was the best you'd get and *bam!* a new window opens to a better world than you ever let yourself imagine.

In the wee hours, I found myself getting teary with happiness, gratitude. Mel gave me a long hug. I didn't have to explain my emotions to her.

By this time, she and I were at the end of the cocktail train, so I sat her at a tiny table and couch at the back of the bar. I bought us glasses of champagne, and Mel lifted one to make a toast.

I stilled her hand. "No, I am the one who will be toasting you." My glass aloft, I said, "To Mel, who has stood by me during my quarter-life crisis."

She laughed, and I swiped away a tear.

"Mel, thank you for encouraging me. Especially to start the blog and such. I have the most amazing news — Marlene has made us a book offer. She wants to publish the *Six-hundred-sixty-six blog* as a love letter to other women about the virtues of not being perfect."

Mel gasped, her champagne slopping. "What?"

"Yes. And it's our book, of course. Hell, it can be your book if you want. You are my best friend and cheerleader and conscience."

"Holy shit!" she screamed in her adorable Southern accent. Several people turned their heads, and we drank from our bubbling glasses of glee. She locked her arms around me, squeezing the breath from my lungs. "I love you, too, sug'. And no way am I doing this alone — fifty-fifty. Then we can be notorious millionairesses together. Deal?"

"Deal." I took another long pull of champagne. "Marlene told us to get an agent and to only take her deal if we wanted to."

"So…she's giving her blessing to shop it."

I nodded. "We can get an agent and consult with them. I certainly don't think that we'd be in poor hands with Marlene."

She danced around in her seat. "Oooooh, I already have

ideas about agents!"

"Me too!" I took one more sip of bubbly and set it down. "Listen, I would love to stay and celebrate, but I need to get back to Skype Y—" I nearly bit my tongue off, for I hadn't—

"Why are you Skyping Yash? Didn't you tell him?"

I suddenly had to find something in the deep, dark recesses of my purse.

Her eyes turned into cartoon saucers. "What *did* you tell him? Because it clearly wasn't the truth."

I whined. "Why do you say that? Maybe he'll think the whole thing is...creative and...funny."

Those saucers narrowed to slits.

"Thanks for the pep talk," I said. I picked up my glass, but—

423. Why is the champagne always gone?

Mel yanked her own glass away from my wandering eye. "Giselle... What. Did. You. Tell. Him?"

I tore my eyes away from her wonderful-looking drink with its inebriative properties. "I'm in Singapore right now."

Mel nodded slowly. "Uh-huh. And why are you there?"

"Because another girl needed me to switch routes."

Mel nodded slowly. "Uh-huh. And when will you return?"

"In a few weeks."

Mel nodded slowly. "Uh-huh. And what the hell is wrong with you?"

"I don't know."

Mel nodded slowly. "Uh-huh. Me neither. How are you convincing him you are in Singapore?"

"I have a whole new collection of curtains. Although one time Myrtle jumped into my lap during a Skype, and I freaked so hard I fell backward out of the chair. The camera was too high for him to see her, thank goodness."

She put her head in her hands. "I'm choosing to call this 'research' for the book, and not your psychotic break."

I nodded slowly. "Uh-huh."

She left me to my machinations then, and I rushed home to put on my uniform blouse and Skype with Yash.

424. *Sometimes I wore new lingerie I'd bought on my travels*

425. *To the Victoria's Secret down the street*

426. *I got on a chair to put up my 'Singapore' hotel curtains (I kept a chart)*

427. *I changed my clothes and made a sweep of the room for any New York items*

428. *A suitcase went behind me*

429. *And the cat went out of the door*

He'd like that last part, anyway.

Finally, I texted Yash that I was awake (noon in Singapore was happening now, eleven p.m. in New York City).

Oh! One more thing. I'd long ago bought a sunlight lamp to use during the winter to chase away the blues.

430. *I put it behind the curtain and pointed it upward, so that 'sunlight' peeked above the window treatment*

431. *Oh, but I was a dirty, dirty whore*

432. *I was no longer Full Austen*

433. *I was Full Wickham*

434. *I had seduced an innocent*

435. *And would soon ruin him*

The Skype ring sounded and I pressed the answer button. With my most charming, rakish smile, I said, "Yash! Aren't you a sight for sore eyes?"

Chapter Seventeen

F*ck-Ups Four-Thirty-Six through Four-Forty-Eight
Vanity Working on a Weak Head Produces Every Sort of
Mischief

The first week at my new job was one of the most exciting and unbelievable of my life. I learned the ropes at Hysterical while brainstorming and researching several books. On Wednesday, I had lunch with Khandye Kardashian, who loved the ideas I pitched for her second book. I left that meeting with a gut feeling that she would fly the coop and crap on Carmichael on the way by.

I also left with a new vibrator and a Mason jar full of avocado vinaigrette.

Mel and I spent our evenings narrowing down our long list of favorite literary agents and, after a couple of sessions, we finalized a list of four we would approach. It took a couple more evenings to work out our query letter, but by Friday, we were ready to pitch the hell out of this blog-slash-book.

It was a fine line to walk, because I definitely wasn't ready publicly to leak my identity as the writer of the blog yet, but hell yes, we wanted our names on that letter so that the agents, all four of whom we knew personally, would be inclined to open the email. We asked for discretion, confident it would be kept.

I drafted the pitch emails and set them to go out Friday morning during business hours. This new venture for Mel and I brought us closer together than ever before, but took away my time with Yash. I missed seeing him in person, and his texts grew increasingly passionate and loving. He was pining.

436. Pining

Truth be told, so was I. Only my surreal new schedule kept me sane.

But no matter how much I missed my false-pretenses boyfriend, I had a much, much, much better week than Taylor Choate.

Taylor had become the punching bag of the Internet— he was the scumbag meme du jour. The public outcry about him had forced the NYPD's hand, who'd pledged to investigate the stories about him.

And the stories were pouring in.

DirtyLinens had published not one, but two features on subsequent days telling anonymous stories from ten women each. They sounded the same, all of them. Met him, the night is a fog, woke up at his apartment in various states of undress. Most had assumed they'd gotten drunk and done something regretful, but others knew what had happened to them.

But with no proof, they'd gotten an STD panel and tried to forget.

These stories filled me with almost a blinding rage. Hot tears sprang into my eyes. To treat innocent women this way… Honestly, no matter what happened to me as a result of stealing those photos, I would never regret doing it.

That piece of shit needed to be shut down.

Two months ago, I probably would have turned my back, afraid to overstep. Worried about the repercussions of making noise.

437. But now I'd started screaming

438. And I didn't intend to stop

Not thirty minutes after our queries went out, we already had a meeting. It can take months to get a response from a busy literary agent, if you get any. We'd gotten lucky that she'd happened to be looking through her queries when ours had come in. She'd called Mel immediately to exclaim excitement over the book idea—she already followed the blog. We had a lunch scheduled for the next day, Saturday!

If we got an offer of representation from her, we could use that as leverage to hopefully move us up the query food chain to get a response from other agents more quickly.

I Skyped Yash that night, and I kept my locale as Singapore because I'd gotten tired of changing curtains. Myrtle was pitching a kitty fit outside the door, and I hoped he couldn't hear her shenanigans.

439. She put me on edge

440. The whole situation put me on edge

441. I sat on the side of a razor

442. I wanted to scream and shout at my amazing week, to share my accomplishments with the man I loved

443. But my biggest accomplishment was a fiction that had nothing to do with the blog

I cried PMS and got off Skype too quickly. Yash could tell something was wrong with me, his eyebrows coming together with deep concern.

"Are you sure you're well?" he asked. "I'm worried about you. It's okay to come home if you need it, right?"

It was all too much. Tears slid down my cheeks and he covered his mouth with his hand.

"No," he said. "Love, tell me what's wrong."

I shook my head. "I miss you. I'm just—it's hormones, nothing more. I'll be okay tomorrow." I stared at my feet rather than at him. His honest, concerned eyes were like the telltale heart.

444. They were driving me mad

I knew I needed to confess, to scream my confession to the heavens. But not like this. I had to take my lumps and plead for his forgiveness face to face.

445. For I was still deluding myself that he would understand and forgive me

446. It could happen

447. It could happen!

448. It could happen…

I signed off and blew him a kiss.

He smiled the sweetest smile I'd ever seen and said, "I love you, Giselle."

And that's how my heart broke.

* * * *

I met Mel at the café fifteen minutes before our prospective agent, Lillian Reynolds, was set to arrive. The day was snowy and brutally cold, but my nerves kept me warm. And my PMS, too. My lies to Yash had only been half-lies.

"Listen to what she has to say first," Mel advised. "We need to be open to ideas."

I nodded, forcing my brain into gear. "I know the drill. We're a commodity that someone wants—we're in the catbird seat."

"You okay?" She squeezed my arm and I put my hand over hers.

"Nope. Yes. I'm amazing! And in the depths of despair."

"Well, you're a writer now." She grinned. "That's normal."

Lillian, a rotund pink jellybean of delight, hurried into the café then. She was a fifty-ish white lady with a laugh that shut down the whole room. I'd helped Carmichael take on a book from one of her clients just before he'd canned me, and I'd loved every moment of working with her.

We both stood, and she rushed over to hug us both at once. "You two!" she said before sitting. "You troublemakers! I was pleased as punch to get your query, and a little shocked, honestly. Dagmar, you seem so straight edge." She threw her head back and cackled, and we couldn't help but do the same.

"I have to ask," she started to *ask*, "is everything in that blog real? Did you really get dumped the same day that Carmichael fired you?"

I nodded, a wry smile creeping onto my face.

"Well!" She waved our waiter over. "Those bastards. That's called dodging a man-sized bullet. Or two."

We ordered drinks and started browsing the menu while making general publishing chit-chat. Once the most important business was done — food choices — we got down to it.

Lillian began. "Obviously, getting an email that Marlene Hodgkins has already expressed interest in a book is a very good email to get." She laughed, and we joined her — you just couldn't help it. "I've been reading the blog since nearly the beginning, and I really love this point of view — that you can't make an omelet without breaking a few eggs. But women are afraid to do that. We have to excel. We have to be the best. And that's just white women — unfortunately, we have an easier time of it than women of color. Even in such a women-dominated industry like publishing, we're still second-class citizens. Look at the proportion of men who get reviews in the *Times* as opposed to women. I don't have to tell you."

We nodded. This was news to nobody paying attention.

"So I really like the idea of breaking out of this 'good girls get ahead' mode."

I said, "We should be able to be as complicated as men."

"Yes. Yes."

"We're already as complicated," Mel said. "We should be able to be humans and still get ahead. We should be able to tell the truth."

Our sandwiches came, and we tucked in with glee. My nervous flutters had fled. No matter what happened here, I felt secure in myself.

Lillian took a thoughtful bite of turkey club and munched. She gave a chubby-cheeked grin. "I stole a peek at your blog stats last night, your Twitter reach. I liked what I saw, as did my partners. We can build the concept into something that's not just an industry-inside point of view, but a general one for all women. 'It's okay to fuck up' is a universal message. And I'd be proud to represent the book. We have the potential for multiple books, merchandise, and I can see it as a movie or TV concept, easy-peasy."

Mel took my hand under the table. We held onto each other and didn't speak for a moment. I couldn't find my voice at all. My partner said, her hand still clasped in mine, "Thank you, that's very exciting. We have queried other agents. Not many — we chose our group very specifically. I mean, we know a lot of agents —"

"Of course, no problem. If you're interested in contracting with me, I think we should shop around even if you're inclined to go with Hysterical. It's better to know what's out there."

I said, "Well, maybe we can catch up in another week? In the meantime, we want to keep our identities secret."

"Sure. Take your time and think of any questions you have for me. I'll be crossing my fingers!" She gave a hearty laugh. "I want to corrupt the female youth of today."

Upon agreeing to this sensible desire, Mel and I paid the bill and left together.

As soon as we'd gotten in a cab, we whooped and hollered until the cabbie turned up his music to drown us out. Mel checked her phone and said, "Holy shit, we got another bite!"

"Really? Who?"

"James Pullings!"

"Oooooooh." He was by far the highest profile of the folks we'd queried. Not that being famous — relatively speaking since we were talking about book nerds — was a necessity, but damn, he'd be a coup if he was the right fit for us. "What does he say?"

"He loves the concept and said that he'd actually been about to approach us."

"No."

"Yes. I'm going to tell him we have an offer of representation, and that we'd like to meet soon. Right?"

"No."

"No?"

I threw my arm around her shoulder. "Just kidding. Yes!"

Mel sent the email and bit her lip. "Should we... We

should email the others and say we have an offer?"

"What do we have to lose? One more email, polite, and then if we don't hear, leave it be." The cab pulled up to my place and I paid for the fare so far. "Two out of four is damn fine work, *sug'*."

"Damn right, *hon*."

I squeezed her again and alit. Once in my apartment, I flopped across the couch and flipped on the TV. I needed a quiet evening of ibuprofen, heating pad, excessive amounts of saturated fats, and my cat.

Myrtle jumped up next to me and immediately turned her kitten butt hole to my face. I gently corrected her position to be the little spoon in front of me, and we settled in to watch *The Golden Girls*.

Maybe we could have sections in the book about inspirational fictional characters — Blanche Deveraux would teach us all a thing or two about going after a hot man whenever you wanted. Or hot tail in general — we couldn't leave out our lesbian sisters. Dorothy would teach us to take no crap. Rose, to be open and loving.

And Sophia — that bullshit stories and lasagna fix everything.

I made a note of this brilliant (?) idea on my phone and settled into stroking Myrtle again.

Contentment fell across me like a snuggly blanket. I'd gotten a new job, was on the way to a book deal and had met a beautiful man who cared for me. Sure, I needed to sort things out with him and my real name, but my heart told me everything would be fine. Right?

Yes, my possibilities were endless! Everything was coming up Dagmar, and all thanks to fucking up!

* * * *

I breezed into the office on Monday morning to start the second week at my fabulous new job. The receptionist and one of our marketing staff stopped talking and gaped at me the moment I walked in. "Good morning," I said. They froze in place and gave me the kind of look that usually follows a very loud, wet fart.

Had I forgotten to put on a blouse today?

"Dagmar," said Jenny, the receptionist, "I am so in love with your blog! I had no idea that was you."

All the air sucked out of the room. "Wh-what?"

"The fuck-up blog! I can't believe how badass you are."

My cell phone rang. Mel. My heart began to pick up into overdrive. I hurried toward my office and answered, "Hello?"

"Dag. Holy shit, Dag. We're on DirtyLinens this morning. They exposed us as the two behind 666. They have photos up and everything!"

"What? No. No!" A staffer turned to stare at me, but I slammed my office door. "How?"

"It must have come from one of these agents' offices."

I collapsed into my chair. "Mel, I have to call Yash. Are our pictures up?"

"Yes."

"Noooooooooooooo!" I screamed it and stomped on the floor over and over again, despair pouring from my very pores.

"Uh...you need a minute?"

I turned my head. Latisha had been sitting there the entire time.

"I'm so sorry," I said. "I just—"

"Yeah, I'm guessing you've seen DirtyLinens?"

I took a deep breath. Two. "We— We did not send that tip. We weren't ready for this."

"Sorry."

"It's okay. I'm sorry for hollering." I threw my purse on my desk with shaking hands. "I have to make a call."

She nodded. "Is that guy you're dating going to see it?"

Shit. Everyone knew about my dirty linens now. "Probably. I need him to hear it from me." My voice came out as a squeak.

She came around my desk and engulfed me into a hug. "Good luck."

I squeezed her back. "I don't really deserve good luck in this circumstance, but you're very sweet."

My phone rang again and my heart fell clean out of my body and squished to the floor.

It was Yash.

A perfunctory knock sounded and Marlene opened the door. "A word, Giselle?" She winked.

"I'm sorry. I know you're my boss, but my boy is calling, and—"

Latisha hurried Marlene out of the door. "We'll give you a minute." She shot our boss an 'oh, shit' look, and they left.

I hit answer. "Hello?" I whispered.

"Hello. *Dagmar.* And goodbye."

He hung up.

Chapter Eighteen

**F*ck-Ups Four-Forty-Nine through Four-Eighty-Four
And Now the Lifetime Original Movie — Pooping Lies:
The Dagmar Kostopoulos Story**

I ran. Like I was in a chick flick starring Kate Hudson
and her four-hundred-dollar blowout. In my red heels, my
black princess wool coat flying behind. I ran from the office.
I ran to the street. I jumped then — into a cab. When the cab
stopped, I ran to Yash's door.

My brain barely functioned. I'd been deluding myself so
very much that when the inevitable happened —

449. It had always been inevitable!

— I simply refused to believe. Mel was blowing up my
phone trying to get me to pick up, but I could do nothing
but try to get him back. To explain. To beg.

I pressed the buzzer for his door. He had to be home. He
always wrote in the morning, in the ugly shirt, because his
brain was freshest then.

Buzz buzz buzz.

My heart *thump thump thumped*. I couldn't breathe.

Buzz buzz buzz.

The tears started then. No answer. Nothing from him.

I dialed his code again and pressed the talk button. "Yash,
please. I'm so sorry. It was just a silly game I was playing
the night we met. An escape from reality." I really started
to sob now. Great, heaving sobs. My knees buckled, but I
leaned against the cold stone wall to reach the button. "I
thought you were a one-time thing. That it wouldn't matter.
But I love you. I did. I have. And by then it was too late! Oh,

God, please just talk to me."

450. Nothing

451. No sound

452. No love

A woman exited the building and shot me a dirty look. I tried to catch the door as it closed, but she yelled at me and threatened to call the police. The door caught my fingers and *slam!*

I screamed and collapsed onto the tile stoop. I held on to my hand and sobbed, the pain ripping what breath was left from my lungs. The tips of three of my fingers had already purpled, one splitting open in a steady stream of blood.

The door opened, nearly hitting me. But it wasn't him. Another man, frowning at me on the way by. "You're getting blood on the tile," he said compassionately.

"Fuck you," I replied with equal respect.

With my bloody fingers, I pulled out my phone. I crawled to the corner of the entrance and crumpled there, tears streaming, entire body numb. I dialed Yash. It went straight to voicemail. I went to text him, but the text went through another color.

453. He'd blocked me

My heart hurt so much, I couldn't breathe. I began gasping, swirling, dying.

Voices started talking. To me? I looked up and two women reached down to me.

"We have to help her," said one.

"Whose buzzer was it?"

The first lady, red hair and blurry face, took my elbow and helped me to my feet. I clung to her, still gasping, gasping. "Do you have somewhere to go?" she asked.

I just stared at her, past her, snot all over my lip.

"Majumdar. Yash Majumdar!" said the other, a super tall blonde. "Oh, my God, he's sexy sex writer guy! Dagmar, you have good taste."

I looked from one to the other. They clearly recognized me from DirtyLinens.com. No. No! I yanked my arm away from the redhead and stumbled toward a cab. Soon I was stop-and-go-ing back toward work. Those women knew me. And now they knew him. No. Please. Please let them not—

My phone rang. I fumbled in my coat pocket again—holy fucking shit did my hand hurt!—to see, to pray it was Yash.

Mel.

I smeared blood across the phone when I hit answer. "It's over, Mel. He won't talk to me. He blocked me. He won't even listen."

She sighed. "Where are you? Marlene called me."

"I-I'm in a cab. I'm going back to work, I guess. Oh, God." I started sobbing again, and the cabbie handed back a grimy tissue pack to me. "Th-th-thank you."

Mel's voice got tougher. "Okay, Missy. So it's a shit day. But... But never say never, 'kay, sug'? Go back to the office and read the article. Our blog is loved. You are a heroine for the book set! And I've gotten five more agent offers of representation in an hour. You probably have too, if you check your email. It's going to be okay, Dag."

"Bu-bu-but—"

"But me no buts!" I could practically hear her stand. She was in general mode now. "You will survive this. You will be strong, like Scarlett O'Hara, but way less racist. The Kostopouloses will rise agayn!" She always got super Southern in these moments.

I was almost back at the office. "Okay." I sniffled and blew my nose into one of the nice cabbie's tissues. "Okay, I can do this. I have to own my fuck-ups, right? That's kinda the point?"

"That's exactly the point! You are a strong woman, and you can do it."

"Do what?"

"Iiiiiiiiiit!"

We pulled up to the high rise. I ended Mel's call, gave the cabbie a ridiculous tip and got out. It would be okay. I loved Yash, but I'd survive this. He'd probably come around—he was just in shock right now. Life was all about choices, right? I could choose to get through this day with dignity. And grace. And poise.

I stepped onto the sidewalk. I straightened my shoulders. And something splatted across my head.

Liquid white dripped down my nose, onto my coat. I wiped my cheek—*poop*.

454. Bird fucking poop

455. A fucking bird

456. Had fucking shit

457. On my fucking head

458. In the fucking middle

459. Of fucking winter!

I screamed. I screamed and screamed and screamed. I got hoarse, but I kept screaming. Rage. Pain. Anger. Heartbreak. Bird shit. I screamed it all, my fists as balled as I could get them with my probably broken fingers. My eyes squeezed shut, mostly to keep the crap from dripping into them.

I used my snot-encrusted tissue to wipe as much shit from my face as possible. This entire day was becoming a joke. "What next?" I screamed to the heavens. A nanny hurried her two charges away from me. I turned to shoot her a dirty look.

Good thing, for I was facing the street when a limo passed and threw a foot-wide puddle of slush all over me.

Freezing. Dripping. Mud. Filth. I just stood there, shivering so hard I bit my cheek. I picked a sodden cigarette butt off my drenched coat. Hey, at least the slush cleaned some of the shit off my head.

I turned and sailed into the building. I splish-splashed my way across the lobby. A security guard stood from behind the desk and opened her mouth to say something. I flicked my gaze to hers. "No worries," she said and sat back down.

460. No worries

A woman stared at me while we rode the elevator up. I smiled at her. It must have come out terrifying, because she backed away as far as possible. "Would you like a hug?" I asked her.

She hit the button for the next closest floor and ran.

I opened the door to the office. Three people gaped this time.

461. I was getting more popular

I waved. I walked. I went into my office. Latisha stood. "Oh, my God," she said.

"Please don't mention that being to me at the moment."

Marlene must have been watching for me. She followed me in. "Wow."

I spit street dirt into my trash can. "Yup."

"You went to his apartment?"

"Yeah, I—" I looked up at her. "How did you know that?" Her eyes filled with pity.

462. Which is such a good look on your new boss

"Come here," she said. "I always keep spare clothes in the office. And you must see something."

The shivers began to rack my body then. I shrugged and followed her. What now? Had Abby given me up? Was Carmichael suing me? Maybe an asteroid was plummeting to earth.

463. I prayed that last one was true

464. Might as well take all these bastards with me

Marlene handed me a pile of expensive, professional wear and shut me in her office to change. She was a little smaller than I, but a wrap dress is forgiving, and it even matched my filthy, wet shoes. Small favors. I went to the bathroom to wash my face and dunk my head to get the poop and whatnot out.

465. Better not think about what's in whatnot

I dried my hair with paper towels until it no longer dripped and returned to Marlene's office, where she awaited me. My body felt…numb. My eyes hurt almost as badly as my hand, which Marlene took one look at and gasped. She pressed her intercom and asked her assistant to get me ice.

Marlene said, "You need to get those examined immediately."

I nodded. I couldn't bend my fingers.

466. Good thing it was my right hand, the one I use for everything

She sat me down at her desk and went to DirtyLinens. I wanted to tell her that I obviously knew about the post, but she was my boss, so I tried to contain myself. And it totally worked.

467. Until she clicked on the second post

468. The video post

469. Taken forty-five minutes ago

470. The one of me begging into Yash's intercom

471. Collapsing onto the ground

472. Sobbing

473. Crushing my hand in the door

I died. I sat there in my boss's chair and died.

Because everything was the worst.

I would now inhabit the world as a ghost. I didn't know what the fuck Casper was so friendly about, because I wanted to murder those two horrible women and hurl bird shit on their ghosts with my ghost hands until we both got dragged into hell by my lord and master, Satan.

Marlene held out her hands to me, as if I were a feral dog. "It's okay. You're very popular on there. The public sees this as romantic! And Yash is so handsome and talented, they all want him to give you a second chance. Well, most of them do. Breathe, Dagmar."

I breathed with my ghost lungs. "Marlene, if you want to fire me, I get it. You didn't sign up for this ridiculous drama. I can't believe — I can't believe someone recognized me at his place and…and…"

I'd run out of tears. This day had lasted a hundred years already.

"No way." She crouched down. "You're just as wonderful as you were yesterday. And I admire you going there to fight for him. Even if it doesn't work, it was worth it to try. Do you love him?"

Oh, look. I did have another tear left. It made a break

down my cheek, and I nodded.

"Love finds a way. Take the rest of the day. Eat a hundred donuts, get the vodka from the freezer and hide from prying eyes. I have a feeling you have a lot of emails coming—hell, agents are taking to Twitter asking to rep your movie rights."

I shook my head. "No. This is my second week on the job, and—"

"I'll charge you a sick day. Go."

Suddenly, I stood and hugged her to me with all my might. She squeezed me back. "Love finds a way, Dagmar. It's going to be okay. Or it won't, and you'll find another man. They're literally everywhere."

"Thanks."

I knew then that I didn't want to shop the book around. I wanted this lovely lady who clothed me in DVF and didn't can me for being ridiculous and stinking of street plague.

My brain barely registered the ride home. The worst part of it all was that Yash wouldn't let me apologize. Then again, why should he? He didn't owe me shit.

474. He didn't even owe me bird shit

I did reach for a bottle the moment I got home.

475. It came with me into the shower

I also ordered a sandwich and a cake from the bakery down the block. An entire cake.

476. It's good to have goals, even in times of great despair

In my ugliest sweatpants, with my bottle of something brown, I opened my laptop. And I wrote, picking letter keys with my one good hand. I didn't blog so much as pour my heart out to him.

No names. Not that it mattered now.

477. Oh, God, poor Yash. To be dealing with my betrayal, and now in the public eye

478. I couldn't even be mad at the bird anymore

479. It had correctly mistaken me for a toilet

I wrote about how I loved him. About how it had all happened so damn fast. How in denial I'd been about my entire life. And, finally, how wrong I'd been to let it go on as long as it had.

And yet...

In a way, I was still happy I'd gone a little crazy there for a while. The pendulum always swings high when it's been tied up. And I'd been double knotted all my life.

At the end of my emotional rant, as an ode to my fucking up, I typed out a hearty *Fuck You* to the asshole who'd filmed my heart breaking and distributed it for all to see. I described them—why should they stay anonymous? I didn't really do it for me even, but for Yash, who in no way deserved this publicity.

I hit Publish.

Finally, I took a deep breath. Another. My cake came. Oh, and also my real food, which I did eat first, thank you very much. First, a bite of sandwich. Then, a bite of cake. Last, ice for my finger. Sandwich. Cake. Ice. Cake. Sandwich. Cake cake cake cake.

Thus infused with comfort food—and a belt of Scotch—I took a look at the blog. Holy shit—the blog's followers had quadrupled. My downfall was an entertainment event for the masses.

But...

But they did support me, just as Marlene had said. Some were telling stories of how they'd played by the rules and gotten screwed. Others, about how they'd messed up their love lives, but it had worked out in the end. Quite a few ladies said I was brave to run and do anything to try to get him back. Some guys said that they'd definitely listen to anyone willing to beg in public when it was so obvious I loved him.

Of course, the inevitable comments about my giant nose and fat butt emerged, but they were jumped on by my loyal gang of fuck-ups, bless them.

Tears dripped into my cake, and yet Yash did not contact me, no matter how many times I refreshed my email.

My fingers had become numb. Not good. I hurried to

the walk-in clinic at the end of the block. Yup — they were fractured. They splinted my middle finger — useful for flipping off purposes — and taped the other two together. This day just got better and better.

As I sat there getting treated, I had nothing to do but hurt and think. I'd formed a thousand arguments in my head for when I came clean. I'd never once considered that the news would come from elsewhere, that he'd just go dark, and I'd never get to tell my side of the story. How much of the blog had he read? Did he see the posts where I said I'd been terrified of losing him? That I was being myself in the relationship, except for the job and the name?

480. This never would have happened if I'd just told him

Mel texted me. *We made Buzzfeed. And CNN.*

481. Uuhfjhdfkajdhjalkfhjsahf

Mel: I have fourteen different agent offers, and that's not counting Lillian.
Mel: We have two of the big five presses coming to us, too. Check your email.

Ugh, my email. Two hundred unread messages sat there. Many friends exclaiming different forms of happiness at my success and sadness for my failures. A few men I didn't know calling me a whore — there were about a thousand of those on my Twitter stream right about now. Also used in a fun way — cunt, bitch, slut, trollop — at least that word was semi-literary — and gold digger (WTF?), along with quite a few colorful offers to murder me. And yes — non-murdery offers. Holy shit, a movie studio. Nope — two.

Me: We need an agent, stat. Anyone good in there besides the four we'd picked?
Mel: I'll come over at lunch to chat about it. You okay? That video was not fucking cool.
Me: I'm exactly how I deserve to be.

Once I got home, I scooped a bite of cake with my good hand and smashed it to my mouth. This was my life now.

482. *Cake without a fork*

483. *Shower Scotch*

484. *Endless regret*

Myrtle jumped into my lap and started licking frosting from my face. I let her do it for a moment until I wondered how healthy buttercream was for cats. Besides, I was totally having a worse day and needed all the fat and butter I could get.

Mel: I'm forwarding an email to you that might cheer you the slightest bit up.

My email refreshed, and, for the first time today, the sun peeked through the clouds. The count of the Big Five publishers was officially up to three.

For Carmichael Burns had just made us an offer on our book.

Chapter Nineteen

F*ck-Ups Four-Eighty-Five through Five-Hundred-Three
Sick Burns

Mel pulled me together enough for us to strategize that night. I told her that I wanted Marlene to have the book and she agreed, provided the dollar signs were lining up. That would be tough, as a small press didn't have quite the funds of a Big Five, but maybe we could work out a higher percentage of sales to compensate for a smaller advance. Momma(s) needed retirement plans.

485. Especially me, as I was probably toxic to the general male populace now and would die alone with Myrtle

486. That reminded me: Time to adopt, like, eight more cats

We arranged three more agent interviews to happen over the phone the following evening. After all was said and done, we'd liked Lillian's sunny attitude and track record the best—there were reasons we'd picked her in the first place—so we signed a contract for the book and all subsequent titles in that series. Agent in hand, we arranged to meet Carmichael at his office on Thursday of that week. He'd asked to take us out to dinner, but I'd said no freaking way.

That entire office would see me strut in there and put him through his paces.

I doubled-down at my own job to make up for the mess earlier in the week. My phone rang off the hook from journalists, well-wishers, and nay-sayers—one of whom mailed a box of severed doll heads to me. Marlene asked reception to start screening my calls and getting rid of anyone who wasn't Hysterical business. I bought Jenny in reception a box of cupcakes as a thank you, and she grew quite fond of getting rid of callers in nice and sometimes extremely nasty ways.

As for me, I was numb. Whenever the black cloud named Yash stormed across my heart, I jumped to edit a manuscript, strategize with an author, or even do the dishes.

My apartment had never been so clean, and Myrtle had taken to running away from me, I tried to brush her so many times.

487. Her food bowl was a mountain of Overcompensation Vittles

Only at night did I let it all out, crying myself to sleep in such a hysterical fashion, I would have slashed it from a manuscript as 'over-dramatic.'

488. My purple prose brings no boys to the yard

Thursday morning, I iced my eyes to de-puff them and took extreme care with my hair and makeup. My hair flowed long and wavy — thank you, hot curlers — just the way Carmichael liked all of *his* women to look. I put on a flirty blue dress with a skirt just on the correct side of too short for business, black tights, and heels. I topped it with a cream princess coat — I looked sexy and every inch the successful cool girl I now was.

Marlene had given her okay to meet Carmichael during work hours, provided, of course, that I recounted it for laughs in the book. She knew hell would freeze into slushies before I rewarded Carmichael with any book I had a hand in.

Mel and I met up in the coffee shop at the bottom of Carmichael's building, and Lillian joined us there.

Lillian flashed the cutest smug smile I'd ever seen. "So, this meeting is a waste of time, right? We're just doing this for the 'fuck you' factor?"

I sat on one side of Lillian, Mel, the other. We enclosed her in a hug, an Oreo of love.

She threw her head back and laughed. "I'll take my cues

from you two. This is going to be the cat's pajamas."

As one, we marched onto Carmichael's floor and informed reception of our exalted presences. I didn't have to tell Matt, at the desk, who we were there to see. He jumped up and swept me into so fierce a hug it took me off the ground. "You look fantastic!" he said. He swiveled around to see if the coast was clear and whispered in my ear, "Give that bastard hell."

I started giggling, and it was exactly what I needed to chase away the nervousness. My stomach had been fluttering like a bird just because I'd set foot in the building. Here, the site of my wimpy past.

Screw that.

And fuck Carmichael.

Ack! Don't fuck Carmichael! The thought was too, too gross.

Matt procured us coffee and ushered us toward Carmichael's office. The entire staff, my former coworkers, stood as we walked by, all of them grinning from ear to ear. They flashed me thumbs-up and whispered praise for the blog. Several said they missed me — I definitely owed a few lunches.

Funny — my most pathetic fuck-up had been filmed for posterity, and it had made me seem like some kind of romance heroine. I was the Meryl Streep of the book-nerd set.

489. Except to Yash, of course

Nope. I pushed his beautiful face from my mind, for we had arrived.

Carmichael opened his door. Jazmine scurried out of the office, the smirk on her face wiped clean when she took a good gander at me.

490. I know it's petty

491. And un-feminist

492. But I was hotter than her now

493. With a better job

494. And I fucking knew it

I ignored her. As did my compatriots.

Carmichael wiped his hands on his pants and shifted a nervous glance from one to the other of us before finally landing on me. A. Nervous. Glance.

Oh, yeah. This man would beg me for my favor.

495. This was gonna be fuuuuuuun

I smiled with my mouth, leaving my eyes out of it, and waited for him to speak. The first one to speak is always the weakest. And no matter what I'd been through, I would never be the weakest ever again.

I faced him down. Well, up. He's a lot taller than I am.

I faced him up. Our eyes met. His slipped down to my tits. I sneered and shook my head, but stayed silent. Ha! Not even his leching would distract me from my up-facing!

Finally, he turned and gestured into his office. "Come in, Dag, Melanie. Hello, Lillian, always a pleasure."

"It's all yours, Carmichael," she replied.

Mel met my eye, as if to say, "We have chosen wisely."

Carmichael laughed, as if what she said had been a joke. Lillian laughed too, but a wicked gleam twinkled in her Mrs. Claus demeanor.

He sat behind the Hemingway desk and said, "Well, who knew little Dagmar had it in her!"

Little Dagmar said, "Who knew that little Carmichael would call me to beg for it?"

A choking noise sounded from my right, followed by a quiet, "Damn, *sug'*," from Mel.

His full-of-shit bluster deflated for a moment, two even, before he puffed it back up again from his reserves. "You'd still have your job with me if you'd displayed this kind of ballsy attitude."

I pulled a face. "Thank goodness it came after."

Lillian sat up straighter. "So, Carmichael. Tell us why we're here."

He sat back in his chair, his feet flying up to perch on the desk. His favorite 'man *grunt* in control' pose. He had about as much in common with Hemingway and real man grunts as Moaning Myrtle did. Finally, he gifted us with his wisdom. "I think the blog is a great example of how when girls decide to behave like men, they get ahead."

Mel stood with a, "Nope."

I had to hide my grin. I put my wounded hand on her shoulder to tap her back down again. I flicked my eyes to my other hand, in which sat my phone. The audio recorder was going. I wanted to be able to recount this stupid meeting in all its glory in the book. I would never name Carmichael.

496. But everyone would know

This appeased her, so she gritted her teeth. Carmichael had watched this while smiling. Oh, how cute we were, right?

He continued taking a crap into the air. "The focus of the book needs to be about how women can start taking control of their lives, finally, and think like a man. Like how Dagmar tried to sleep with that guy from the coffee shop to get ahead."

I cleared my throat. "Wouldn't that be acting like Jazmine? Is she a man, Carmichael?" I leaned in closer. "Is there something you want to tell us?"

"Ha ha." He did not laugh. "The idea clearly came from me, and I promise, Dag, I'm all man."

Mel bristled, and I shot her a sideways glance to keep her still.

Wait a minute... Perhaps my take-down of Carmichael Burns should consist of killing with kindness. Everyone in the office understood the way to Carmichael's heart — telling him exactly what he wanted to hear.

I smiled my sweetest smile and said, in my most adorable tone, "Yeah, I think I see what you're getting at. So, you took control of the situation like a man and told her that she'd get a promotion if she slept with you? That's why you're the boss."

He pointed at me. "Finally, you're fucking figuring out life. I knew you had potential. It took me canning you to really bring out the best in you, but then again, I knew that."

"Canning me because I was too naive to sleep with you?"

"I can see you're learning. I think it's fantastic the way you took that guy...Mahatma, for a ride. Although that blubbering thing was... Well, I guess you can't take all the girl out of the girl. And who would want to?" He bestowed us with a wink. "Men are men, women are women. You can borrow some of our traits, but you still need to act like a lady." His massive head nodded. "The book can talk about applying things learned from men for business, but keeping it womanly at home. No guy wants to *sleep* with a bitchy boss. There's a place for everything."

By this point, Lillian's mouth hung wide open.

Carmichael scratched at his belly. "I don't really like the whole 'mistake' concept, though. Women need to keep their shit together. If you're anything less than ideal at work or at home, you'll fall further behind than you already are. It's a self-improvement book, after all. You're trying to *improve women*."

I nodded. "You're right. But what about men's mistakes?"

He laughed. "Dagmar, you're cute. Women are so much more forgiving than men. You're better than us!" There went that wink again, with a side of casual sexism.

Lillian swallowed—no doubt around the bad taste in her mouth. "Uh, well, we'll take what you've said here and... and think about it. I'll email you the auction details."

"You're the hot bitches in town right now," he said, addressing me and Mel, "but don't get caught up in it. You need a star to really make a breakout book. You need me. I can bring you the male readership you desperately need. I'm seeing you, Dag, on the cover. Bikini and neck tie. *Six-Hundred-Sixty-Six Ways to Succeed Like a Man (While Being the Ultimate Woman)*. Like it?"

Mel choked on her own spit.

I stood. "Oh, I love it, Carmichael. I'll start a diet today."

He stood. "Good! For every ten pounds, you'll go up a slot on the *NYT*. Remember, my experience is worth at least quadruple the bid I make."

We made our way outside and stood on the sidewalk,

gob-freaking-smacked.

"So" — I turned to Lillian — "we'll wait until he's made an offer to tell the CEO and board that he admitted to trading a position for sex with an underling, right? And also that he fired me for not doing so? We can send them the recording." I held up my phone. "After all, women are supposed to be helpful!"

Lillian rubbed her hands together. "Why, yes! I think it's only right to let them know why they won't be getting this holiday's nonfic bestselling title."

"Provided Dag drops two hundred pounds," Mel joked.

"I'll stop eating immediately and for all of time," I promised.

As one, we threw our heads back and cackled. Dagmar, Melanie, Lillian — The Witch Bitch Coven of Publishing.

Lillian wrapped her arms around our waists, me on one side, Mel on the other. "Ladies, I feel honored that you chose me to run around town and cause trouble with."

I squeezed her back. "You are a welcome addition to the coven."

Mel said, "Lillian, you don't know the half of it."

Her eyebrows rose. "I bet. Dag, I cannot believe you goaded him into saying all that."

I turned to face them both. "His ego is the size of Jupiter. You can't imagine the stuff he says to his inner circle. Enough drugs and sexual harassment to choke a coke-head horse."

We parted ways then with a promise to have a call at the end of the day to begin parsing interested parties and go to auction. That way we would see all the bids, with the final choice being ours.

I worked, worked, worked, didn't eat —

497. Because of emotions, not bikini cover

498. Which would never happen

Worked, and worked some more. Anything not to stew about *you know who*. Not to send my itchy fingers to my phone to text him. To email him. The struggle lasted through every minute — *tick* email him, *tock* think of another way to say sorry, *tick* I loved him, *tock* maybe today he'd unblocked me?

Finally, I asked Latisha to take my phone away. I couldn't be trusted.

499. Obviously

Sometimes I would sit there and edit, tears streaming down my face.

500. My poor Latisha

501. What a shitty surprise I turned out to be

502. She'd probably request a transfer to a toilet stall

503. It couldn't possibly stink worse than I

Chapter Twenty

F*ck-Ups Five-Hundred-Four through Five-Thirty-Three
February without Yash

The money from Marlene wasn't as great as some other offers, but she did cut us excellent merchandise and film takes, plus book percentages that made up for the smaller advance.

And just like that, Mel and I were semi-wealthy young women. Everyone in town wanted to know us. Book parties, lunches, everyone wanted to see us and be seen with us.

My heartbreak blogs seemed to be the most popular. Although the one about the bird shitting on my head was the best traffic we'd ever had. I got asked on dates every day of the week, but I turned them all down. Mel, however, was drowning in more dick than a male prison.

Her words.

In my heart of hearts, I hoped Yash read the blog. He had to, right? He had to.

504. If the situation were reversed, I'd be hate-reading the shit out of me!

One time, I made a post so that the first letters on the left side of the page spelled out a message. "Please forgive me, Yash."

505. It was so clever

506. That commenters on the blog figured it out immediately

507. Then they debated about whether or not it was pathetic

508. Newsflash. It was.

On the other hand, Mel loved it when I pathetic'd up the place. Our hits skyrocketed. On those days, she'd post a teaser for the book.

It seemed to make people feel better, though, when I screwed up. Because let's face it, we're all piles of ego-driven lumpy animal cells just shitting and fucking and pissing our way through our pathetic lives until we die in some stupid, meaningless way and sink into a dark abyss from which there is no return.

509. I might be depressed

We sold the TV rights to my ongoing shit show to a premier paid cable network—the Holy Grail of deals. A movie comes and goes, but six seasons of syndicated goodness would perform as a girl's 401K for a lifetime.

One side-effect of the publicity:

510. My father had been horrified by all the shitass language

But my sister was the Official Designated Family Expresser of Dissatisfaction. One Saturday, as I sat in the long-cold bathtub at home while licking the inside of a Häagen-Dazs container, she called.

511. I answered on speaker

Me: Sigh.
Vanessa: "Pardon if it's noisy. I have kids!"
Me: "What, you have what? Since when?"
Vanessa: "Is that you being funny?"

I examined my ice cream container, but it was empty.

512. Like my bed

Ugh, I didn't feel like playing this tennis match with her today. She lobbed the balls straight at my head, and had trained her hell spawn to do the same. Not that I didn't love my niece and nephew.

513. But they were little assholes
514. Then again, so was I

Vanessa: "Dagmar! Are you still there? No. No, don't do that. Renesmee, don't do that! Renesmee, put it down. Put it down. Renesmee, put it down. Put it down. Renesmee. Renesmee. Renesmee. Put it down. Put it down. P—"

241

I hung up. 'Renesmee, put it down' could go on for ten minutes. I'd clocked it once. Why Vanessa didn't just go grab the thing to be put down, I'd never know. I asked once and was told I couldn't understand unless I was a mom.

Another thing I didn't understand?

515. Naming her daughter after a Twilight book character who ate her way out of her mother

She'd chosen it while midway through peeing on the stick. Seemed like bad karma to me and, indeed, the epidural hadn't worked. And, no shit, Renesmee had been born with two teeth.

516. The horrifying name 'Renesmee,' of Twilight fame, wasn't strictly my fuck-up

517. But a fuck-up by and for humanity

518. So on the list it went

519. Ooooh! Maybe I'd blog about it

520. Although imagine the angry rants

The phone rang again, right as I was wiping bathwater off my butt. I put it on speaker and waited.

Vanessa: "Why did you hang up?"

Me: "You weren't talking to me."

Vanessa: "You'll understand when you have kids, Dagmar."

Me: "*If.*"

Vanessa: "When."

She continued —

521. "What kind of woman doesn't want kids?"

522. "Is that why that guy dumped you?"

523. "The foreigner?"

524. "Because you wouldn't give him kids?"

I ground my teeth as I threw on my brand new aqua chenille robe. It was the best thing in my life right now, and I needed it for protection.

She just. Kept. Talking.

Vanessa: "Dad would flip if he knew he was Middle Eastern, anyway."

525. I didn't bother to correct her
526. He'd dumped me, so it's not as if I'd ever bring him to Thanksgiving dinner

Vanessa: "Wait, what did I call about?"

Me: "There was a reason for all these compliments?"

Vanessa: "Ah, yes. That's it—it's the attitude, Dagmar. That blog thing is horrifying. Are you on drugs? Because it reads like you're high on goof-offs. Dad practically cried when he read some of that. And now our family's life is going to be some sort of slutty television show? Horrifying. If Renesmee ever embarrassed the family that way, I'd—"

I hung up on her.

What the hell was a 'goof off'? That word had totally come from Dad. Sounded like slang from 1962.

527. Where would I even get these 'goof-offs'?
528. No, really, it was totally the time in my depression-slash-success to start a lovely drug habit

Of course I wouldn't include any of my family in the book or TV show. Not even to mock Renesmee's name. It wasn't her fault. It was Vanessa's. And, to an equal extent, Stephenie Meyer's.

Slowly, I slumped into the kitchen for a new pint of ice cream.

529. I was on a butterfat cleanse

Ugh, I wasn't such a monster that I didn't understand why they were upset at some of the stuff on the blog. But really, to not feel pride in me at all? They hadn't congratulated me. Neither of them. Not once.

The fact that I wasn't following the Kostopoulos woman life script was the biggest sin I'd ever commit. The worst part? Say I did get married and even pop out a little monster of my own. I would have done it for me, but they'd all nod and say 'I knew she'd figure out her true purpose eventually.'

Although... My kids would never be treated as well by their grandpa as Vanessa's were. I knew that. Children of the scapegoat would forever be grandscapegoats.

Marriage and kids didn't bug me—it was the idea that nothing else had meaning for a woman that made me want to run an all-female criminal commune on the beach where we'd do goof-offs and never shave again.

530. New business idea — Goof-Off Island

My phone rang. I ignored it. A while later, when I sat down to a lonely evening of Netflix with Myrtle, I finally listened to the message. Vanessa informed me, for four long minutes, that if I was going to make bank off her life story, I should at least give her all the money from it because she had children and needed money more than I. That if I spent the money I'd earned on me, a childless person, it was a waste.

Wow.

No matter that Vanessa's husband brought home more money than they knew what to do with. Nope.

531. Congrats on your pay day, but sign it over to someone more worthy, and also you're a piece of crap

I had already decided to help my niece and nephew with college, but I'd probably keep it a secret for a while. Couldn't have Vanessa think that her demands worked.

I made a bet with myself that the next message would be my dad demanding that I give Vanessa all my money while telling me the reason for my success was embarrassing.

532. The call came fifteen minutes later

533. New business idea — Add a psychic to Goof-Off Island

Dad had totally gotten his wish, though. I fell onto the couch and sobbed about my worthlessness while the cat ate my hair.

Chapter Twenty-One

F*ck-Ups Five-Thirty-Four through Five-Forty-Eight
March without Yash

I spent a week in Palm Springs with Mel and Khandye Kardashian. We partied like rock stars by night, and by day invented new and interesting ways to put quinoa into Mason jars. I finally experienced an evening of naked hot-tubbing! I shucked knickers with the two ladies (bonding) and two male members of the Avengers (lusting) while surrounded by a bunch of gorgeous rich people who had no pursuits besides working out and snorting coke.

534. I barely remembered it

535. But it had been hella fun

536. I hadn't ended up in bed with movie stars, though

537. My own fault

The Avengers had been really sweet. They listened to the whole story about Yash and told me that he must have really cared about me to be so upset. If he hadn't cared, he would have just kept banging me. So they said. They added that they would love to bang me.

538. I'd cried then, which was a super boner killer. So much for my reputation as a bad, bad girl

Although I had let one of the Avengers grab my boob. Because *come on*.

On the plus side, Khandye and I had created a new Mason jar salad. We called it the Breakup Bonanza — three donuts slid over a rabbit vibrator. Once you ate all the donuts. And washed the vibrator —

539. You could cry into the empty jar so it caught your tears

At least my work life was going well.

Khandye was a nice lady, but the week had been surreal. At the pool parties, the hottest ticket in town at our rented bungalow, I was the person most folks wanted to meet. Me. I was told that I'd inspired someone to end a bad relationship, or try for a dream job, or to start painting again. It meant a lot that my —

540. *Literal*

Shitshow had made a positive difference to others, and their stories helped to shape the book as I wrote it. I also blogged about these testimonials.

541. *Yash had to read the blog, right?*

542. *R*

543. *I*

544. *G*

545. *H*

546. *T*

547. *?*

A blizzard hit New York the night we returned from the west coast. I hid in my now-crusty bathrobe and tried to cry, but it appeared that I was already shriveling up into a dry spinsterhood.

So I chose a different pursuit. I reached into the bowels of my email and pulled out the one thing I'd been avoiding — Yash's second book. He'd sent it just before our relationship had pulled a Titanic. In this scenario, he is Leonardo DiCaprio, and I'm the iceberg. I hadn't opened the book because I figured I didn't have the right to read it anymore.

But he wasn't talking to me, and I would never share it, so what the hell. What was the harm? I'd already ripped his heart out. Might as well take a stiletto to it.

I dived into a new tub of ice cream while dithering. Dither dither dither. Although how I still had the wherewithal for one dither — never mind three — was a mystery. My emotions had churned themselves into a lather, and the lather had solidified, like congealed fat on top of a pot roast.

My heart yearned for him my every moment of waking.

Yearn yearn yearn. Hell, even when I slept, my heart made pictures of him for my mind. I yearned to hear him again, and I couldn't fight it anymore.

548. I opened the book just to hear his voice

Ooh, it was action-packed and heartfelt and funny at times — about three Indian women who cleaned a scientific facility. They came across a time machine and used it to try to prevent the Sikh genocide of 1984. The women were middle-aged, brave, and struggling to get by, and they risked their lives to try to save their families.

I didn't put it down for two hours.

After that, sleep escaped me completely. After flailing in bed for a while, I pulled out my laptop and dicked around in the comment section of the last blog I'd put up. I answered people's questions and snarked at meanies.

But then one username jumped out at me. It was called 'Scully's Tentacles.' I yelped into the empty apartment, and Myrtle ran to the other end of the bed.

It was him it was him it was him…and he wanted me to know it!

I searched for other comments from this user, but there was only one.

I don't understand why you couldn't just tell Sexy Sex Writer Guy the truth. Why go so far with the deception? Did you think so little of him that he didn't deserve the truth? To make a decision on his own? Do you think he'd never been through a tough time in his life? If he was half as great as you've said here, then he deserved to be in the know. PS: Good for the bird.

It was only after I fell back against the headboard that I realized I'd been curled around the computer, tense as a growling dog. I started laughing — PS — Good for the bird. Ha ha ha! My laughter brought Myrtle back to me, and she walked right onto my lap, half covering the keyboard.

I shooed her off so I could type a response. Better just do it before I overthought it to death.

Dear Scully's Tentacles,

You sound awesome, and I will pass your good wishes to the bird. It was a very smart and accurate bird, and I, a worthy target.

Truth was, I was a coward. I thought I would lose SSWG if he knew I'd lied. The lie was silly and innocent on the first night. A silly bar lie to escape my life, which had bottomed out from under me not three days before. SSWG is wonderful – the most wonderful man I've ever met – and losing him terrified me. Although the lies guaranteed he'd be angry enough to dump me, I'd deluded myself into hoping otherwise.

He deserved more, he deserved better, and I'll regret my stupidity always. And now, I just pray he'll be happy, because he deserves that. I love him so much, and I always will.

I hit Publish and didn't sleep a wink.

Chapter Twenty-Two

F*ck-Ups Five-Forty-Nine through Five-Sixty-Eight
Ppppphhhhppbbbbbbbtttttttttttt

In late April, I got a tattoo — something I'd always dreamed of doing, but had been too chicken to pull the trigger on. I'd Tweeted out a question about great female tattoo artists in NYC. Among the responses was DirtyLinens, asking for an exclusive interview while I got tattooed. Mel and Marlene flipped over the amazing free publicity. Marlene made sure to put the book on super early pre-order to capitalize on my inking.

My tattoo wasn't going to be any wild piece of surrealist art — I'd decided on quotation marks on the backs of my shoulders. Probably too stupidly literal, as several Twitter followers had said, but they would look amazing with a tank top, and would remind me to never again keep quiet when I wanted to shout from the rooftops.

The day of reckoning came. A Saturday. I woke up on the weekend and, as I did most non-work days, reached for a breakfast beer. Then it occurred to me.

549. Breakfast beers were probably bad

550. When they happened ten times a month

Having fun or drowning sorrows was one thing, alcoholism was another.

551. Alcoholism was for old-timey male literary authors

Ew, right? So I made a demonstrably un-fucking-up decision to stop day drinking.

552. I still cried in my shower, though

553. Let's not get crazy with the good progress, for

554. 'Scully's Tentacles' had not left another comment

Despite assuring myself I would not bring up Yash in the interview...

555. She totally brought up Yash in the interview

I lay on my squished boobs on the medical-ish bed at the tattoo parlor, my palms sweating. As the needle buzzed in the hand of a super-tattooed lady named, of all things, Giselle, I talked about how badly I'd fucked up my dream relationship. I'd sabotaged myself because I'd convinced myself it could end no other way.

556. Then I fretted out loud about taking further advantage of him just by talking

My nerves already jumped because Anna was the one interviewing me. I'd made sure not to wear the same coat to meet her this time.

And I left my unicorn head at home.

The needle made my tongue loose, for talking helped distract me from the pain. We discussed fear in relationships, choosing a path our family didn't approve of — her family was made of lawyers...until her — and about behaving like good little girls. She got death and rape threats regularly online, just as I did. It's the accepted cost of doing business if you're a woman on the Internet.

557. Ha ha ha no, the world is terrible and shouldn't be that way

Soon, one completed quotation mark throbbed on my shoulder! We took a break so that I could take a break from the pain. *Seriously — I was a wimp.* I sat up and squeezed my eyes shut. Seemed I was always tired and hung over from either booze or emotions lately. Sometimes both. It had been months, and my heart was still a raw piece of steak chewed on by a mangy mutt. How could I let him go when he hadn't ever been mine?

558. That made no sense, but whatever

My palms started to sweat anew, and I pulled Anna aside. "I-I shouldn't be talking about him in this interview. It's so disrespectful. He didn't ask for any of this, and I —"

"Okay, okay." She yanked on my arms and pulled me in for a hug. My face landed between her tits. It was a very comforting place, I could tell why people liked it. "We'll have a general conversation about relationships, not a conversation about *one* relationship."

I sniffled, fighting with all my might not to cry or mucus on her boobies, from which I dislodged myself. "Thanks. This has been, without question, the weirdest year of my life."

She grinned. "I sure hope so."

"I have to have something left over for the book. Let's get back to the inking. You can spend five hundred words mocking my low tolerance for pain."

"Oh, I don't know. Seems to me you have a pretty big capacity for taking tough shit and turning it into gold."

We started on the other shoulder with a new ease between us, and we cracked open beers to help me with the pain and her with the need for a beer.

My phone dinged. Anna was closest to it, and her eyes flicked to the source of the beep before going very wide. Trepidation seizing my belly, I took the phone as she handed it over to me. The lock screen lit up again with four words.

The first word was *Yash*.

I almost fell off the table. He'd texted me. He'd texted me!

The next three were *That's your explanation?*

My bottom dropped out. I jerked up, and the tattoo artist's needle stabbed me. She called out, and I mumbled a "Sorry" while cradling the phone, the blessed phone. The text color had changed—he'd unblocked me!

I made it to my feet and jumped up and down, my boobs bouncing perilously in the bandeau bra I'd worn.

Anna opened her mouth and I fell to my knees at her feet. I was a drama queen—so what? "Please. Please don't publish that you saw that. If I have any hope in hell of even making him my friend again, I can't have people knowing this. It's the first word he's said directly to me since it all went down. Please, please, pl — "

"Okay." She held up her hands. "Okay, I believe in the cause of true, fucked-up love. But if you two crazy kids actually work out, I expect an exclusive on the wedding."

"You can take the first born I probably won't have."

"Uh…that's okay."

She and the tattoo artist stared at me, still on the floor. What to do? Should I answer now? Keep getting the tattoo? Act cool, calm, collected?

Hahahahahaha *what the fuck* no. My innards were about to explode like an alien out of John Hurt's chest.

I scrambled to standing. "I-I have to go. I'm so sorry, can we continue the appointment at a later date?"

Giselle gave me that eyebrows-together-you're-a-loon face I often received from Mel. "Yeah, sure. You look like a dangling thought now, though."

I held a mirror in front of me and examined my partial tattoos in the mirror behind. One quote on the right, a partial outline on the left. She was right — I was the beginning of a sentence that yet had no end. She affixed clear plastic over the tattoos, such as they were.

I yanked on my shirt while babbling. "Thank you. Thank you both. It's just that I — I have to — He — I never thought I'd hear from hi — "

"Go," Anna said.

"Go," Giselle said. "Get him back. He seems like a cool guy, and his first book was great."

I smiled. "Thank you." Then I kept talking like an idiot.

559. "You should read the sec — "

560. I bit my tongue to hold in the fact that I'd started his next book, which had made me weep in its heartbreaking wit

He'd gotten better. The beautiful bastard had gotten better.

Anna raised an eyebrow, clearly having almost heard my almost slip. I waved and ran from the building before I said or did anything else stupid.

A few blocks down, under a weak streetlight, I stared at

my phone. Seven minutes had passed since he'd sent the three words. I stood there, a pebble in the stream of people coming and going on either side.

In my urgency to answer the blessed text, it hadn't even occurred to me—

561. What do I say now?

A minute passed under the streetlight. Three. My head swam, and my shoulder hurt like the blazes. How could I form a proper sentence with only one quotation mark?

I'd rehearsed the speech a thousand times in my mind. Infinite variations of explanation, all of which had fled my cerebellum at the crucial moment. All I could think of was his laugh. All I could see was his face. All I could hear was the murmured sounds of his words in my ear as he made love to me.

Six minutes passed. Finally, terrified he would block me again, I responded.

Me: Because I was an idiot. And then I was an idiot who cared about you, and I was in too deep. The lie was too big, so I got desperate for any time I could spend with you. You must believe me when I say I'm so sorry. And I never in a million years thought anyone would ferret you out. Please see beginning of message about me being an idiot.

My stomach flipping into my throat, I hit Send.

I stood there. The message had been read. I waited for those little ellipse marks that show you the other end is writing. I waited.

562. I waited…

563. Dot dot dot

Nothing.

I shivered. Spring had not yet sprung in New York, and my too-light jacket did not cut the mustard. Chill puffed from my mouth. I wound my arms around myself, phone still in my hand, and started walking home. The cold felt nice, actually.

564. In the cold, I could pretend my shaking was from the temperature, not from terror

I came to a dead stop under another light, the person behind me running me over with a "Move!" Ugh. I picked myself off the ground, brushed the grit off my hand, and sent three more words to Yash, because I couldn't not.

Me: I love you.

565. I waited…
566. I waited… Tears sprang to my eyes
567. I waited…my heart breaking in two

No, it had already split. My heart lay in fractions in my chest—a game of Plinko wherein they fell down, down, down.

Nothing.

That night was the worst in a long time, because before there may have been the tiniest glimmer of hope, but I'd said the wrong damn thing, and he'd responded with exactly nothing.

There wasn't enough buttercream in the world.

* * * *

The next day, my eyes puffy from being punched by feelings, I managed to drag myself to work. My phone had become a permanent fixture in my hand, just in case he sent another word.

But one thing was different today from yesterday. Today I was still unblocked. He hadn't shut the door. Oh, the thought made my heart race, not to mention my love-starved body. He hadn't shut the door on me, even if he wasn't taking a step through it.

I mentioned none of this in my blog. A new piece had gone up today, about getting the tattoo. I'd written it before I'd gone to get inked, and people were demanding pictures. Latisha graciously took a photo of the one completed quote tattoo and I updated the post with it. The *666* blog was publishing company business now because we'd profit off the eventual book. The commenters wanted to know why I had only one quote.

I thought my half-finished art was deep, in a high school poetry class sort of way. What would the end of my dialogue be?

568. As of today, I think it probably sounded like a long dog fart
However that was spelled.

Chapter Twenty-Three

F*ck-Ups Five-Sixty-Nine through Six-Thirty-Five
May with/out Yash

569. May 1–5: Ate too many Mason jar salads and got the runs

570. May 7: Tried six-inch high heels

571. I now wear ankle brace. Ouch

572. May 8: Wrote Yash a love song

573. Was halfway to posting it on the blog when Mel wrestled my laptop away from me

574–577. May 10–17: Adopted four kittens on four separate days

Mel took two off my hands while she muttered about my spinsterhood.

I named mine Gray Lady and Peeves. Peeves enjoyed annoying me and peeing everywhere, so his name was most apt. Gray was gray — *I'm smart* — and loved to hide, so very ghostly she was.

578. May 18: Started hanging out in the flower shop across the street from Yash's apartment

579. Spent two hundred dollars on flowers in two weeks

580. Spotted Yash once

581. Dived behind a rickety table of bonsai

582. Spent two hundred and fifty dollars on broken bonsai

583. By the time I stopped being dizzy from the pot cracked across my skull, Yash had gone

584. I hadn't talked to him

585. And thereafter my ankle and *head were injured*

586. May 19: Attended a book launch party at Yash's publisher

587. Received sneers from Yash's friends

588. *Tried talking to them anyway with a bright smile and tons of hair flips*

589. *Accidentally flipped my hair in one guy's mouth*

590. *He cussed me out, and they scurried away while laughing that they didn't want to end up in my shitty book*

591. *May 20: Tried writing more of my shitty book, but cried instead*

592. *Facebook-stalked Yash's mean friends with Mel*

We printed their ugliest pictures and drew neckbeards on them. That was pretty fun.

593. *May 22: After resisting for weeks and weeks, I texted Yash. I sent him a link to a funny news article about the downfall of a mutually hated celebrity*

594. *He didn't reply*

595. *May 23: He didn't reply*

596. *May 24: He didn't reply*

597. *May 25: Mel took my phone away*

598. *Also —*

599. *He didn't freaking reply*

On May 27th Mel and I spoke on a panel at a book conference. Ours was a session on women breaking the rules in publishing and forging new directions. The place was packed, and my urge to barf nearly won. Somehow, I made it onto the stage without yakking on the audience. Win! Unfortunately, I hadn't planned my outfit very well, and —

600. *Wore too short a skirt to sit on the high stool they'd put out for us*

601. *Seriously, this thing perched eight feet off the ground*

602. *Or so*

603. *Had to sit twisted sideways with my legs crossed*

604. *Mel kept shooting me dirty looks because my feet were in her space*

605. *Fell off the stool once*

606. *When the moderator asked me a question about Yash that they'd agreed not to ask*

607. *Stupid moderator! He'd totally done that on purpose!*

Once I climbed back onto the stool—good thing I'd worn cute undies—the audience sat quiet and waiting. For me. The moderator repeated the question. Do you regret putting your former boyfriend in the spotlight?

My mouth went dry. My tongue melted into some kind of glue, sticking my talk hole closed. Mel reached over and took my hand. With a squeeze of support, and using her for ballast, I stood to answer.

I licked my lips. "I was an asshole. So yes, I regret it."

The audience tittered a little. Mel gave me a proud-friend smile, and I kept talking. "Not really sure why that question is relevant. We're here today to talk about women breaking barriers, and you ask me a question about a boyfriend. But here's the thing—women have been out there, being awesome, redefining books and the world throughout all time. We on this stage aren't new. Virginia Woolf said, 'For most of history, anonymous was a woman.'"

I started pacing now, a wireless mic on my dress. "We invented science fiction. We invented superheroes. We're amazing, and, who knew—we're *people*. We do groundbreaking things, but we also fuck up. When dudes fuck up, it can be considered romantic. Oh, look—he tried hard. Give him a second, third, fourth chance. Give him more money—shit, how many times has Donald Trump gone broke? But when women screw up, it's the end of the world, and the world loves vilifying us. I'd worked my whole life to be a perfect woman, and it's not possible. I failed anyway. So I did a one-eighty, and I wrote about my imperfections, hence my being here today. And yeah, I really screwed up my relationship with the best man I've ever known. He didn't deserve it. He didn't deserve to be outed in a video on fucking YouTube. Thanks, fellow asshole, for doing that." I flipped the bird at the audience, and they broke into applause.

I started to laugh, as did the panel behind me. "Maybe things really are changing for women, because I have a following for fucking up. I have thousands and thousands

259

of fans even though I've made some pretty huge mistakes. The women especially tell me that I've inspired them to be less afraid of failure. That makes me proud. But fans of a mistake don't make it any less of a mistake, and yes, again, I'm really sorry to that beautiful man who allowed me to be his friend for a while."

I turned to the moderator. "I only came on this panel under the agreement that you wouldn't bring him into this—I want that known. You fucked up. And now I'll ask—Do *you* regret putting my former boyfriend in the spotlight here today?"

The room went wild. The moderator at least had the temerity to look abashed.

I wandered back toward my Stool O' Doom. "Men are told to achieve. Women are told to behave." The panel around me broke into agreeing murmurs. "It's true! And while I regret hurting someone I love, I don't regret my fuck-up adventures. Because, for better or worse, I'm less afraid now. I'm more apt to take wild chances. I care about outside opinions less now, and more about my own. If I have one thing to tell this audience, it's to not just behave to please others—behave in a way that pleases you. Because the mistake that comes from *your* heart is a helluva lot easier to live with than a mistake that comes from someone else's."

The room applauded and whooped and hollered. I sat back down again and gave the floor to the other awesome ladies on the panel, many of whom gave a similar message— Listen to your own voice, be true to yourself, and help empower other women to do the same.

Months ago, I'd never have stalked around this stage calling people assholes and telling a famous author moderator to, basically, shut up. But today, I wore a yellow wiggle dress and spoke my truth, good and bad.

Not a mistake.

As the other women talked, I scanned the audience for familiar faces. There were many. Marlene had come out, too, and had whooped the loudest of all. I met her gaze, and she winked at me. Whew. My boss-slash-editor, today with orange hair, approved of my rant.

I smiled at a few more people behind her, and —

And —

Holy shit, it was Yash. Yash!

608. I teetered into Mel, who shoved me upright again with a frown

I clutched her arm and squeezed my apologies while trying not to attract attention. But him being here had literally thrown me.

Yash wore a cap pulled very low, tinted eyeglasses, and a scarf he didn't need inside. On the aisle, halfway back. He'd turned away from the people sitting next to him, but I'd recognize that chin, that nose anywhere.

I swiveled my gaze to the floor, lest he catch me noticing.

Holy moly.

Holy cheese.

Holy donut wrapped around a vibrator!

Hope — a dry riverbed pocked with my millions of salty, dried tears — sprang forth with fresh, clean water. My heart tried to dance and barf at the same time, like a drunk girl at a bachelorette party.

The rest of the talk flew by in a blur of lustful hope.

609. It probably doesn't say much about my feminism that I was thinking about a boy instead of the important philosophical discussion of women in the workplace

As soon as the house applauded the end of the talk, I slipped gracefully — er…

610. Fell

Off my stool and beelined to Marlene under the guise of talking to her. While I gave her a hug, I stood on tiptoe to spy Yash's location over her shoulder. Oh no! He'd made it to the exit already!

611. No

612. No

613. Noooooooo!

With a quick "I'll explain later" to Marlene, I followed him out of the door. Some folks wanted to chat—aw, so nice—and I waved at them. "I'll be right back!" I said while continuing to follow him a ways down the block. No way I'd let anyone witness this and film it.

614. Fucking social media

615. Except when it helped me

"Hey!" I called, not even wanting to use his name.

He stopped in the middle of the sidewalk. He stopped! Oh, hell—my heart had thumped out of my chest and was currently humping his leg.

I approached slowly, as I did with my cat, Gray Lady.

616. Of course, she always ran away

617. Made me insecure, honestly

"Yash," I whispered. His head turned, and even from his profile, I saw the struggle to stay or go.

I held my breath, so afraid to do the wrong thing, it paralyzed me.

He finally turned all the way around and I nearly burst into tears. I held my chest with both hands—he was too beautiful.

With a little head shake, he took off his glasses and slapped me with a look of hurt mixed with anger.

"I'm sorry," I said.

He waved a hand. "Enough with the apologies. What you did can't be fixed that way."

A single tear spilled onto my cheek.

618. It would have been poetic if I weren't the villain

I said, "I understand that. Please know that everything that happened between us was the real me. Just…a different name. And occupation. And curtains…"

He laughed.

He. Laughed!

My knees buckled with happiness, but I snapped those slutty joints back into place so I could stand. "When we met, I'd been fired for not fucking the boss. My cheater boyfriend had just abandoned me with an apartment I couldn't afford. So I escaped into Giselle. It was supposed to be temporary."

His face clouded over. "I was nice to *a cat* for you. I keep finding cat hair on my stuff..." He took a step forward. "You flashed the whole audience in that sexy dress."

"I...sorry...thanks?"

"Sexy sex writer guy? Really?"

I couldn't seem to draw breath into my lungs. "It was a compliment?"

"Are you asking or telling me?"

"Uh—"

"People are harassing me on your behalf. Telling me what you did was *romantic*." He tossed off the word as if it tasted rancid. "Lying isn't romantic, Gis—Dagm—Whoever!"

"I kno—"

"But it rather was!"

"What?"

With a grunt, he put his hands on his hips and stared at his shoes. "I mean...you went to all that effort. Just to... keep seeing me."

My heart flip-flopped. "Yes, I did."

"But you can't just make up sexy, wonderful identities to suit you!"

"I kno—"

"Do you even have a twin? Or was all that family drama just fodder for the eventual book?"

"No!" Now I was starting to get angry. "No, that was all one hundred percent real. They hate the blog and the book and the everything just as much as you do." I laughed— short and bitter. "Maybe you all should compare notes on how I'm the worst."

His demeanor cracked. I watched him pity me, hate me, lust for me. He then began to back away.

No no no! He was bending, I could feel it. And also he couldn't tear his eyes away from my tits.

I talked in a torrent of word vomit. "Look, Yash. It just... spiraled. When I found out who you were, and that we were in the same business of all things…I didn't want to be my normal, no-job, sensible-underwear loser. Blade had said nobody would ever want to stay with a boring nothing like me, so how could I be Dagmar with you, when she was—"

I completely lost my breath then and my face went numb. That was it. That was why I *never came clean to Yash* —

619. Deep, deep down…I'd believed every hateful thing Blade had said to me

620. I thought if I were me with Yash, he'd never want to stay with such a piece of crap

"Oh, my God," I whispered. The horrible defeatism of it all nearly knocked me off my feet.

"What the hell is…a Blade?"

I looked at Yash again. "My ex. He told me nobody would ever love me…because I was boring and naive and—"

"Boring?" His eyes nearly bugged out. "You're a smoking hot con artist with a book and a TV deal!"

"You think I'm smoking hot?"

He threw his hands up. "Ugh, what am I doing? I— This is nuts. You might be nuts. And cats suck!"

He huffed away, and I didn't run after him. Reality had walloped me in the shins, and I couldn't make my legs work anymore. I might have been 'smoking hot,' but I was also a complete and total fool *still* under the thumb of a man I'd let convince me I was worthless.

Yash was long gone when my phone rang—

"Hey, Mel."

"You ran off."

"Yeah… Yash was here. I talked to him for a second, and I've come to a major realization—"

"I'm sure it's super deep, sug', but your friend Latisha is, I think, sick with the flu, and can you help me take her home?"

I turned on my heel and started back. "Of course! I owe her a lot—she's been putting up with my bullshit since I got that job."

Mel laughed. "She can join my club."

621. I hung up on such truths.

* * * *

Hours later, Mel and I sat on Latisha's living room floor while she bundled on her couch. We'd urged her to rest in bed, but she'd been there for hours and wanted human company. Most likely it was a twenty-four-hour flu — poor lady shook and shivered, fit to tear herself apart.

Latisha sat up and took the chicken soup I offered her. "Thanks for staying with me. My girlfriend is in Hawaii for a week with her family, the turd."

"She should have taken all of us with her," Mel observed, and we nodded in mute agreement.

"That was some speech today, Dag." Latisha managed to crack a small smile. "I'm glad you told that moderator off. He shouldn't have asked it."

I nodded. Mel started on a rant about what a jerk he was while searching the Internet to see if anyone had filmed my sermon.

"You're quiet," Latisha said to me.

"I just want to make sure you feel okay, office buddy."

"Eh, I've had worse."

Mel inclined her head to me. "She's introspecting about Yash. He was there today."

Latisha sat up. Well, she tried to. It was a very forceful twitch. "Tell me what happened!"

My face fell. "No, no. Not my drama today. You're sick, and you—"

"Oh, hush." Sickie collapsed onto the couch again. "I'm sick and unhappy — not that you two aren't entertaining — and I order you to tell me about your stupid drama. I have to hear about it anyway, as your editor. So spill. My relationship is smooth-sailing and full of love."

I shook my head. "That's just awful."

"Yeah," added Mel.

Latisha grinned through a coughing fit. "So did he talk to

you?"

I sat back and nibbled on a bagel. "Yes. I made him laugh, and he called me smoking hot."

"Really?" Latisha gasped.

"It's not so far-fetched that I'm hot, okay?" I threw half a bagel at her, and she caught it and took a bite. "But I ended the talk abruptly…because — ugh."

"What?" Mel punched me in the arm.

"Ow!" I scooted away from her. "I suddenly realized why I sabotaged my relationship with Yash."

Two sets of eyebrows raised with expectation.

"My ex said many hateful things the day he left. He told me I was boring and worthless and nobody would want me. And, even though I never acknowledged it to myself…I believed him." I stared at the floor and tried to squish my eyes shut to keep the tears at bay.

Mel's arm closed around my shoulder, and I leaned on her. "So," she said, "you kept up Giselle…"

"Because Dagmar was too shitty for Yash to stay interested in."

"That's fucked up," Latisha said, saying it all. "You've spent months feeling sorry for yourself. What you gonna do about it?"

I looked up into her red, tired eyes.

"What you gonna do about it?" She set her container of soup on the table. "If he called you hot and stuff, and he came to the talk today, then he wants you back! What are you gonna do about it? Don't make me ask again. We need an ending to this book, and it had better be happy. I want a yacht before I'm forty."

My mouth dropped open, bewilderment robbing me of words.

Mel sat back on her arms. "It seems to me you can go on as you have, leaving him pathetic messages on the blog and praying to your shrine."

622. *"It's not a shrine!" I lied about my shrine of Yash, containing*

623. An old tee he'd worn

624. Selfies of us

625. And the dirty wine glass he'd used last time he was over

626. Not pathetic

627. I said not!

"Or!" Mel said with a friendly kick in my direction. "Or you can go get him."

"Yes!" Latisha said. Then she coughed, and we shoved more blankets around the poor girl.

"How do I get him? You want me to play 'In Your Eyes' on a boom box while I stand under his window?"

"Hell yes!" Mel said, leaping to her knees.

"No, no, no." I waved my hands. "Noooooo. Someone would put it on fucking YouTube. People are the worst."

Mel took me by the shoulders. "Yash fell for a weird, brash, hot weirdo who had guts and fire. Who exposed a date rapist to all the world!"

"What now?" asked Latisha.

628. "Nothing," we replied

"If you want him back," Mel said, "you need to be Giselle again. Wild, grifting cats, jetting off to Hawaii Giselle. Make a gesture. Let him know that you are she."

They both looked at me with hope. And maybe a little greed. But mostly hope!

"He's obviously been reading the blog, Dag," Latisha said. "He came to the panel. He unblocked your number. He wants you back. You have to let him know you're all in."

"No." I shook my head and squeezed my eyes shut. "No! I got myself into this mess by being her."

Mel escalated from shaking me to punching me in the arm. Again. "You got him in the first place by lying! You wouldn't have gotten him and lost him and had a chance to get him back without lying."

I rubbed the owie on my arm while I parsed through that sentence to understand it. "But...aren't I supposed to be learning a lesson about lying, and honesty...and...shit like

267

that?"

"Nah," Latisha said. "Good girls never succeed. You gotta have a little devil in you somewhere, even if it's just enough to not let people walk all over you."

"Amen," Mel agreed.

A swamp of indecision swirled in my guts. I shook Mel off me and lay back on the floor. Wow, Latisha really kept her hardwood spotless. I was so afraid of turning Yash off with more deviousness.

629. *But then again*

630. *What did I really have to lose?*

631. *My life was sex and loveless anyway*

I stood. "Okay. I'll do it. What's the worst that can happen?"

632. *"He could tell you to go to hell," Mel said*

633. *"Marry someone else to spite you," Latisha added*

634. *"Throw you into the ocean"*

635. *"Get a forehead tattoo saying, 'I hate Dagmar!'"*

"Okay!" I said. "I get it, you're both very funny."

"Now get me more crackers, cracker," Latisha said. "And get me the best ending to a book since *Bridget Jones's Diary*."

"Mr. Darcy," said Mel.

We all sighed.

And when I was done sighing, I started forming a plan. Well, Giselle started forming a plan.

Chapter Twenty-Four

F*ck-Ups Six-Thirty-Six through Six-Sixty-Four—
Love Is Composed of a Dual Soul Inhabiting One Body

My plan had many facets — most of them ridiculous — and all accompanied by a wardrobe of the mini-est minis I could wear without being arrested for solicitation.

636. Although that would be a very Giselle thing to do…

I wrote a blog post about Moaning Myrtle, accompanied by many photographs. In one of them, I forced her to lie on the DVD of *Talladega Nights*, the movie Yash and I had watched in bed together.

637. It took an hour

638. And two visits with my antiseptic before I accomplished that photo

I also posed a photo of Myrtle sitting on a pair of men's shoes (procured from my neighbor).

639. Heh heh heh

640. I hopefully would cause him to wonder… Whose shoes are those?

641. Bwaahahahahahaaa!

642. That laugh was more evil than laugh number 639

I'd gotten him while devious, and I would take him back while being the same. A little less devious than before, but the goal remained. I needed that giant, sweet, amazing man in my bed forever and ever. Amen.

The day after my painful cat photo shoot went live, I reached out on Facebook to one of Yash's friends. This was the most precarious portion of the plan. This fellow, Tim, was one of those who mocked me at the book party, so I was most excited to rekindle our robust and beautiful friendship.

He agreed to chat on the phone, and I told him my plan, as well as basically groveling about how much I loved Yash, how I wanted to make it up to him, on and on...until he finally confessed that Yash had been miserable without me!

"No!" I said.

"Yes," he countered begrudgingly. "I gotta admit, your blog is fun to read. Did a bird really poop on your head?"

"Yes. Yes, it did."

He laughed. "Yeah, cool. That sexual harassment stuff you went through, though—that's not cool."

"Thanks, Tim. So you'll help me?"

He blew really loudly into the phone. "Yeah. I want him to be happy. And I think you're the good kind of crazy."

"Thanks?"

"You're welcome. He's not a good flyer, so get him a little drunk. Maybe I'll pack him a Valium or two."

"Thank you. Let me know when the prep is done on your end."

"Ya, okay, bye. Oh, hey—"

"Yes?" I asked.

"So, whose shoes was that cat sitting on? At your place?"

I clapped my hand over my mouth to stifle the laugh—the evil one. "Just a neighbor's. Why?"

"Oh, man. That picture drove Yash nuts. He emailed all of us that cat post, going crazy over it."

643. Yes!

644. Yes yes yes yes yes yes yes!

He hung up then, and I knew it... I knew I *had* Yash.

I *hoped* I had him.

Oh, God, I still had him, right?

645. Riiiiiiight?

Tim, and by extension Yash, in hand, I began making my own arrangements. These nefarious plans would take a chunk of my advance, but if my scheme worked, the money would mean nothing.

Time flew over the next few days. I arranged vacation off work with Marlene's blessing, especially seeing as it was in pursuit of Yash—and, thereby, her book investment. She even got me a deal at the airline for better seats than I could afford.

I went to the dry cleaner's, the bank, the bikini waxer. Boring and painful, the lot of them, but a girl's got to cover all her bases, especially when her base has been out of commission for a while.

Finally, I spent time at the Civil Court. For personal reasons.

Mel would take my cats for a couple of weeks. Hopefully. Unless my plan went horribly awry, and I returned early in need of cat fur to cry and sneeze into.

At least I'd never again have a relationship with Yash based on fear. I would be honest, and myself—my best self, my worst self, and all versions in between.

I barely slept that night, for the next morning would be my salvation or my undoing. But then Peeves jumped up on the bed and settled onto my forehead. Didn't help me sleep, but at least the purring was nice.

* * * *

Mel waited with me on a bright, gorgeous morning near the water at the southern tip of Manhattan. She clasped my sweaty hand in hers with only minimum grumbling. The air smelled of sea, and I breathed it in, converted it to fear, and released it again.

"He's not going to say no," Mel said.

I nodded to her with a head so light and weak, it might plop off and splash around the island.

Finally, fifteen minutes late, a limo pulled up to the helipad.

I stood, adjusted the pillbox hat on my head, and tottered on unsteady heels toward it.

646. Here goes nothing

Tim was the first out of the limo. He shot me a leer that told me they were at least one morning cocktail into the day. That was probably good.

Yash emerged next—somebody pushed him into Tim, who twirled him around to face me.

I flashed a smile that probably looked twenty-three-percent green with terror. "Welcome to Dagmar-Giselle airlines. Uh, helicopter…lines. I can't afford a plane. Would you like to be seated in first class, sir?"

647. I should not have worn a bra if I wanted this to work

Yash's jaw dropped, so I cocked a hip and tried to appear alluring. He turned to Tim and his other boys. "What's going on? Are we flying a helicopter to Vegas?"

"Nah, bro." Tim clapped him on the back and testosterone leaped into the air. "I think Giselle…uh…whoever airlines is a better fit for you."

I smiled and waved my hand into the helicopter. "Would you like to see the first-class cabin? It's the only cabin, and it's a two seater, but it's very nice."

My darling's face both fell and spread into a small smile as he figured out we were all in on it. "Why are you helping her?" he asked Tim.

Tim flipped back his sandy hair and said, "Well… I think she loves you. And she'll never be boring—you have to admit that."

Never be boring? I grinned.

Yash turned his velvet-brown eyes to mine, almost as if he didn't want to, but couldn't help it. He'd heard my apologies. He'd read my explanations, save one.

One of his buds tossed a second piece of luggage at his feet. "What's this?" Yash asked.

"It's the rest of your stuff," Tim said. "You're going away for longer than three days. Dude, we wouldn't have picked through your underwear drawer for her sake if we didn't like her."

The burly guy who'd carried luggage pointed at Mel. "Are you as weird as she is?"

"More," Mel said with a wink. "I think I know who my ride's going to be."

"You mean *what* it's going to be," I said.

She shrugged.

Yash stared at the new bag at his feet. The guys behind him waved Mel over, so she gave me a whack on the butt and left with the fellas. Through it all, Yash didn't speak to me, didn't look at me.

The helicopter pilot gave a quizzical eyebrow and I shrugged. He smiled and left us beside the helicopter to have a smoke.

648. I'd made my plans

649. I'd put on my ridiculous costume

650. And now, I waited

Yash took three steps toward me before he deigned to turn that marvelous face down to mine. "Dagmar?" he said, so faintly I almost didn't hear it.

"Do you see why maybe I'd want a sexier name?"

He laughed then, and hope shone a light bright as the sun in my eye. Ow. No, it was just a reflection off one of the nearby building's windows. I stepped into Yash's shadow. "My friends call me Dag."

"So..." He took a step forward. "Dagmar is yet another lie."

I bit my lip and nodded.

He nodded. He took another step. He was not yet close enough to touch, but every inch of my skin had leaped to attention at this tantalizing proximity. "Where are we headed? Theoretically?"

"Well, I thought I'd make at least part of my lies a truth—we're flying first-class Lufthansa to Paris. Two weeks, all expenses paid by *moi*. And they'll even let me serve you drinks if you want. Although not in the uniform—they were not amused by my modifications and—"

He closed the distance between us and kissed me. And kissed me. And kissed me, like some kind of Disney prince—except dirtier, and with tongues. After a minute or two, we were both breathless, and his fingers ground into my shoulders, pulling me close. I didn't care about the bruises. He could alpha-male me any day of the week, and thrice on Sunday. I threw my arms around his neck, happier in that moment than maybe I'd ever been in my entire life. Being pressed against that body sure didn't hurt.

By the time he let me up, my mouth hurt, but my heart felt as light as the ray of sun blinding my eye, *damn it*, again. I turned his back to the glare.

"Say it to me," he said. "*You* say it—weird, funny, crazy cat lady Dag. Say it."

Tears sprang to my eyes. "I love you, Yash."

He shook his head. "That's not my name."

I took a step back. "What?"

His face crept into a smile. "See? It's not fun. Yes, it's my name, barmy lady."

"I take that as a compliment." I waved my arm again in my best air hostess, and he climbed into the helicopter. After a quick fetch of the pilot, we were about to leave for JFK.

Yash gripped the sides of his seat after putting on his headphones. His knuckles blanched to white and his breathing revved into overdrive. "I've never been in a helicopter."

"Me, neither." I pried one of his hands off and held it to my heart. "Did Tim give you a Valium?"

"Yes."

"Take it. God invented drugs so that we don't have to deal with our fears by ourselves."

He took it.

The blades whirred to life and Yash threw one arm all the way around me in a death grip.

651. Uh…'death grip' sounds awful in a flying contraption

In a life grip. As we began to rise into the sky, I told him through our mic channel, "I love you, Yash. Just look at me. Look in my eyes, baby."

He did, his own peepers full of sheer panic as we pitched

a little to the side.

"It's fine," I assured him. "We're supposed to be going up."

"Uuuuuhhh-kay," he said, not sounding very confident in my stewardess abilities.

I smiled. "I'm going to tell you a deep, dark secret, okay? You're going to hear all of them now."

"Good," he said. His arm around me loosened just enough to decompress my vertebrae.

"It's something I didn't even realize until the last time we spoke. I didn't then know exactly why I kept up this ridiculous charade for you."

His eyebrows rose expectantly and his arm loosened once again. Excellent. If I kept his brain occupied elsewhere, maybe he wouldn't be as afraid.

I ran a gentle hand along his arm as I spoke. "When my ex dumped me—and he cheated on and *dumped* me—he moved to L.A. without me and without even telling me until he packed…he said horrible things. He told me I was too boring for any man to stay with. That I'd never have real love because I wasn't spontaneous or wild enough. That I deserved the treatment I'd gotten, that I deserved to be walked all over."

"That's awful," he said.

"Yes. My dad spent my whole life telling me basically the same thing. And, well, I believed them. Not in so many words. I didn't think to myself 'I'm worthless and boring' but obviously my extreme one-eighty proved that I did believe it. My behavior wasn't completely 'Hey, I'll make lemonade from these lemons'… It was more 'If I don't change drastically forever, I'll die alone.'" His arm unwound from me and he took my hand. "After I met you, I knew I had to come clean sooner or later, but…"

"You thought the real you was deficient."

"Yes! Worthless, stupid, ugly. But I see now that Blade was both right and wrong. Look, he was a dickbag, so who cares about his opinions? He probably would have cheated on

275

me even if I'd been a Kardashian. However, he was partly right. I did need to start learning how to assert myself and not care so much about the judgments of others. So, while many of my changes were positive, you got caught in the middle of my quarter-life crisis, which I'm kind of ashamed actually happened to me."

He shook his head. "Don't be. Life is change. You took chances, and that's a lot further than most ever get. I'm proud of you, Gis—uh, Dag. You sat me in a roller coaster without a seatbelt, but I'm proud of you for…for having this wild adventure."

My face scrunched into pain. "Can I make it up to you?"

"No."

I gasped and pulled back.

He yanked me to him once again. "You don't have to make it up to me—

652. *"Your public humiliations have been very satisfying"*

653. *"Very satisfying"*

"Yes, okay," I agreed.

654. *"Do you have a picture of you with the bird shite on your head?"*

"Okay!"

He stuck out his tongue at me like an adult. "Hey, you broke my heart. I'm entitled to some schadenfreude."

I nodded. "I know. You didn't deserve any of this." I slid my phone from my pocket and texted Latisha. "I'm pretty sure Latisha took a photo that day. I shall supply it—spread it far and wide however you wish."

"Nah." He shot me a half-smile. "I just want it to look at it from time to time. To remind me of how we met. I can see you've been sorry, and that you were going through difficulties. I read your blog, and sometimes, I felt like you were talking only to me. Especially the weird hidden messages. Seriously, you are an odd, dorky woman."

"Wait'll I tell you how Mel and I took down a date rapist on the Internet."

His eyes turned to saucers. "I'm glad you like me. I can't

imagine the fuck-ups I'd have been on the other end of otherwise."

"You remember that."

"Yes, madam." He squeezed my hand. "You must promise me, though, that you'll never lie to me again."

"Never. Never ever. You'll hear the good, the bad, and the Dagmar. Although…" I reached into my bag and pulled out an envelope. "Here."

His eyebrows shot up, but he opened the thing and read the paper inside. After a minute, he started laughing. "You're really doing this?"

"I think I need both Dag and Giselle, so Dagmar Giselle Kostopoulos is who I shall forever be. And you can call me Giselle when you're feeling randy." I shot him a leer and he pulled me into his arms for a kiss.

Well, he tried, but we clinked microphones. "Nope. It's Dag when I want to get some of that sweet ass. I'll call you Giselle when I'm angry."

You couldn't have wiped my smile off with a sledgehammer. "Deal."

"In actuality…" He licked his lips and blinked a lot—the meds were kicking in, and his knuckles had turned his normal, lovely shade of brown. "My mother can never, ever know about our…interesting meeting story. And if she ever hears about your book, we'll have to lie and say it was about another brilliant, young, fine-ass writer. In fact, maybe we can just pretend you're Indian."

"Uh…" I snickered. "I'll let you be in charge of those lies."

"Good, yes. Desi children lie to their folks regularly. And their folks probably lied to their folks. A line of lies stretching back a thousand years. But that's a story for another day."

I grinned, my face nearly hurting from the sheer volume of joy. "Well, we have a long flight to Paris. And two weeks to snuggle in bed." I leaned closer. "I can't wait to hear about all of it."

He slid his hand up my miniskirt and teased my thigh.

Unnnnnfffff, how I'd missed this!

I said, breathlessly, "Have I mentioned that your new book is brilliant?"

"No, but feel free to now."

"It's the best book ever written by any person on earth or in any other parts of the universe!"

He got all bashful — so cute. He batted his lashes as he looked at his hands. "You can give me that exact cover quote, since you're a much more famous author than I am. You're the voice of a generation."

655. God help us all

"Yash?" I said.

"Yes, lovely girl?"

"Say it to me. I said it to you, but you haven't said…the words…" My heart thumped, waiting to see if he felt —

"I love you, Dagmar Giselle Fuck-up Kostopoulos. God help us all." He lifted my hand and kissed it, sending me into a shiver from both his words and his actions. Could it be real? Did a fuck-up like me really have a storybook ending? My phone dinged —

656. Latisha had sent the photo of me, the voice of a generation, covered in bird poo and slush

I guess it wasn't every girl's storybook, but hell, it was mine. I handed the phone to Yash, who burst into laughter and immediately texted the photo to himself.

657. I had better be nice to him for all of eternity now

658. Because that was a baaaaad picture

659. Bird shit crusted into my nose

660. Dirty, wet hair all over my forehead, and

661. Worst of all

662. She'd taken the photo from a downward angle!

663. Hello, double chin

Maybe not the cover of the storybook.

Yash was still laughing. Like, wildly. I figured it was his drugs, but he wasn't afraid anymore — or mad at me — so I let it go.

He deserved to laugh at Dag, at Giselle, at whoever I was

tomorrow.

The helicopter descended at JFK airport, and I held my Yash throughout the wobbly touchdown.

664. Certain that my days of making mistakes were over

Epilogue

F*ck-Ups Six-Sixty-Five through Six-Sixty-Seven — A Happy Ending Leadeth to a Yacht

Eight months later

"So when can we expect the next installment of Dagmar Kostopoulos' fuck-ups?"

Marlene asked me that question as we stood at one end of the book release party for *Six-Hundred-Sixty-Six*. Her hair shone bright red for the occasion, and our agent Lillian stood on the other side of her, a cherub of happiness. Right next to me bobbed my Mel, too happy to stand still.

A little spotlight shone on us and the overcrowded room waited with bated breath for my answer. My fabulous boss had bought out this entire wine bar for the night just to celebrate our book, and I couldn't believe all this was for me and Mel. Yash stood just off to the side, champagne in hand, grinning like a Looney Tune. A handsome Looney Tune whose clothes I wanted to rip off with my teeth.

I held our book in my hand. Our very own book. With my photo on the front. The bird shit photo. It seemed much too fitting not to be used, and hell, it was funnier than bird shit, and it enticed people to buy. A sexy, fabulous pic of me and Mel looking like *Sex and the City* actresses graced the back flap, and that was good enough for me. And I'd finally dyed my hair a fun color — my long, dark tresses transitioned to deep blue at the ends now.

My stomach fluttered at all the people expecting me to say the perfect thing in the perfect moment. I set the book aside on a catering table to my right. In seeming slow motion, I saw the book fall. I saw the folder I had mistaken for the table edge flip upward. I saw the drink on the other end of that folder slide, slide, I ducked, too late! Whoops, noooooooooo!

665. Champagne splashed all over my silk-clad crotch

The entire room burst into applause and Yash almost had to take a knee from laughing. Mel rushed to help, hysterical tears in her eyes, and started to dry off my lady bits with a napkin.

666. And that's the photo the New York Post *took. Mel rubbing my crotch while I peed champagne*

"Well," I said to the crowd. "That depends on what kind of fuck-ups you mean, Marlene." The crowd laughed. I laughed. "Uh… Obviously, I'll continue being a total mess, no effort required."

"Hear, hear!" Latisha called out.

I grinned. "I think, though, that I only have one more formal mistake to make:

667. "I hereby cease being a fuck-up"

The assemblage started saying "Nooooo," and "Boooo," and I hushed them. "Hear me out. My days of trying to sleep with the boss are over —"

"Hear, hear," muttered Marlene.

"As well as lying to wonderful men about being anything or anyone other than who I am. But, as I've said in the book, learning to stand up for myself, what I believe in, what I want… Those things aren't fuck-ups. They're not. They're being brave, even if the result is not great. It's the intent, sometimes, that can make a fuck-up an act of bravery, not the result. You can be amazing and brave and talented and still fail. But that doesn't make *you* a failure — it happens to everyone. You'll notice that none of my family are here. That's because they don't believe in the person I am — they want me to be someone else. I love them, but I will stay true to me. Even if that 'me' changes over time. I think that's the best any of us can do. So" — I raised my glass — "don't toast being a fuck-up — toast being brave. And toast my soaked hoo-ha and ruined dress."

"Hear, hear!" yelled Yash. He ran to me and lifted me into his arms. His kiss lasted so long that everyone had dissipated by the time he released me, breathless, buoyant. "I love you, D," he said.

"I love you, Y." His beautiful, proud face was the thing I needed in this world to make it past the mistakes and the hurts. The last few months had been the best of my entire life — dream job, dream boyfriend, too many dream cats, amazing friends. I thought him everything that was worthy and amiable — yup, he still sent me Full Austen. My very soul soared above the crowd, scarcely believing what it saw. Nothing could go wrong now!

"Dagmar, wow — you look great, babe."

I gasped and turned. Blade. *Blade.* "How the hell did you get in here, Blade?"

He gave Yash an unfriendly once-over while chewing on a baby carrot. "Is this the guy?"

Yash's face took on a cast I'd never seen before. Dark, nostrils flaring — and sexy as hell. "This guy is with her, and you're not welcome here."

Blade rolled his eyes. "So you're all hot shit now, Dag? I have to admit, I can't believe how you look. I called up your dad and was asking about you, and he told me they were throwing you a party for your book tonight."

That's what I got for inviting Dad...

"He didn't seem to think too much of the book." Blade started laughing.

Yup — that's what I got.

My wonderful ex just kept talking. "So anyway, what say you and me find a nice quiet corner, huh? You seem a lot better now, sexy." He leaned down to me, liquor on his breath. "You might be a L.A. kind of girl now."

"*An* L.A. kind of girl," I corrected, just because I could.

Yash bristled, his muscles rumbling in his tight button-down. Rawr! "I feel a fuck-up coming over me," he growled.

I put a hand on his arm. "No, my love. Let me. And it's not a fuck-up when they deserve it."

I cocked my high-heeled foot, looked Blade in the eyes, and kneed him right in the balls. He screamed and imploded faster than my old life.

Not. A. Mistake.

The Dimple of Doom

Excerpt

Chapter One

It's a Not-So-Wonderful Life

Accountants should not be so sexy.

It all started at the office Christmas party, as many terrible hangovers do.

My palms began to sweat at the sight of The Accountant walking in my direction. His shining eyes said, I wanna spread your sheet, his masterful gait said, Damn, I'm masterful, and his tantalising smirk said, I've read the Kama Sutra—all the way through.

I swallowed the lump of lust in my throat and twiddled with the tablecloth of the catered buffet table. My usual party plan involved making winsome eyes at the food, but tonight I salivated over more than just the pigs in a blanket.

"Potato ball?" he asked. Sam Turner, aka The Accountant, held the fried offering palm up on a festive red and green paper plate.

I had the hots for a dude named Sam. My name is Samantha. Samantha 'n' Sam. It was the stuff of obnoxious wedding invitations.

What colour were his hazel eyes today? Glancing up, I slid into hormone heaven. He stood, eyes mossy green pools of sensual seductiveness, and offered me the Garden of Eden apple. Except it was a potato ball.

Cocking my head, I posed in an alluring manner that I hoped brought Marilyn Monroe to mind. I should say something. Something not stupid.

"I love balls." Oh, damn. "And potatoes!" *Did I just tell him I loved to eat balls?* "I mean I love to eat food! In ball form. You know. Because it's easy. To eat. Except when it rolls. Then it can be hard to catch."

Stop.

Talking.

"Okay." Sam's lips turned upward in mockery on his almost handsome, totally charming face, topped in curling, floppy, please-run-your-hands-through-me brown hair.

Yes, I absolutely had told him I loved to eat balls. I decided I should smile through this faux pas. Everyone knew a bright grin made unpleasant things go away. Ask Judy Garland.

"I like food in stick or chip form myself," he said, munching a piece of celery in stick form.

I couldn't come up with anything to say about sticks that wasn't dirty. "Chips are good." Really, I impressed even myself with the brilliance of my witty banter. At any moment my clothes would be ripped off my quivering body by Sam, my same-named accounting crush.

I hated the office Christmas party.

Sam blinked and appraised me in what I chose to interpret as a captivated manner. A girl could dream. Instead he said, "So, Scott told me you entertained the employees at last year's party."

"Yes. I fell down the steps." My cheeks burned like the

carpet at the end of two flights of stairs. I wasn't clumsy too often, but when I made the effort, I really won at it. "You can still see the splotch on the floor from the blood. I lost a tooth, but gained a reputation."

"That's gross." He grinned. One wouldn't call him drop-dead gorgeous or anything. At first, you might consider him kinda ordinary-looking. Then the naughty glimmer in his eye caught your breath. The smile appeared, emphasising the lickable curve of his bottom lip. Charm emanated from his very pores.

And, of course, he possessed the nuclear weapon of facial features. The dimple. Only one — on the left side of his face — deep enough to bury yourself in. One flicker and panties fell at thirty paces.

My body temperature had suddenly shot upward to somewhere near surface of the sun levels. I'd disconnected completely from the conversation and reverted to teenage-girl-like gawking.

I took a steadying breath and jumped back into the fray. "So, accounting? Is that as glamorous as it sounds?" I had, apparently, decided that deriding his profession was the way to go, flirt-wise. Plays like this were risky, but desperation had sunk in. His temp job in the finance department ended today — I would have no more chances to bend and snap at the water cooler for his benefit.

The corners of his sometimes green, sometimes brown, always dreamy eyes crinkled. "Of course. Usually I have eight models in my accounting entourage, but I gave them the night off."

Uh-oh. He was funny, too. It just wasn't fair. "How kind of you. You could say you're a model boss! Ha ha!" Yes, I laughed at my own joke, which was a behaviour shared by the most sophisticated of ladies. Then I remembered I turned a horrid shade of blotchy red when I got too excited. I choked off my laughter and forced down some potato.

"I could say that, but I won't."

"No, you really shouldn't."

The dimple chose that moment to come out and play. Oh, Sam — let's retire to the supply room and hump. It had been so long since I had humped anyone. Or anywhere. I shoved more mmmmm-yummy potato ball into my mouth and almost didn't get it on my festive sweater, the beautiful red one I'd spent way too much money on in the hopes of getting Sam to notice me.

He noticed now. "You have a blob of — "

Then he grabbed my boob.

"Jesus, I'm sorry!" His eyes became saucers, and he jerked his hand back, leaving my skin scorched and feverish. "There's a bunch of potato on your...sweater. Let's, um, let's go to the kitchen. There's a sink."

My stomach dropped three storeys — I'd just accidentally got to second base in public. He grabbed my arm, and we hurried past a maze of monochrome cubes draped in twinkle lights to the break room. This was the most exciting event in the office since they had switched the carpeting from taupe to tan.

Sam stood there while I applied a paper towel to my tit. Actually, he didn't merely stand there — he stared, turned away, blinked and stared again. I couldn't blame the guy. The girls were rather ravishing — perky from the cold water, encased in a formidable push-up bra, eager for more inappropriate fondling.

"I'm sorry about...that." He slumped and shoved his hands in his pockets.

"It's okay. It happens." I smiled, brimming with reassurance.

The tension finally broke when he snickered. "It does? How often does it happen? You should avoid potato balls."

"And accountants."

We laughed at each other. For once I wasn't laughing by myself.

More books from Lucy Woodhull

If you can't beat them, join them… and then beat them.

It's like a freaking
princess movie.
Well, an R-rated one.

Samantha Lytton
BOOK THREE
The Wrath
of Dimple
LUCY WOODHULL

Unforgettable. That's what she's not.

About the Author

Lucy Woodhull

Lucy Woodhull has always loved le steamy romance. And laughing. And both things at the same time, although that can get awkward. Her motto is "Laugh and the world laughs with you, cry and you'll short-circuit your Kindle."

That's why she writes funny books, because goodness knows we all need to escape the real world once in a while.

She believes in red lipstick, equality, and the interrobang. Lucy daydreams in Los Angeles with her husband and a very fat cat who doesn't like you.

Lucy Woodhull loves to hear from readers. You can find contact information, website details and an author profile page at https://www.totallybound.com/

Home of Erotic Romance

www.ingramcontent.com/pod-product-compliance
Lightning Source LLC
Chambersburg PA
CBHW020602260626
47157CB00003B/832